Nora Roberts is the *New York Times* bestselling author of more than one hundred and ninety novels. A born storyteller, she creates a blend of warmth, humour and poignancy that speaks directly to her readers and has earned her almost every award for excellence in her field. The youngest of five children, Nora Roberts lives in western Maryland. She has two sons.

Visit her website at www.noraroberts.com.

Also available by

Nora Roberts

Nora Roberts

Winter Dreams

Silhouette and Colophon are registered trademarks of
Harlequin Books S.A., used under licence.
Silhouette Books, Eton House, 18-24 Paradise Road,
Richmond, Surrey TW9 1SR

WINTER DREAMS © Nora Roberts 2009

The publisher acknowledges the copyright holder
of the individual works as follows:

Blithe Images © 1981 by Nora Roberts.
Song of the West © 1982 by Nora Roberts.

ISBN: 978 0 263 87715 1

026-1109

Silhouette Books' policy is to use papers that are
natural, renewable and recyclable products and made from
wood grown in sustainable forests. The logging and
manufacturing processes conform to the legal environmental regulations
of the country of origin.

Printed in Great Britain
by Clays Ltd, St Ives plc

CONTENTS

Blithe Images

To Ron's Patience

Chapter 1

The girl twisted and turned under the lights, her shining black hair swirling around her as various expressions flitted across her striking face.

"That's it, Hillary, a little pout now. We're selling the lips here." Larry Newman followed her movements, the shutter of his camera clicking rapidly. "Fantastic," he exclaimed as he straightened from his crouched position. "That's enough for today."

Hillary Baxter stretched her arms to the ceiling and relaxed. "Good, I'm beat. It's home and a hot tub for me."

"Just think of the millions of dollars in lipstick your

face is going to sell, sweetheart." Switching off lights, Larry's attention was already wavering.

"Mind-boggling."

"Mmm, so it is," he returned absently. "We've got that shampoo thing tomorrow, so make sure your hair is in its usual gorgeous state. I almost forgot." He turned and faced her directly. "I have a business appointment in the morning. I'll get someone to stand in for me."

Hillary smiled with fond indulgence. She had been modeling for three years now, and Larry was her favorite photographer. They worked well together, and as a photographer he was exceptional, having a superior eye for angles and detail, for capturing the right mood. He was hopelessly disorganized, however, and pathetically absentminded about anything other than his precious equipment.

"What appointment?" Hillary inquired with serene patience, knowing well how easily Larry confused such mundane matters as times and places when they did not directly concern his camera.

"Oh, that's right, I didn't tell you, did I?" Shaking her head, Hillary waited for him to continue. "I've got to see Bret Bardoff at ten o'clock."

"*The* Bret Bardoff?" Hillary demanded, more than a

little astonished. "I didn't know the owner of *Mode* magazine made appointments with mere mortals—only royalty and goddesses."

"Well, this peasant's been granted an audience," Larry returned dryly. "As a matter of fact, Mr. Bardoff's secretary contacted me and set the whole thing up. She said he wanted to discuss plans for a layout or something."

"Good luck. From what I hear of Bret Bardoff, he's a man to be reckoned with—tough as nails and used to getting his own way."

"He wouldn't be where he is today if he were a pushover," Larry defended the absent Mr. Bardoff with a shrug. "His father may have made a fortune by starting *Mode,* but Bret Bardoff made his own twice over by expanding and developing other magazines. A very successful businessman, and a good photographer—one that's not afraid to get his hands dirty."

"You'd love anyone who could tell a Nikon from a Brownie," Hillary accused with a grin, and pulled at a lock of Larry's disordered hair. "But his type doesn't appeal to me." A delicate and counterfeit shudder moved her shoulders. "I'm sure he'd scare me to death."

"Nothing scares you, Hil," Larry said fondly as he

watched the tall, willowy woman gather her things and move for the door. "I'll have someone here to take the shots at nine-thirty tomorrow."

Outside, Hillary hailed a cab. She had become quite adept at this after three years in New York. And she had nearly ceased to ponder about Hillary Baxter of a small Kansas farm being at home in the thriving metropolis of New York City.

She had been twenty-one when she had made the break and come to New York to pursue a modeling career. The transition from small-town farm girl to big-city model had been difficult and often frightening, but Hillary had refused to be daunted by the fast-moving, overwhelming city and resolutely made the rounds with her portfolio.

Jobs had been few and far between during the first year, but she had hung on, refusing to surrender and escape to the familiar surroundings of home. Slowly, she had constructed a reputation for portraying the right image for the right product, and she had become more and more in demand. When she had begun to work with Larry, everything had fallen into place, and her face was now splashed throughout magazines and, as often as not, on the cover. Her life was proceeding according to plan, and the fact that she now commanded a top model's salary had enabled her to move from the third-floor walk-up in which she had started her New York life to a comfortable high rise near Central Park.

Modeling was not a passion with Hillary, but a job. She had not come to New York with starry-eyed dreams of fame and glamour, but with a resolution to succeed, to stand on her own. The choice of career had seemed inevitable, since she possessed a natural grace and poise and striking good looks. Her coal black hair and high cheekbones lent her a rather exotic fragility, and large, heavily fringed eyes in deep midnight blue contrasted appealingly with her golden complexion. Her mouth was full and shapely, and smiled beautifully at the slightest provocation. Along with her stunning looks, the fact that she was inherently photogenic added to her current success in her field. The uncanny ability to convey an array of images for the camera came naturally, with little conscious effort on her part. After being told the type of woman she was to portray, Hillary became just that—sophisticated, practical, sensuous—whatever was required.

Letting herself into her apartment, Hillary kicked off her shoes and sank her feet into soft ivory carpet. There was no date to prepare for that evening, and she was looking forward to a light supper and a few quiet hours at home.

Thirty minutes later, wrapped in a warm, flowing azure robe, she stood in the kitchen of her apartment preparing a model's feast of soup and unsalted crackers. A ring of the doorbell interrupted her far-from-gourmet activities.

"Lisa, hi." She greeted her neighbor from across the hall with an automatic smile. "Want some dinner?"

Lisa MacDonald wrinkled her nose in disdain. "I'd rather put up with a few extra pounds than starve myself like you."

"If I indulge myself too often," Hillary stated, patting a flat stomach, "I'd be after you to find me a job in that law firm you work for. By the way, how's the rising young attorney?"

"Mark still doesn't know I'm alive," Lisa complained as she flopped onto the couch. "I'm getting desperate, Hillary. I may lose my head and mug him in the parking lot."

"Tacky, too tacky," Hillary said, giving the matter deep consideration. "Why not attempt something less dramatic, like tripping him when he walks past your desk?"

"That could be next."

With a grin, Hillary sat and lifted bare feet to the surface of the coffee table. "Ever hear of Bret Bardoff?"

Lisa's eyes grew round. "Who hasn't? Millionaire, incredibly handsome, mysterious, brilliant businessman and still fair game." These attributes were counted off carefully on Lisa's fingers. "What about him?"

Slim shoulders moved expressively. "I'm not sure. Larry has an appointment with him in the morning."

"Face to face?"

"That's right." Amusement dawned first, then dark blue eyes regarded Lisa with curiosity. "Of course, we've both done work for his magazines before, but I can't imagine why the elusive owner of *Mode* would want to see a mere photographer, even if he is the best. In the trade, he's spoken of in reverent whispers, and if gossip columns are to be believed, he's the answer to every maiden's prayer. I wonder what he's really like." She frowned, finding herself nearly obsessed with the thought. "It's strange, I don't believe I know anyone who's had a personal dealing with him. I picture him as a giant phantom figure handing out monumental corporate decisions from *Mode*'s Mount Olympus."

"Maybe Larry will fill you in tomorrow," Lisa suggested, and Hillary shook her head, the frown becoming a grin.

"Larry won't notice anything unless Mr. Bardoff's on a roll of film."

Shortly before nine-thirty the following morning, Hillary used her spare key to enter Larry's studio. Prepared for the shampoo ad, her hair fell in soft, thick waves, shining and full. In the small cubicle in the rear she applied her makeup with an expert hand, and at nine forty-five she was impatiently switching on the lights required for indoor shots. As minutes slipped by, she began to entertain the annoying suspicion that Larry had neglected to arrange for a substitute. It was nearly ten when the door to the studio opened, and Hillary immediately pounced on the man who entered.

"It's about time," she began, tempering irritation with a small smile. "You're late."

"Am I?" he countered, meeting her annoyed expression with raised brows.

Pausing a moment, she realized how incredibly handsome the man facing her was. His hair, the color of corn silk, was full and grew just over the collar of his casual polo-necked gray sweater, a gray that exactly matched large, direct eyes. His mouth was quirked in a half smile, and there was something vaguely familiar about his deeply tanned face.

"I haven't worked with you before, have I?" Hillary asked, forced to look up to meet his eyes since he was an inch or more over six feet.

"Why do you ask?" His evasion was smooth, and she felt suddenly uncomfortable under his unblinking gray glance.

"No reason," she murmured, turning away, feeling compelled to adjust the cuff of her sleeve. "Well, let's get to it. Where's your camera?" Belatedly, she observed he carried no equipment. "Are you using Larry's?"

"I suppose I am." He continued to stand staring down at her, making no move to proceed with the task at hand, his nonchalance becoming thoroughly irritating.

"Well, come on then, let's not be all day. I've been ready for half an hour."

"Sorry." He smiled, and she was struck with the change it brought to his already compelling face. It was a carelessly slow smile, full of charm, and the thought passed through her mind that he could use it as a deadly weapon. Pivoting away from him, she struggled to ignore its power. She had a job to do. "What are the pictures for?" he asked her as he examined Larry's cameras.

"Oh, Lord, didn't he tell you?" Turning back to him, she shook her head and smiled fully for the first time. "Larry's a tremendous photographer, but he is the most exasperatingly absentminded man. I don't know how he remembers to get up in the morning." She tugged a lock of raven hair before giving her head a dramatic toss. "Clean, shiny, sexy hair," she explained in the tone of a commercial. "Shampoo's what we're selling today."

"O.K.," he returned simply, and began setting equipment to rights in a thoroughly professional manner that did much to put Hillary's mind at ease. At least he knows his job, she assured herself, for his attitude had made her vaguely uneasy. "Where is Larry, by the way?" The question startled Hillary out of her silent thoughts.

"Didn't he tell you anything? That's just like him." Standing under the lights, she began turning, shaking her head, creating a rich black cloud as he clicked the camera, crouching and moving around her to catch different angles. "He had an appointment with Bret Bardoff," she continued, tossing her hair and smiling. "Lord help him if he forgot that. He'll be eaten alive."

"Does Bret Bardoff consume photographers as a habit?" the voice behind the camera questioned with dry amusement.

"Wouldn't be surprised." Hillary lifted her hair above her head, pausing for a moment before she allowed it to fall back to her shoulders like a rich cloak. "I would think a ruthless businessman like Mr. Bardoff would have little patience with an absentminded photographer or any other imperfection."

"You know him?"

"Lord, no." She laughed with unrestrained pleasure. "And I'm not likely to, far above my station. Have you met him?"

"Not precisely."

"Ah, but we all work for him at one time or another, don't we? I wonder how many times my face has been in one of his magazines. Scillions," she calculated, receiving a raised-brow look from behind the camera. "Scillions," she repeated with a nod. "And I've never met the emperor."

"Emperor?"

"How else does one describe such a lofty individual?" Hillary demanded with a gesture of her hands. "From what I've heard, he runs his mags like an empire."

"You sound as though you disapprove."

"No," Hillary disagreed with a smile and a shrug. "Emperors just make me nervous. I'm plain peasant stock myself."

"Your image seems hardly plain or peasant," he remarked, and this time it was her brow that lifted. "That should sell gallons of shampoo." Lowering his camera, he met her eyes directly. "I think we've got it, Hillary."

She relaxed, pushed back her hair, and regarded him curiously. "You know me? I'm sorry, I can't quite seem to place you. Have we worked together before?"

"Hillary Baxter's face is everywhere. It's my business to recognize beautiful faces." He spoke with careless simplicity, gray eyes smoky with amusement.

"Well, it appears you have the advantage, Mr.—?"

"Bardoff, Bret Bardoff," he answered, and the camera clicked to capture the astonished expression on her face. "You can close your mouth now, Hillary. I think we've got enough." His smile widened as she obeyed without thinking. "Cat got your tongue?" he mocked, pleasure at her embarrassment obvious.

She recognized him now, from pictures she had seen of him in newspapers and his own magazines, and she was busily engaged in cursing herself for the stupidity she had just displayed. Anger with herself spread to encompass the man in front of her, and she located her voice.

"You let me babble on like that," she sputtered, eyes and cheeks bright with color. "You stood there taking pictures you had no business taking and just let me carry on like an idiot."

"I was merely following orders." His grave tone and sober expression added to her mounting embarrassment and fury.

"Well, you had no right following them. You should have told me who you were." Her voice quavered with indignation, but he merely moved his shoulders and smiled again.

"You never asked."

Before she could retort, the door of the studio opened and Larry entered, looking harassed and confused. "Mr. Bardoff," he began, advancing on the pair standing under the lights. "I'm sorry. I thought I was to meet you at your office." Larry ran a hand through his hair in agitation. "When I got there, I was told you were coming here. I don't know how I got it so confused. Sorry you had to wait."

"Don't worry about it," Bret assured him with an easy smile, "The last hour's been highly entertaining."

"Hillary." Her existence suddenly seeped into Larry's consciousness. "Good Lord, I knew I forgot something. We'll have to get those pictures later."

"No need." Bret handed Larry the camera. "Hillary and I have seen to them."

"You took the shots?" Larry looked at Bret and the camera in turn.

"Hillary saw no reason to waste time." He smiled and added, "I'm sure you'll find the pictures suitable."

"No question of that, Mr. Bardoff." His voice was tinged with reverence. "I know what you can do with a camera."

Hillary had an overwhelming desire for the floor to open up and swallow her. She had to get out of there quickly. Never before in her life had she felt such a fool. Of course, she reasoned silently, it was his fault. The nerve of the man, letting her believe he was a photographer! She recalled the fashion in which she had ordered him to begin, and the things she had said. She closed her eyes with an inward moan. All she wanted to do now was disappear, and with luck she would never have to come face to face with Bret Bardoff again.

She began gathering her things quickly. "I'll leave you to get on with your business. I have another session across town." Slinging her purse over her shoulder, she took a deep breath. "Bye, Larry. Nice to have met you, Mr. Bardoff." She attempted to brush by them, but Bret put out his hand and captured hers, preventing her exit.

"Goodbye, Hillary." She forced her eyes to meet his,

feeling a sudden drain of power by the contact of her hand in his. "It's been a most interesting morning. We'll have to do it again soon."

When hell freezes over, her eyes told him silently, and muttering something incoherent, she dashed for the door, the sound of his laughter echoing in her ears.

Dressing for a date that evening, Hillary endeavored, without success, to block the events of the morning from her mind. She was confident that her path would never cross Bret Bardoff's again. After all, she comforted herself, it had only been through a stupid accident that they had met in the first place. Hillary prayed that the adage about lightning never striking twice would hold true. She had indeed been hit by a lightning bolt when he had casually disclosed his name to her, and her cheeks burned again, matching the color of her soft jersey dress as her careless words played back in her mind.

The ringing of the phone interrupted her reflections, and she answered, finding Larry on the other end. "Hillary, boy, I'm glad I caught you at home." His excitement was tangible over the wire, and she answered him quickly.

"You just did catch me. I'm practically out the door. What's up?"

"I can't go into details now. Bret's going to do that in the morning."

She noted the fact that *Mr. Bardoff* had been discarded since that morning and spoke wearily. "Larry, what are you talking about?"

"Bret will explain everything in the morning. You have an appointment at nine o'clock."

"What?" Her voice rose and she found it imperative to swallow twice. "Larry, what are you talking about?"

"It's a tremendous opportunity for both of us, Hil. Bret will tell you tomorrow. You know where his office is." This was a statement rather than a question, since everyone in the business knew *Mode*'s headquarters.

"I don't want to see him," Hillary argued, feeling a surge of panic at the thought of those steel gray eyes. "I don't know what he told you about this morning, but I made a total fool of myself. I thought he was a photographer. Really," she continued, with fresh annoyance, "you're partially to blame, if—"

"Don't worry about all that now," Larry interrupted confidently. "It doesn't matter. Just be there at nine tomorrow. See you later."

"But, Larry." She stopped, there was no purpose in arguing with a dead phone. Larry had hung up.

This was too much, she thought in despair, and sat down heavily on the bed. How could Larry expect her to go through with this? How could she possibly face that man after the things she had said? Humiliation, she decided, was simply something for which she was not suited. Rising from the bed, she squared her shoulders. Bret Bardoff probably wanted another opportunity to laugh at her for her stupidity. Well, he wasn't going to get the best of Hillary Baxter, she told herself with firm pride. She'd face him without cringing. This peasant would stand up to the emperor and show him what she was made of!

Hillary dressed for her appointment the next morning with studious care. The white, light wool cowl-necked dress was beautiful in its simplicity, relying on the form it covered to make it eye-catching. She arranged her hair in a loose bun on top of her head in order to add a businesslike air to her appearance. Bret Bardoff would not find her stammering and blushing this morning, she determined, but cool and confident. Slipping on soft leather shoes, she was satisfied with the total effect, the heels adding to her height. She would not be forced to look up quite so high in order to meet those gray eyes, and she would meet them straight on.

Confidence remained with her through the taxi ride and all the way to the top of the building where Bret Bardoff had his offices. Glancing at her watch on the elevator, she was pleased to see she was punctual. An attractive brunette was seated at an enormous reception desk, and Hillary stated her name and business. After a brief conversation on a phone that held a prominent position on the large desk, the woman ushered Hillary down a long corridor and through a heavy oak door.

She entered a large, well-decorated room where she was greeted by yet another attractive woman, who introduced herself as June Miles, Mr. Bardoff's secretary. "Please go right in, Miss Baxter. Mr. Bardoff is expecting you," she informed Hillary with a smile.

Walking to a set of double doors, Hillary's eyes barely had time to take in the room with its rather fabulous decor before her gaze was arrested by the man seated at a huge oak desk, a panoramic view of the city at his back.

"Good morning, Hillary." He rose and approached her. "Are you going to come in or stand there all day with your back to the door?"

Hillary's spine straightened and she answered coolly. "Good morning, Mr. Bardoff, it's nice to see you again."

"Don't be a hypocrite," he stated mildly as he led her to a seat near the desk. "You'd be a great deal happier if you never laid eyes on me again." Hillary could find no comment to this all-too-true observation, and contented herself with smiling vaguely into space.

"However," he continued, as if she had agreed with him in words, "it suits my purposes to have you here today in spite of your reluctance."

"And what are your purposes, Mr. Bardoff?" she demanded, her annoyance with his arrogance sharpening her tone.

He leaned back in his chair and allowed his cool gray eyes to travel deliberately over Hillary from head to toe. The survey was slow and obviously intended to disconcert, but she remained outwardly unruffled. Because of her profession, her face and form had been studied before. She was determined not to let this man know his stare was causing her pulses to dance a nervous rhythm.

"My purposes, Hillary"—his eyes met hers and held—"are for the moment strictly business, though that is subject to change at any time."

This remark cracked Hillary's cool veneer enough to

bring a slight blush to her cheeks. She cursed the color as she struggled to keep her eyes level with his.

"Good Lord." His brows lifted with humor. "You're blushing. I didn't think women did that anymore." His grin widened as if he were enjoying the fact that more color leaped to her cheeks at his words. "You're probably the last of a dying breed."

"Could we discuss the business for which I'm here, Mr. Bardoff?" she inquired. "I'm sure you're a very busy man, and believe it or not, I'm busy myself."

"Of course," Bret agreed. He grinned reflectively. "I remember—*'Let's not waste time.'* I'm planning a layout for *Mode,* a rather special layout." He lit a cigarette and offered Hillary one, which she declined with a shake of her head. "I've had the idea milling around in my mind for some time, but I needed the right photographer and the right woman." His eyes narrowed as he peered at her speculatively, giving Hillary the sensation of being viewed under a microscope. "I've found them both now."

She squirmed under his unblinking stare. "Suppose you give me some details, Mr. Bardoff. I'm sure it's not usual procedure for you to interview models personally. This must be something special."

"Yes, I think so," he agreed suavely. "The idea is a layout—a picture story, if you like—on the Many Faces of Woman." He stood then and perched on the corner of the desk, and Hillary was affected by his sheer masculinity, the power and strength that exuded from his lean form clad in a fawn-colored business suit. "I want to portray all the facets of womanhood: career woman, mother, athlete, sophisticate, innocent, temptress, et cetera—a complete portrait of Eve, the Eternal Woman."

"Sounds fascinating," Hillary admitted, caught up in the backlash of his enthusiasm. "You think I might be suitable for some of the pictures?"

"I know you're suitable," he stated flatly, "for *all* of the pictures."

Finely etched brows raised in curiosity. "You're going to use one model for the entire layout?"

"I'm going to use *you* for the entire layout."

Struggling with annoyance and the feeling of being submerged by very deep water, Hillary spoke honestly. "I'd be an idiot not to be interested in a project like this. I don't think I'm an idiot. But why me?"

"Come now, Hillary." His voice mirrored impatience, and he bent over to capture her surprised chin in his hand. "You do own a mirror. Surely you're intelligent enough to know that you're quite beautiful and extremely photogenic."

He was speaking of her as if she were an inanimate object rather than a human being, and the fingers, strong and lean on her chin, were very distressing. Nevertheless, Hillary persisted.

"There are scores of beautiful and photogenic models in New York alone, Mr. Bardoff. You know that better than anyone. I'd like to know why you're considering me for your pet project."

"Not considering." He rose and thrust his hands in his pockets, and she observed he was becoming irritated. She found the knowledge rewarding. "There's no one else I would consider. You have a rather uncanny knack for getting to the heart of a picture and coming across with exactly the right image. I need versatility as well as beauty. I need honesty in a dozen different images."

"In your opinion, I can do that."

"You wouldn't be here if I weren't sure. I never make rash decisions."

No, Hillary mused, looking into his cool gray eyes, you calculate every minute detail. Aloud, she asked, "Larry would be the photographer?"

He nodded. "There's an affinity between the two of

you that is obvious in the pictures you produce. You're both superior alone, but together you've done some rather stunning work."

His praise caused her smile to warm slightly. "Thank you."

"That wasn't a compliment, Hillary—just a fact. I've given Larry all the details. The contracts are waiting for your signature."

"Contracts?" she repeated, becoming wary.

"That's right," he returned, overlooking her hesitation. "This project is going to take some time. I've no intention of rushing through it. I want exclusive rights to that beautiful face of yours until the project's completed and on the stands."

"I see." She digested this carefully, unconsciously chewing on her bottom lip.

"You needn't react as if I've made an indecent proposal, Hillary." His voice was dry as he regarded her frowning concentration. "This is a business arrangement."

Her chin tilted in defiance. "I understand that completely, Mr. Bardoff. It's simply that I've never signed a long-term contract before."

"I have no intention of allowing you to get away. Contracts are obligatory, for you and for Larry. For the next few months I don't want you distracted by any other jobs. Financially, you'll be well compensated. If you have any complaints along those lines, we'll negotiate. However, my rights to that face of yours for the next six months are exclusive."

He lapsed into silence, watching the varied range of expressions on her face. She was working out the entire platform carefully, doing her best not to be intimidated by his overwhelming power. The project appealed to her, although the man did not. It would be fascinating work, but she found it difficult to tie herself to one establishment for any period of time. She could not help feeling that signing her name was signing away liberation. A long-term contract equaled a long-term commitment.

Finally, throwing caution to the winds, she gave Bret one of the smiles that made her face known throughout America.

"You've got yourself a face."

Chapter 2

Bret Bardoff moved quickly. Within two weeks contracts had been signed, and the shooting schedule had been set to begin on a morning in early October. The first image to be portrayed was one of youthful innocence and unspoiled simplicity.

Hillary met Larry in a small park selected by Bret. Though the morning was bright and brisk, the sun filtering warm through the trees, the park was all but deserted. She wondered a moment if the autocratic Mr. Bardoff had arranged the isolation. Blue jeans rolled to mid-calf and a long-sleeved turtleneck in scarlet were

Hillary's designated costume. She had bound her shining hair in braids, tied them with red ribbons, and had kept her makeup light, relying on natural, healthy skin. She was the essence of honest, vibrant youth, dark blue eyes bright with the anticipation.

"Perfect," Larry commented as she ran across the grass to meet him. "Young and innocent. How do you manage it?"

She wrinkled her nose. "I am young and innocent, old man."

"O.K. See that?" He pointed to a swing set complete with bars and a slide. "Go play, little girl, and let this old man take some pictures."

She ran for the swing, giving herself over to the freedom of movement. Stretching out full length, she leaned her head to the ground and smiled at the brilliant sky. Climbing on the slide, she lifted her arms wide, let out a whoop of uninhibited joy, and slid down, landing on her bottom in the soft dirt. Larry clicked his camera from varying angles, allowing her to direct the mood.

"You look twelve years old." His laugh was muffled, his face still concealed behind the camera.

"I am twelve years old," Hillary proclaimed, scurrying onto the crossbars. "Betcha can't do this." She hung up by her knees on the bar, her pigtails brushing the ground.

"Amazing." The answer did not come from Larry, and she turned her head and looked directly into a pair of well-tailored gray slacks. Her eyes roamed slowly upward to the matching jacket and further to a full, smiling mouth and mocking gray eyes. "Hello, child, does your mother know where you are?"

"What are you doing here?" Hillary demanded, feeling at a decided disadvantage in her upside-down position.

"Supervising my pet project." He continued to regard her, his grin growing wider. "How long do you intend to hang there? The blood must be rushing to your head."

Grabbing the bar with her hands, she swung her legs over in a neat somersault and stood facing him. He patted her head, told her she was a good girl, and turned his attention to Larry.

"How'd it go? Looked to me as if you got some good shots."

The two men discussed the technicalities of the morning's shooting while Hillary sat back down on the swing, moving gently back and forth. She had met with Bret a handful of times during the past two weeks, and each time she had been unaccountably uneasy in his presence. He was a vital and disturbing individual, full of raw, masculine power, and she was not at all sure she wanted to be closely associated with him. Her life was well ordered now, running smoothly along the lines she designated, and she wanted no complications. There was something about this man, however, that spelled complications in capital letters.

"All right." Bret's voice broke into her musings. "Setup at the club at one o'clock. Everything's been arranged." Hillary rose from the swing and moved to join Larry. "No need for you to go now, little girl— you've an hour or so to spare."

"I don't want to play on the swings anymore, Daddy," she retorted, bristling at his tone. Picking up her shoulder bag, she managed to take two steps before he reached out and took command of her wrist. She rounded on him, blue eyes blazing.

"Spoiled little brat, aren't you?" he murmured in a mild tone, but his eyes narrowed and met the dark blue blaze with cold gray steel. "Perhaps I should turn you over my knee."

"That would be more difficult than you think, Mr. Bardoff," she returned with unsurpassable dignity. "I'm twenty-four, not twelve, and really quite strong."

"Are you now?" He inspected her slim form dubiously. "I suppose it's possible." He spoke soberly, but she recognized the mockery in his eyes. "Come on, I want some coffee." His hand slipped from her wrist, and his fingers interlocked with hers. She jerked away, surprised and disconcerted by the warmth. "Hillary," he began in a tone of strained patience. "I would like to buy you coffee." It was more a command than a request.

He moved across the grass with long, easy strides, dragging an unwilling Hillary after him. Larry watched their progress and automatically took their picture. They made an interesting study, he decided, the tall blond man in the expensive business suit pulling the slim, dark woman-child behind him.

As she sat across from Bret in a small coffee shop, Hillary's face was flushed with a mixture of indignation and the exertion of keeping up with the brisk pace he had set. He took in her pink cheeks and bright eyes, and his mouth lifted at one corner.

"Maybe I should buy a dish of ice cream to cool you off." The waitress appeared then, saving Hillary from formulating a retort, and Bret ordered two coffees.

"Tea," Hillary stated flatly, pleased to contradict him on some level.

"I beg your pardon?" he returned coolly.

"I'll have tea, if you don't mind. I don't drink coffee; it makes me nervous."

"One coffee and one tea," he amended before he turned back to her. "How do you wake up in the morning without the inevitable cup of coffee?"

"Clean living." She flicked a pigtail over her shoulder and folded her hands.

"You certainly look like an ad for clean living now." Sitting back, he took out his cigarette case, offering her one and lighting one before going on. "I'm afraid you'd never pass for twenty-four in pigtails. It's not often one sees hair that true black—certainly not with eyes that color." He stared into them for a long moment. "They're fabulous, so dark at times they're nearly purple, quite dramatic, and the bone structure, it's rather elegant and exotic. Tell me," he asked suddenly, "where did you get that marvelous face of yours?"

Hillary had thought herself long immune to comments and compliments on her looks, but somehow his words nonplussed her, and she was grateful that the waitress returned with their drinks, giving her time to gather scattered wits.

"I'm told I'm a throwback to my great-grandmother."

She spoke with detached interest as she sipped tea. "She was an Arapaho. It appears I resemble her quite strongly."

"I should have guessed." He nodded his head continuing his intense study. "The cheekbones, the classic bone structure. Yes, I can see your Indian heritage, but the eyes are deceiving. You didn't acquire eyes like cobalt from your great-grandmother."

"No." She struggled to meet his penetrating gaze coolly. "They belong to me."

"To you," he acknowledged with a nod, "and for the next six months to me. I believe I'll enjoy the joint ownership." The focus of his study shifted to the mouth that moved in a frown at his words. "Where are you from, Hillary Baxter? You're no native."

"That obvious? I thought I had acquired a marvelous New York varnish." She gave a wry shrug, grateful that the intensity of his examination appeared to be over. "Kansas—a farm some miles north of Abilene."

He inclined his head, and his brows lifted as he raised his cup. "You appear to have made the transition from wheat to concrete very smoothly. No battle scars?"

"A few, but they're healed over." She added quickly, "I hardly have to point out New York's advantages to you, especially in the area of my career."

His agreement was a slow nod. "It's very easy to picture you as a Kansas farm girl or a sophisticated New York model. You have a remarkable ability to suit your surroundings."

Hillary's full mouth moved in a doubtful pout. "That makes me sound like I'm no person on my own, sort of…inconspicuous."

"Inconspicuous?" Bret's laughter caused several heads to turn, and Hillary stared at him in dumb amazement. "Inconspicuous," he said again, shaking his head as if she had just uttered something sublimely ridiculous. "What a beautiful statement. No, I think you're a very complex woman with a remarkable affinity with her surroundings. I don't believe it's an acquired talent, but an intrinsic ability."

His words pleased Hillary out of all proportion, and she made an issue of stirring her tea, giving it her undivided attention. Why should a simple, impersonal compliment wrap around my tongue like a twenty-pound chain? she wondered, careful to keep a frown from forming. I don't think I care for the way he always manages to shift my balance.

"You do play tennis, don't you?"

Again, his rapid altering of the conversation threw her

into confusion, and she stared at him without comprehension until she recalled the afternoon session was on the tennis court of an exclusive country club.

"I manage to hit the ball over the net once in a while." Annoyed by his somewhat condescending tone, she answered with uncharacteristic meekness.

"Good. The shots will be more impressive if you have the stance and moves down properly." He glanced at the gold watch on his wrist and drew out his wallet. "I've got some things to clear up at the office." Standing, he drew her from the booth, again holding her hand in his oddly familiar manner, ignoring her efforts to withdraw from his grip. "I'll put you in a cab. It'll take you some time to change from little girl to female athlete." He looked down at her, making her feel unaccustomedly small at five foot seven in her sneakers. "Your tennis outfit's already at the club, and I assume you have all the tricks of your trade in that undersized suitcase?" He indicated the large shoulder bag she heaved over her arm.

"Don't worry, Mr. Bardoff."

"Bret," he interrupted, suddenly engrossed with running his hand down her left pigtail. "I don't intend to stop using your first name."

"Don't worry," she began again, evading his invitation. "Changing images is my profession."

"It should prove interesting," he murmured, tugging the braid he held. Then, shifting to a more professional tone he said, "The court is reserved for one. I'll see you then."

"You're going to be there?" Her question was accompanied by a frown as she found herself undeniably distressed at the prospect of dealing with him yet again.

"My pet project, remember?" He nudged her into a cab, either unaware of or unconcerned by her scowl. "I intend to supervise it very carefully."

As the cab merged with traffic, Hillary's emotions were in turmoil. Bret Bardoff was an incredibly attractive and distracting man, and there was something about him that disturbed her. The idea of being in almost daily contact with him made her decidedly uneasy.

I don't like him, she decided with a firm nod. He's too self-assured, too arrogant, too... Her mind searched for a word. *Physical.* Yes, she admitted, albeit unwillingly, he was a very sexual man, and he unnerved her. She had no desire to be disturbed. There was something about the way he looked at her, something about the way her body reacted whenever she came into contact with him.

Shrugging, she stared out the window at passing cars. She wouldn't think of him. Rather, she corrected, she would think of him only as her employer, and a temporary one at that—not as an individual. Her hand still felt warm from his, and glancing down at it, she sighed. It was imperative to her peace of mind that she do her job and avoid any more personal dealings with him. Strictly business, she reminded herself. Yes, their relationship would be strictly business.

The tomboy had been transformed into the fashionable tennis buff. A short white tennis dress accented Hillary's long, slender legs and left arms bare. She covered them, as she waited on the court, with a light jacket, since the October afternoon was pleasant but cool. Her hair was tied away from her face with a dark blue scarf, leaving her delicate features unframed. Color had been added to her eyes, accenting them with sooty fringes, and her lips were tinted deep rose. Spotless white tennis shoes completed her outfit, and she held a lightweight racket in her hands. The pure white of the ensemble contrasted well with her golden skin and raven hair, and she appeared wholly feminine as well as capable.

Behind the net, she experimented with stances, swinging the racket and serving the balls to a nonexistent partner while Larry roamed around her, checking angles and meters.

"I think you might have better luck if someone hit back."

She spun around to see Bret watching her with an amused gleam in his eyes. He too was in white, the jacket of his warm-up suit pushed to the elbows. Hillary, used to seeing him in a business suit, was surprised at the athletic appearance of his body, whipcord lean, his shoulders broad, his arms hard and muscular, his masculinity entirely too prevalent.

"Do I pass?" he asked with a half smile, and she flushed, suddenly aware that she had been staring.

"I'm just surprised to see you dressed that way," she muttered, shrugging her shoulders and turning away.

"More suitable for tennis, don't you think?"

"We're going to play?" She spun back to face him, scowling at the racket in his hand.

"I rather like the idea of action…shots," he finished with a grin. "I won't be too hard on you. I'll hit some nice and easy."

With a good deal of willpower, she managed not to stick out her tongue. She played tennis often and well.

Hillary decided, with inner complacency, that Mr. Bret Bardoff was in for a surprise.

"I'll try to hit a few back," she promised, her face as ingenuous as a child. "To give the shots realism."

"Good." He strode over to the other side of the court, and Hillary picked up a ball. "Can you serve?"

"I'll do my best," she answered, coating honey on her tongue. After glancing at Larry to see if he was ready, she tossed the ball idly in the air. The camera had already replaced Larry's face, and Hillary moved behind the fault line, tossed the ball once more, connected with the racket, and smashed a serve. Bret returned her serve gently, and she hit back, aiming deep in the opposite corner.

"I think I remember how to score," she called out with a thoughtful frown. "Fifteen-love, Mr. Bardoff."

"Nice return, Hillary. Do you play often?"

"Oh, now and again," she evaded, brushing invisible lint from her skirt. "Ready?"

He nodded, and the ball bounced back and forth in an easy, powerless volley. She realized with some smugness that he was holding back, making it a simple matter for her to make the return for the benefit of Larry's rapidly snapping camera. But she too was holding back, hitting the ball lightly and without any style. She allowed a few more laconic lobs, then slammed the ball away from him, deep in the back court.

"Oh." She lifted a finger to her lips, feigning innocence. "That's thirty-love, isn't it?"

Bret's eyes narrowed as he approached the net. "Why do I have this strange feeling that I'm being conned?"

"Conned?" she repeated, wide-eyed, allowing her lashes to flutter briefly. He searched her face until her lips trembled with laughter. "Sorry, Mr. Bardoff, I couldn't resist." She tossed her head and grinned. "You were so patronizing."

"O.K." He returned her grin somewhat to Hillary's relief. "No more patronizing. Now I'm out for blood."

"We'll start from scratch," she offered, returning to the serving line. "I wouldn't want you to claim I had an unfair advantage."

He returned her serve with force, and they kept each other moving rapidly over the court in the ensuing volley. They battled for points, reaching deuce and exchanging advantage several times. The camera was forgotten in the focus of concentration, the soft click of the shutter masked by the swish of rackets and thump of balls.

Cursing under her breath at the failure to return a

ball cleanly, Hillary stooped to pick up another and prepared to serve.

"That was great." Larry's voice broke her concentration, and she turned to gape at him. "I got some fantastic shots. You look like a real pro, Hil. We can wrap it up now."

"Wrap it up?" She stared at him with incredulous exasperation. "Have you lost your mind? We're at deuce." She continued to regard him a moment as if his brain had gone on holiday, and shaking her head and muttering, she resumed play.

For the next few minutes, they fought for the lead until Bret once more held the advantage and once more placed the ball down the line to her backhand.

Hillary put her hands on her hips and let out a deep breath after the ball had sailed swiftly past her. "Ah, well, the agony of defeat." She smiled, attempted to catch her wind, and approached the net. "Congratulations." She offered both hand and smile. "You play a very demanding game."

He accepted her hand, holding it rather than shaking it. "You certainly made me earn it, Hillary. I believe I'd like to try my luck at doubles, with you on my side of the net."

"I suppose you could do worse."

He held her gaze a moment before his eyes dropped

to the hand still captive in his. "Such a small hand." He
lifted it higher and examined it thoroughly. "I'm astonished it can swing a racket like that." He turned it palm
up and carried it to his lips.

Odd and unfamiliar tingles ran up her spine at his kiss,
and she stared mesmerized at her hand, unable to speak
or draw away. "Come on." He smiled into bemused
eyes, annoyingly aware of her reaction. "I'll buy you
lunch." His gaze slid past her. "You too, Larry."

"Thanks, Bret." He was already gathering his equipment. "But I want to get back and develop this film. I'll
just grab a sandwich."

"Well, Hillary." He turned and commanded her attention. "It's just you and me."

"Really, Mr. Bardoff," she began, feeling near to panic
at the prospect of having lunch with him and wishing
with all her heart that he would respond to the effort she
was currently making to regain sole possession of her
hand. "It's not necessary for you to buy me lunch."

"Hillary, Hillary." He sighed, shaking his head. "Do
you always find it difficult to accept an invitation, or is
it only with me?"

"Don't be ridiculous." She attempted to maintain a
casual tone while she became more and more troubled

by the warmth of his hand over hers. She stared down at the joined hands, feeling increasingly helpless as the contact continued. "Mr. Bardoff, may I please have my hand back?" Her voice was breathless, and she bit her lip in vexation.

"Try Bret, Hillary," he commanded, ignoring her request. "It's easy enough, only one syllable. Go ahead."

The eyes that held hers were calm, demanding, and arrogant enough to remain steady for the next hour. The longer her hand remained in his, the more peculiar she felt, and knowing that the sooner she agreed, the sooner she would be free, she surrendered.

"Bret, may I please have my hand back?"

"There, now, we've cleared the first hurdle. That didn't hurt much, did it?" The corner of his mouth lifted as he released her, and immediately the vague weakness began to dissipate, leaving her more secure.

"Nearly painless."

"Now about lunch." He held up his hand to halt her protest. "You do eat, don't you?"

"Of course, but—"

"No buts. I rarely listen to buts or nos."

In short order Hillary found herself seated across from Bret at a small table inside the club. Things were not going as she had planned. It was very difficult to maintain a businesslike and impersonal relationship when she was so often in his company. It was useless to deny that she found him interesting, his vitality stimulating, and he was a tremendously attractive man. But, she admonished herself, he certainly wasn't her type. Besides, she didn't have time for entanglements at this point of her life. Still, the warning signals in her brain told her to tread carefully, that this man was capable of upsetting her neatly ordered plans.

"Has anyone ever told you what a fascinating conversationalist you are?" Hillary's eyes shot up to find Bret's mocking gaze on her.

"Sorry." Color crept into her face. "My mind was wandering."

"So I noticed. What will you have to drink?"

"Tea."

"Straight?" he inquired, his smile hovering.

"Straight," she agreed, and ordered herself to relax. "I don't drink much. I'm afraid I don't handle it well. More than two and I turn into Mr. Hyde. Metabolism."

Bret threw back his head and laughed with the appearance of boundless pleasure. "That's a transformation I would give much to witness. We'll have to arrange it."

Lunch, to Hillary's surprise, was an enjoyable meal, though Bret met her choice of salad with open disgust and pure masculine disdain. She assured him it was adequate, and made a passing comment on the brevity of overweight models' careers.

Fully relaxed, Hillary enjoyed herself, the resolution to keep a professional distance between herself and Bret forgotten. As they ate, he spoke of the next day's shooting plans. Central Park had been designated for more outdoor scenes in keeping with the outdoor, athletic image.

"I've meetings all day tomorrow and won't be able to supervise. How do you exist on that stuff?" He changed the trend of conversation abruptly, waving a superior finger at Hillary's salad. "Don't you want some food? You're going to fade away."

She shook her head, smiling as she sipped her tea, and he muttered under his breath about half-starved models before resuming his previous conversation. "If all goes according to schedule, we'll start the next segment Monday. Larry wants to get an early start tomorrow."

"Always," she agreed with a sigh. "If the weather holds."

"Oh, the sun will shine." She heard the absolute confidence in his voice. "I've arranged it."

Sitting back, she surveyed the man across from her

with uninhibited curiosity. "Yes." She nodded at length, noting the firm jaw and direct eyes. "I believe you could. It wouldn't dare rain."

They smiled at each other, and as the look held, she experienced a strange, unfamiliar sensation running through her—something swift, vital, and anonymous.

"Some dessert?"

"You're determined to fatten me up, aren't you?" Grateful that his casual words had eliminated the strange emotion, she summoned up an easy smile. "You're a bad influence, but I have a will of iron."

"Cheese cake, apple pie, chocolate mousse?" His smile was wicked, but she tossed her head and lifted her chin.

"Do your worst. I don't break."

"You're bound to have a weakness. A little time, and I'll find it."

"Bret, darling, what a surprise to see you here." Hillary turned and looked up at the woman greeting Bret with such enthusiasm.

"Hello, Charlene." He granted the shapely, elegantly dressed redhead a charming smile. "Charlene Mason, Hillary Baxter."

"Miss Baxter." Charlene nodded in curt greeting, and green eyes narrowed. "Have we met before?"

"I don't believe so," Hillary returned, wondering why she felt a surge of gratitude at the fact.

"Hillary's face is splashed over magazines covers everywhere," Bret explained. "She's one of New York's finest models."

"Of course." Hillary watched the green eyes narrow further, survey her, and dismiss her as inferior merchandise. "Bret, you should have told me you'd be here today. We could have had some time."

"Sorry," he answered with a casual move of his shoulders. "I won't be here long, and it was business."

Ridiculously deflated by his statement, Hillary immediately forced her spine to straighten. Didn't I tell you not to get involved? she reminded herself. He's quite right, this was a business lunch. She gathered her things and stood.

"Please, Miss Mason, have my seat. I was just going." She turned to Bret, pleased to observe his annoyance at her hasty departure. "Thanks for lunch, Mr. Bardoff," she added politely, flashing a smile at the frown that appeared at her use of his surname. "Nice to have met you, Miss Mason." Giving the woman occupying the seat she had just vacated a professional smile, Hillary walked away.

"I didn't realized taking employees to lunch was part

of your routine, Bret." Charlene's voice carried to Hillary as she made her exit. Her first instinct was to whirl around and inform the woman to mind her own business, but grasping for control, she continued to move away without hearing Bret's reply.

The following day's session was more arduous. Using the brilliant fall color in Central Park for a backdrop, Larry's ideas for pictures were varied and energetic. It was a bright, cloudless day, as Bret had predicted, one of the final, golden days of Indian summer. Gold, russet, and scarlet dripped from the branches and covered the ground. Against the varied fall hues, Hillary posed, jogged, threw Frisbees, smiled, climbed trees, fed pigeons, and made three costume changes as the day wore on. Several times during the long session she caught herself looking for Bret, although she knew he was not expected. Her disappointment at his absence both surprised and displeased her, and she reminded herself that life would run much more smoothly if she had never laid eyes on a certain tall, lean man.

"Lighten up, Hil. Quit scowling." Larry's command broke into her musings. Resolutely, she shoved Bret Bardoff from her mind and concentrated on her job.

That evening she sank her tired body into a warm tub, sighing as the scented water worked its gentle magic on aching muscles. Oh, Larry, she thought wearily, with a camera in your hands you become Simon Legree. What you put me through today. I know I've been snapped from every conceivable angle, with every conceivable expression, in every conceivable pose. Thank heavens I'm through until Monday.

This layout was a big assignment, she realized, and there would be many more days like this one. The project could be a big boost to her career. A large layout in a magazine of *Mode*'s reputation and quality would bring her face to international recognition, and with Bret's backing she would more than likely be on her way to becoming one of the country's top models.

A frown appeared from nowhere. Why doesn't that please me? The prospect of being successful in my profession has always been something I wanted. Bret's face entered her mind, and she shook her head in fierce rejection.

"Oh, no you don't," she told his image. "You're not going to get inside my head and confuse my plans. You're the emperor, and I'm your lowly subject. Let's keep it that way."

* * *

Hillary was seated with Chuck Carlyle in one of New York's most popular discos. Music filled every corner, infusing the air with its vibrancy, while lighting effects played everchanging colors over the dancers. As the music washed over them, Hillary reflected on her reasoning for keeping her relationship with Chuck platonic.

It wasn't as though she didn't enjoy male companionship, she told herself. It wasn't as though she didn't enjoy a man's embrace or his kisses. A pair of mocking gray eyes crept into her mind unbidden, and she scowled fiercely into her drink.

If she shied away from more intimate relationships, it was only because no one had touched her deeply enough or stirred her emotions to a point where she felt any desire to engage in a long-term or even a short-term affair. Love, she mused, had so far eluded her, and she silently asserted that she was grateful. With love came commitments, and commitments did not fit into her plans for the immediate future. No, an involvement with a man would bring complications, interfere with her well-ordered life.

"It's always a pleasure to take you out, Hillary." Thoughts broken, she glanced over to see Chuck grin and look pointedly down at the drink she had been nursing ever since their arrival. "You're so easy on my paycheck."

She returned his grin and pushed soul-searching aside. "You could look far and wide and never find another woman so concerned about your financial welfare."

"Too true." He sighed and adopted a look of great sadness. "They're either after my body or my money, and you, sweet Hillary, are after neither." He grabbed both of her hands and covered them with kisses. "If only you'd marry me, love of my life, and let me take you away from all this decadence." His hand swept over the dance floor. "We'll find a vine-covered cottage, two-point-seven kids, and settle down."

"Do you know," Hillary said slowly, "if I said yes, you'd faint dead away?"

"When you're right, you're right." He sighed again. "So instead of sweeping you off your feet to a vine-covered cottage, I'll drag you back to the decadence."

Admiring eyes focused on the tall, slim woman with the dress as blue as her eyes. Hillary's skirt was slit high to reveal long, shapely legs as she turned and spun with the dark man in his cream-colored suit. Both dancers possessed a natural grace and affinity with the music, and they looked spectacular on the dance floor. They ended the dance with Chuck lowering Hillary into a deep, dramatic dip, and when she stood again, she was laughing and flushed with the excitement of the dance. They wove their way back to their table, Chuck's arm around her shoulders, and Hillary's laughter died as she found herself confronted with the gray eyes that had disturbed her a short time before.

"Hello, Hillary." Bret's greeting was casual, and she was grateful for the lighting system, which disguised her change of color.

"Hello, Mr. Bardoff," she returned, wondering why her stomach had begun to flutter at the sight of him.

"You met Charlene, I believe."

Her eyes shifted to the redhead at his side. "Of course, nice to see you again." Hillary turned to her partner and made quick introductions. Chuck pumped Bret's hand with great enthusiasm.

"Bret Bardoff? *The* Bret Bardoff?" Hillary cringed at the undisguised awe and admiration.

"The only one I know," he answered with an easy smile.

"Please"—Chuck indicated their table—"join us for a drink."

Bret's smile widened as he inclined his head to

Hillary, laughter lighting his eyes as she struggled to cover her discomfort.

"Yes, please do." She met his eyes directly, and her voice was scrupulously polite. She was determined to win the silent battle with the strange, uncommon emotions his mere presence caused. Flicking a quick glance at his companion, her discomfort changed to amusement as she observed Charlene Mason was no more pleased to share their company than she was. Or perhaps, Hillary thought idly as they slid behind the table, she was not pleased with sharing Bret with anyone, however briefly.

"A very impressive show the two of you put on out there," Bret commented to Chuck, indicating the dance floor with a nod of his head. His gaze roamed over to include Hillary. "You two must dance often to move so well together."

"There's no better partner than Hillary," Chuck declared magnanimously, and patted her hand with friendly affection. "She can dance with anyone."

"Is that so?" Bret's brows lifted. "Perhaps you'll let me borrow her for a moment and see for myself."

An unreasonable panic filled Hillary at the thought of dancing with him and it was reflected in her expressive eyes.

She rose with a feeling of helpless indignation as Bret came behind her and pulled out her chair without waiting for her assent.

"Stop looking like such a martyr," he whispered in her ear as they approached the other dancers.

"Don't be absurd," she stated with admirable dignity, furious that he could read her so effortlessly.

The music had slowed, and he turned her to face him, gathering her into his arms. At the contact, an overpowering childish urge to pull away assailed her, and she struggled to prevent the tension from becoming noticeable. His chest was hard, his basic masculinity overwhelming, and she refused to allow herself the relief of swallowing in nervous agitation. The arm around her waist held her achingly close, so close their bodies seemed to melt together as he moved her around the floor. She had unconsciously shifted to her toes, and her cheek rested against his, the scent of him assaulting her senses, making her wonder if she had perhaps sipped her drink too quickly. Her heart was pounding erratically against his, and she fought to control the leaping of her pulses as she matched her steps to his.

"I should have known you were a dancer," he murmured against her ear, causing a fresh flutter of her heartbeat.

"Really," she countered, battling to keep her tone careless and light, attempting to ignore the surge of excitement of his mouth on the lobe of her ear. "Why?"

"The way you walk, the way you move. With a sensuous grace, and effortless rhythm."

She intended to laugh off the compliment and tilted her head to meet his eyes. She found herself instead staring wordlessly into their gray depths. His hold on her did not lessen as they faced, their lips a breath apart, and she found the flip remark she had been about to make slip into oblivion.

"I always thought gray eyes were like steel," she murmured, hardly aware she was voicing her thoughts. "Yours are more like clouds."

"Dark and threatening?" he suggested, holding her gaze.

"Sometimes," she whispered, caught in the power he exuded. "And others, warm and soft like an early mist. I never know whether I'm in for a storm or a shower. Never know what to expect."

"Don't you?" His voice was quiet as his gaze dropped to her lips, tantalizingly close to his. "You should by now."

She struggled with the weakness invading her at his softly spoken retort and clutched for sophistication. "Really, Mr. Bardoff, are you attempting to seduce me in the middle of a crowded dance floor?"

"One must make use of what's available," he answered, then lifted his brow. "Have you somewhere else in mind?"

"Sorry," she apologized, and turned her head so their faces no longer met. "We're both otherwise engaged, and," she added, attempting to slip away, "the dance is over."

He did not release her, pulling her closer and speaking ominously in her ear. "You'll not get away until you drop that infuriatingly formal Mr. Bardoff and use my name." When she did not reply, he went on, an edge sharpening his voice. "I'm perfectly content to stay like this. You're a woman who was meant for a man's arms. I find you suit mine."

"All right," Hillary said between her teeth. "Bret, would you please let me go before I'm crushed beyond recognition?"

"Certainly." His grip slacked, but his arm remained around her. "Don't tell me I'm really hurting you." His smile was wide and triumphant as he gazed into her resentful face.

"I'll let you know after I've had my x rays."

"I doubt if you're as fragile as all that." He led her back to the table, his arm still encircling her waist.

They joined their respective partners, and the group spoke generally for the next few minutes. Hillary felt unmistakable hostility directed toward her from the other woman, which Bret was either blissfully unaware of or ignored. Between frosty green eyes and her own disquieting awareness of the tall, fair man whose arms had held her so intimately, Hillary was acutely uncomfortable. It was a relief when the couple rose to leave, and Bret refused Chuck's request that they stay for another round. Charlene looked on with undisguised boredom.

"Charlene's not fond of discos, I'm afraid," Bret explained, grinning as he slipped an arm casually around the redhead's shoulders, causing her to look up at him with a smile of pure invitation. The gesture caused a sudden blaze of emotions to flare in Hillary that she refused to identify as jealousy. "She merely came tonight to please me. I'm thinking of using a disco background for the layout." Bret gazed down at Hillary with an enigmatic smile. "Wasn't it a stroke of luck that I was able to see you here tonight. It gives me a much clearer picture of how to set things up."

Hillary's gaze narrowed at his tone, and she caught the gleam of laughter in his eyes. Luck nothing, she thought suddenly, realizing with certainty that Bret rarely depended on luck. Somehow he had known she would be here tonight, and he had staged the accidental meeting. This layout must be very important to him, she mused, feeling unaccountably miserable. What other reason would he have for seeking her out and dancing with her while he had the obviously willing Charlene Mason hanging all over him?

"See you Monday, Hillary," Bret said easily as he and his lady made to leave.

"Monday?" Chuck repeated when they were once more alone. "Aren't you the fox." His teeth flashed in a grin. "Keeping the famous Mr. Bardoff tucked in your pocket."

"Hardly," she snapped, irritated by his conclusion. "Our relationship is strictly business. I'm working for his magazine. He's my employer, nothing more."

"O.K., O.K." Chuck's grin only widened at her angry denial. "Don't take my head off. It's a natural mistake, and I'm not the only one who made it."

Hillary looked up sharply. "What are you talking about?"

"Sweet Hillary," he explained in a patient tone, "didn't you feel the knives stabbing you in the back when you were dancing with your famous employer?" At her blank stare, he sighed deeply. "You know, even after three years in New York, you're still incredibly naive." The corners of his mouth lifted, and he lay a brotherly hand on her shoulder. "A certain redhead was shooting daggers into you from her green eyes the entire time you were dancing. Why, I expected you to keel over in a pool of blood at any second."

"That's absurd." Hillary swirled the contents of her glass and frowned at them. "I'm sure Miss Mason knew very well Bret's purpose in seeing me was merely for research, just background for his precious layout."

Chuck regarded her thoroughly and shook his head. "As I said before, Hillary, you are incredibly naive."

Chapter 3

Monday morning dawned, cool, crisp, and gray. In the office of *Mode,* however, threatening skies were not a factor. Obviously, Hillary decided, Bret had permitted nature to have a tantrum now that shooting had moved indoors.

At his direction, she was placed in the hands of a hairdresser who would assist in the transformation to smooth, competent businesswoman. Jet shoulder-length hair was arranged in a sleek chignon that accented classic bone structure, and the severely tailored lines of the three-piece gray suit, instead of appearing masculine, only heightened Hillary's femininity.

Larry was immersed in camera equipment, lighting, and angles when she entered Bret's office. Giving the room a quick survey, she was forced to admit it was both an elegant and suitable background for the morning's session. She watched with fond amusement as Larry, oblivious to her presence, adjusted lenses and tested meters, muttering to himself.

"The genius at work," a voice whispered close to her ear, and Hillary whirled, finding herself staring into the eyes that had begun to haunt her.

"That's precisely what he is," she retorted, furious with the way her heart began to drum at his nearness.

"Testy this morning, aren't we?" Bret observed with a lifted brow. "Still hung over from the weekend?"

"Certainly not." Dignity wrapped her like a cloak. "I never drink enough to have a hangover."

"Oh, yes, I forgot, the Mr. Hyde syndrome."

"Hillary, there you are." Larry interrupted Hillary's search for a suitable retort. "What took you so long?"

"Sorry, Larry, the hairdresser took quite some time."

The amused gleam in Bret's eyes demanded and received her answer. As their gaze met over Larry's head with the peculiar intimacy of a shared joke, a sweet weakness washed over her, like a soft, gentle wave washing over a waiting shore. Terrified, she dropped her eyes, attempting to dispel the reaction he drew from her without effort.

"Do you always frighten so easily?" Bret's voice was calm, with a tint of mockery, the tone causing her chin to lift in defiance. She glared, helplessly angry with his ability to read her thoughts as if they were written on her forehead. "That's better," he approved fending off the fire with cool composure. "Anger suits you. It darkens your eyes and puts rose in your cheeks. Spirit is an essential trait for women and"—his mouth lifted at the corner as he paused—"for horses."

She choked and sputtered over the comparison, willing her temper into place with the knowledge that if she lost it she would be powerless against him in a verbal battle. "I suppose that's true," she answered carelessly after swallowing the words that had sprung into her head. "In my observation, men appear to fall short of the physical capacity of one and the mental capacity of the other."

"Well, that hairstyle certainly makes you look competent." Larry turned to study Hillary critically, oblivious to anything that had occurred since he had last spoken. With a sigh of defeat, Hillary gazed at the ceiling for assistance.

"Yes," Bret agreed, keeping his features serious. "The woman executive, very competent, very smart,"

"Assertive, aggressive, and ruthless," Hillary interrupted, casting him a freezing look. "I shall emulate you, Mr. Bardoff."

His brows rose fractionally. "That should be fascinating. I'll leave you then to get on with your work, while I get on with mine."

The door closed behind him, and the room was suddenly larger and strangely empty. Hillary shook herself and got to work, attempting to block out all thoughts of Bret Bardoff from her mind.

For the next hour Larry moved around the room, clicking his camera, adjusting the lighting, and calling out directions as Hillary assumed the poses of a busy woman executive.

"That's a wrap in here." He signaled for her to relax, which she did by sinking into a soft leather chair in a casual, if undignified, pose.

"Fiend!" she cried as he snapped the camera once more, capturing her as she sprawled, slouched in the chair, legs stretched out in front of her.

"It'll be a good shot," he claimed with an absent smile. "weary woman wiped-out by woesome work."

"You have a strange sense of humor, Larry," Hillary retorted, not bothering to alter her position. "It comes from having a camera stuck to your face all the time."

"Now, now, Hil, let's not get personal. Heave yourself out of that chair. We're going into the board room, and you, my love, can be chairman of the board."

"Chairperson," she corrected, but his mind was already involved with his equipment. Groaning, she stood and left him to his devices.

The remainder of the day's shooting was long and tedious. Dissatisfied with the lighting, Larry spent more than half an hour rearranging and resetting until it met with his approval. After a further hour under hot lights, Hillary felt as fresh as week-old lettuce and was more than ready when Larry called an end to the day's work.

She found herself searching for Bret's lean form as she made her way from the building, undeniably disappointed when there was no sign of him and angry with her own reaction. Walking for several blocks, she breathed in the brisk autumn air, determined to forget the emotions stirred by the tall man with sharp gray eyes. Just a physical attraction, she reasoned, tucking her hands in her pockets and allowing her feet to take her farther down the busy sidewalk. Physical attraction happens all the time; it would pass like a twenty-four-hour virus.

A diversion was what she required, she decided—something to chase him from her mind and set her thoughts back on the track she had laid out for herself. Success in the field she had chosen, independence, security—these were her priorities. There was no room for romantic entanglements. When the time came for settling down, it certainly would not be with a man like Bret Bardoff, but with someone safe, someone who did not set her nerves on end and confuse her at every encounter. Besides, she reminded herself, ignoring the sudden gloom, he wasn't interested in her romantically in any case. He seemed to prefer well-proportioned redheads.

Shooting resumed the next morning, once again in *Mode*'s offices. Today, dressed in a dark blue shirt and boot-length skirt of a lighter shade, Hillary was to take on the role of working girl. The session was to take place in Bret's secretary's office, much to that woman's delight.

"I can't tell you how excited I am, Miss Baxter. I feel like a kid going to her first circus."

Hillary smiled at the young woman whose eyes were alight with anticipation. "I'll admit to feeling like a trained elephant from time to time—and make it Hillary."

"I'm June. This is all routine to you, I suppose." Her head shook, causing chestnut curls to bounce and sway. "But it seems very glamorous and exciting to me." Her eyes drifted to where Larry was setting up for the shooting with customary absorption. "Mr. Newman's a real expert, isn't he? He's been fiddling with all those dials and lenses and lights. He's very attractive. Is he married?"

Hillary laughed, glancing carelessly at Larry. "Only to his Nikon."

"Oh." June smiled, then frowned. "Are you two, ah, I mean, are you involved?"

"Just master and slave," Hillary answered, seeing Larry as an attractive, eligible man for the first time. Looking back at June's appealing face, she smiled in consideration. "You know the old adage, 'The way to a man's heart is through his stomach.' Take my advice. The way to that man's heart is through his lenses. Ask him about f-stops."

Bret emerged from his office. He broke into a slow, lazy smile when he saw Hillary. "Ah, man's best friend, the efficient secretary."

Ignoring the pounding of her heart, Hillary forced her voice into a light tone. "No corporate decisions today. I've been demoted."

"That's the way of the business world." He nodded understandingly. "Executive dining room one day, typing pool the next. It's a jungle out there."

"All set," Larry announced from across the room. "Where's Hillary?" He turned to see the trio watching him and grinned. "Hello, Bret, hi, Hil. All set?"

"Your wish is my command, O master of the thirty-five millimeter," Hillary said, moving to join him.

"Can you type, Hillary?" Bret inquired cheerily. "I'll give you some letters, and we can kill two birds with one stone."

"Sorry, Mr. Bardoff," she replied, allowing herself to enjoy his smile. "Typewriters and I have a longstanding agreement. I don't pound on them, and they don't pound on me."

"Is it all right if I watch for a while, Mr. Newman?" June requested. "I won't get in the way. Photography just fascinates me."

Larry gave an absent assent, and, after casting his secretary a puzzled look, Bret turned to reenter his office. "I'll need you in a half hour, June—the Brookline contract."

The session went quickly with Larry and Hillary progressing with professional ease. The model followed the photographer's instructions, often anticipating a mood before he spoke. After a time, June disappeared unobtrusively through the heavy doors leading to Bret's office. Neither Hillary nor Larry noticed her silent departure.

Sometime later, Larry lowered his camera and stared fixedly into space. Hillary maintained her silence, knowing from experience this did not signal the end, but a pause while a fresh idea formed in his mind.

"I want to finish up with something here," he muttered, staring through Hillary as if she were intangible. His face cleared with inspiration. He focused his eyes. "I know. Change the ribbon in the typewriter."

"Surely you jest." She began an intense study of her nails.

"No, it'll be good. Go ahead."

"Larry," she protested in patient tones. "I haven't the foggiest notion how to change a ribbon."

"Fake it," Larry suggested.

With a sigh, Hillary seated herself behind the desk and stared at the typewriter.

"Ever harvested wheat, Larry?" she hazarded, attempting to postpone his order. "It's a fascinating process."

"Hillary," he interrupted, drawing his brows together.

With another sigh, she surrendered to artistic temperament. "I don't know how to open it," she muttered, pushing buttons at random. "It has to open, doesn't it?"

"There should be a button or lever under it," Larry returned patiently. "Don't they have typewriters in Kansas?"

"I suppose they do. My sister… Oh!" she cried, and grinned, delighted out of all proportion, like a small child completing a puzzle, when the release was located. Lifting the lid, she frowned intently at the inner workings. "Scalpel," she requested, running a finger over naked keys.

"Keep going, Hil," Larry commanded. "Just pretend you know what you're doing."

She found herself falling into the spirit of things and attacked the thin black ribbon threaded through various guides with enthusiasm. Her smooth brow was puckered in concentration as she forgot the man and his camera and gave herself over to the job of dislodging ribbon from machine. The more she unraveled, the longer the ribbon became, growing with a life of its own. Absently, she brushed a hand across her cheek, smearing it with black ink.

An enormous, ever-growing heap tangled around her fingers. Realization dawned that she was fighting a losing battle. With a grin for Larry, she flourished the mess of ribbon as he clicked a final picture.

"Terrific." he answered her grin as he lowered his camera. "A classic study in ineptitude."

"Thanks, friend, and if you use any of those shots, I'll sue." Dumping the mass of loose ribbon on the open typewriter, she expelled a long breath. "I'll leave it to you to explain to June how this catastrophe came about. I'm finished."

"Absolutely." Bret's voice came from behind, and Hillary whirled in the chair to see both him and June staring at the chaos on the desk. "If you ever give up modeling, steer clear of office work. You're a disaster."

Hillary attempted to resent his attitude, but one glance at the havoc she had wrought brought on helpless giggles. "Well, Larry, get us out of this one. We've been caught red-handed at the scene of the crime."

Bret closed the distance between them with lithe grace and gingerly lifted one of Hillary's hands. "Black-handed, I'd say." Putting his other hand under her chin, he smiled in the lazy way that caused Hillary's reluctant heart to perform a series of somersaults. "There's quite a bit of evidence on that remark-able face as well."

She shook off the sweet weakness invading her and peered down at her hands. "Good Lord, how did I manage that? Will it come off?" She addressed her question to June, who assured her soap and water would do the trick. "Well, I'm going to wash away the evidence, and I'm leaving you"—she nodded to Larry—"to make amends for the damage." She encompassed June's desk with a sweeping gesture. "Better do some fast talking, old man," she added in a stage whisper, and gave June the present of her famous smile.

Reaching the door before her, Bret opened it and took a few steps down the long hall beside her. "Setting up a romance for my secretary, Hillary?"

"Could be," she returned enigmatically. "Larry could do with more than cameras and darkrooms in his life."

"And what could you use in yours, Hillary?" His question was soft, putting a hand on her arm and turning her to face him.

"I've…I've got everything I need," she stammered, feeling like a pinned butterfly under his direct gaze.

"Everything?" he repeated, keeping her eyes locked on his. "Pity I've an appointment, or we could go into this in more detail." Pulling her close, his lips brushed her, then formed a crooked smile that was devastatingly appealing. "Go wash your face—you're a fine mess." Turning, he strode down the hall, leaving Hillary to deal with a mixture of frustration and unaccustomed longing.

She spent her free afternoon shopping, a diversionary tactic for soothing jangled nerves, but her mind constantly floated back to a brief touch of lips, a smile lighting gray eyes. The warmth seemed to linger on her mouth, stirring her emotions, arousing her senses. A cold blast of wind swirling in her face brought her back to reality. Cursing her treacherous imagination, she hailed a cab. She would have to hurry in order to make her dinner date with Lisa.

It was after five when Hillary entered her apartment and dumped her purchases on a chair in the bedroom. She released the latch on the front door for Lisa's benefit and made her way to the bath, filling the tub with hot, fragrant water. She intended to soak for a full twenty minutes. Just as she stepped from the tub and grabbed a towel, the bell sounded at the front door.

"Come on in, Lisa. Either you're early, or I'm late." Draping the towel saronglike around her slim body, she walked from the room, the scent of strawberries clinging to her shining skin. "I'll be ready in a minute. I got carried away in the tub. My feet were…" She stopped dead in her tracks, because instead of the small, blond Lisa, she was confronted by the tall, lean figure of Bret Bardoff.

"Where did you come from?" Hillary demanded when she located her voice.

"Originally or just now?" he countered, smiling at her confusion.

"I thought you were Lisa."

"I got that impression."

"What are you doing here?"

"Returning this." He held up a slim gold pen. "I assumed it was yours. The initials H.B. are engraved on it."

"Yes, it's mine," she concurred, frowning at it. "I must have dropped it from my bag. You needn't have bothered. I could have gotten it tomorrow."

"I thought you might have been looking for it." His eyes roamed over the figure scantily clad in the bath towel and lingered on her smooth legs, then rested a moment on the swell of her breast. "Besides, it was well worth the trip."

Hillary's eyes dropped down to regard her state of disarray and widened in shock. Color stained her cheeks as his eyes laughed at her, and she turned and ran from the room. "I'll be back in a minute."

Hastily, she pulled on chocolate brown cords and a beige mohair sweater, tugged a quick brush through her hair, and applied a touch of makeup with a deft hand. Taking a deep breath, she returned to the living room, attempting to assume a calm front that she was far from feeling. Bret was seated comfortably on the sofa, smoking a cigarette with the air of someone completely at home.

"Sorry to keep you waiting," she said politely, fighting back the embarrassment that engulfed her. "It was kind of you to take the trouble to return the pen to me." He handed it to her and she placed it on the low mahogany table. "May I…would you…" She bit her lip in frustration, finding her poise had vanished. "Can I get you a drink? Or maybe you're in a hurry—"

"I'm in no hurry," he answered, ignoring her frown. "Scotch, neat, if you have it."

Her frown deepened. "I may have. I'll have to check." She retreated to the kitchen, searching through cupboards for her supply of rarely used liquor. He had followed her, and she turned, noting with a quickening of pulse how his presence seemed to dwarf the small room. She felt an intimacy that was both exciting and disturbing. She resumed her search, all too conscious of his casual stance as he leaned against the refrigerator, hands in pockets.

"Here." Triumphantly, she brandished the bottle. "Scotch."

"So it is."

"I'll get you a glass. Neat, you said?" She pushed at her hair. "That's with no ice, right?"

"You'd make a marvelous bartender," he returned, taking both bottle and glass and pouring the liquid himself.

"I'm not much of a drinker," she muttered.

"Yes, I remember—a two-drink limit. Shall we go sit down?" He took her hand with the usual familiarity, and her words of protest died. "A very nice place, Hillary," he commented as they seated themselves on the sofa. "Open, friendly, colorful. Do the living quarters reflect the tenant?"

"So they say."

"Friendliness is an admirable trait, but you should know better than to leave your door unlatched. This is New York, not a farm in Kansas."

"I was expecting someone."

"But you got someone unexpected." He looked into her eyes, then casually swept the length of her. "What do you think would have happened if someone else had come across that beautiful body of yours draped in a very insufficient towel?" The blush was immediate and impossible to control, and she dropped her eyes. "You should keep your door locked, Hillary. Not every man would let you escape as I did."

"Yes, O mighty emperor," Hillary retorted before she could bite her tongue, and his eyes narrowed dangerously. He captured her with a swift movement, but whatever punishment he had in mind was postponed by the ringing of the phone. Jumping up in relief, Hillary hurried to answer.

"Lisa, hi. Where are you?"

"Sorry, Hillary." The answering voice was breathless. "The most wonderful thing happened. I hope you don't mind, but I have to beg off tonight."

"Of course not—what happened?"

"Mark asked me to have dinner with him."

"So you took my advice and tripped him, right?"

"More or less."

"Oh, Lisa," Hillary cried in amused disbelief, "you didn't really!"

"Well, no," she admitted. "We were both carrying all these law books and ran smack into each other. What a beautiful mess."

"I get the picture." Her laughter floated through the room. "It really has more class than a mugging."

"You don't mind about tonight?"

"Do you think I'd let a pizza stand in the way of true love?" Hillary answered. "Float along and have fun. I'll see you later."

She replaced the receiver and turned to find Bret regarding her with open curiosity. "I must admit that was the most fascinating one-ended conversation I've ever heard." She flashed him a smile with full candlepower and told him briefly of her friend's long unrequited love affair.

"So your solution was to land the poor guy on his face at her feet," he concluded.

"It got his attention."

"Now you're stood up. A pizza, was it?"

"My secret's out," she said, carefully seating herself in a chair across from him. "I hope I can trust you never to breathe a word of this, but I am a pizza junkie. If I don't have one at well-ordered intervals, I go into a frenzy. It's not a pretty sight."

"Well, we can't have you foaming at the mouth, can we?" He set down his empty glass and stood with a fluid motion. "Fetch a coat, I'll indulge you."

"Oh, really, there's no need," she began with quick panic.

"For heaven's sake, let's not go through this again. Get a coat and come on," he commanded, pulling her from her chair. "I could do with some food myself."

She found herself doing his bidding, slipping on a short suede jacket as he picked up his own brown leather. "Got your keys?" he questioned, reengaging the latch and propelling her through the door.

Soon they were seated in the small Italian restaurant that Hillary had indicated. The small table was covered with the inevitable red and white checkered cloth, a candle flickering in its wine bottle holder.

"Well, Hillary, what will you have?"

"Pizza"

"Yes, I know that," he countered with a smile. "Anything on it?"

"Extra cholesterol."

White teeth flashed as he grinned at her. "Is that all?"

"I don't want to overdo—these things can get out of hand."

"Some wine?"

"I don't know if my system can handle it." She considered, then shrugged. "Well, why not, you only live once."

"Too true." He signaled the waiter and gave their order. "You, however," he continued when they were once more alone, "look as though you had lived before. You are a reincarnation of an Indian princess. I bet they called you Pocahontas when you were a kid."

"Not if they were smart," Hillary returned. "I scalped a boy once for just that."

"Do tell?" Bret's attention was caught, and he leaned forward, his head on his hands as his elbows rested on the table. "Please elaborate."

"All right, if you can handle such a bloodthirsty subject over dinner." Pushing back her hair with both hands, she mirrored his casual position. "There was this boy, Martin Collins. I was madly in love with him, but he preferred Jessie Winfield, a cute little blond number with soulful brown eyes. I was mad with jealousy. I was also too tall, skinny, all eyes and elbows, and eleven years old. I passed them one day, devastated because he was carrying her books, and he called out 'Head for the hills, it's Pocahontas.' That did it, I was a woman scorned. I planned my revenge. I went home and got the small scissors my mother used for mending, painted my face with her best lipstick, and returned to stalk my prey.

"I crept up behind him stealthily, patiently waiting for the right moment. Springing like a panther, I knocked my quarry to the ground, holding him down with my body and cutting off as much hair as I could grab. He screamed, but I showed no mercy. Then my brothers came and dragged me off and he escaped, running like the coward he was, home to his mother."

Bret's laughter ran out as he threw back his head. "What a monster you must have been!"

"I paid for it." She lifted the glass of wine that Bret had poured during her story. "I got the tanning of my life, but it was worth it. Martin wore a hat for weeks."

Their pizza arrived, and through the meal their conversation was more companionable and relaxed than Hillary would have believed possible. When the last piece was consumed, Bret leaned back and regarded her seriously.

"I'd never have believed you could eat like that."

She grinned, relaxed by the combination of wine, good food, and easy company. "I don't often, but when I do, I'm exceptional."

"You're a constant amazement. I never know what to expect. A study of contradictions."

"Isn't that why you hired me, Bret?" She used his

name for the first time voluntarily without conscious thought. "For my versatility?"

He smiled, lifted his glass to his lips, and left her question unanswered.

Hillary felt her earlier nervousness return as they walked down the carpeted hall toward her apartment. Determined to remain calm, she bent her head to fish out her keys, using the time to assume a calm veneer.

"Would you like to come in for coffee?"

He took the keys from her hand, unlocked the door, and gave her a slow smile. "I thought you didn't drink coffee."

"I don't, but everyone else in the world does, so I keep some instant."

"With the Scotch, no doubt," he said leading her into the apartment.

Removing her jacket, Hillary assumed the role of hostess. "Sit down. I'll have coffee out in a minute."

He had shed his own coat, carelessly dropping it down over the arm of a chair. Once more she was aware of the strong build beneath the dark blue rib-knit sweater and close-fitting slacks. She turned and made for the kitchen.

Her movements were deft and automatic as she set the kettle on the burner and removed cups and saucers from cupboards. She set a small sugar bowl and creamer on the glass and wicker tray, and prepared tea for herself and coffee for the man in her living room. She moved with natural grace to the low table, to set the ladened tray down. She smiled with professional ease at the tall man who stood across the room leafing casually through her collection of record albums.

"Quite an assortment." He addressed her from where he stood, looking so at ease and blatantly masculine that Hillary felt her veneer cracking rapidly and fought back a flutter of panic. "Typical of you though," he went on, sparing her from the necessity of immediate comment. "Chopin when you're romantic, Denver when you're homesick, B. B. King when you're down, McCartney when you're up."

"You sound like you know me very well." She felt a strange mixture of amusement and resentment that he had pinpointed her mood music with such uncanny accuracy.

"Not yet," he corrected, putting down an album and coming over to join her. "But I'm working on it."

Suddenly, he was very close, and there was an urgent need in Hillary to be on a more casual footing. "Your coffee's getting cold." She spoke quickly and bent to remove the clutter from the tray, dropping a spoon in her agitation. They bent to retrieve it simultaneously, his strong, lean fingers closing over her fine-boned hand. At the contact a current of electricity shot down her arm and spread through her body, and her eyes darkened to midnight. She raised her face to his.

There were no words as their eyes met, and she realized the inevitability of the movement. She knew they had been drifting steadily toward this since the first day in Larry's studio. There was a basic attraction between them, an undefinable need she did not pause to question as he lifted her to her feet, and she stepped into his arms.

His lips were warm and gentle on hers as he kissed her slowly, then with increasing pressure, his tongue parted her lips, and his arms tightened around her, crushing her breasts against the hardness of his chest. Her arms twined around his neck. She responded as she had never responded to any man before. The thought ran through her clouded brain that no one had ever kissed her like this, no one had ever held her like this. Then all thought was drowned in a tidal wave of passion.

She made no resistance as she felt herself lowered onto the cushions of the couch, her mouth still the captive of his. The weight of his body pushed hers deep into the sofa as his legs slid between hers, making no secret of his desire. His mouth began to roam, exploring the smooth skin of her neck. The fire of a new and ageless need raged through her veins. She felt the thudding of a heart—hers or his, she could not tell—as his lips caressed her throat and face before meeting hers with possessing hunger. His hand moved under her sweater to cup the breast that swelled under his touch. She sighed and moved under him.

She was lost in a blaze of longing such as she had never known, responding with a passion she had kept buried until that moment, as his lips and hands moved with expertise over her warm and willing body.

His hands moved to the flatness of her stomach, and when she felt his fingers on the snap of her jeans, she began to struggle against him. Her protests were ignored, his mouth devouring hers, then laying a trail of heat along her throat.

"Bret, please don't. You have to stop."

He lifted his head from the curve of her neck to look into the deep pools of her eyes, huge now with fear and desire. His own breathing was ragged. She knew a sharp fear that the decision to stop or go on would be taken out of her hands.

"Hillary," he murmured, and bent to claim her lips again, but she turned her head and pushed against him.

"No, Bret, no more."

A long breath escaped from his lips as he removed his body from hers, standing before removing a cigarette from the gold case he had left on the table. Hillary sat up, clutching her hands together in her lap, keeping her head lowered to avoid his eyes.

"I knew you were many things, Hillary," he said after expelling a swift and violent stream of smoke. "I never thought you were a tease."

"I'm not!" she protested, her head snapping up at the harshness of his tone. "That's unfair. Just because I stopped, just because I didn't let you…" Her voice broke. She was filled with confusion and embarrassment, and a perverse longing to be held again in his arms.

"You are not a child," he began with an anger that caused her lips to tremble. "What is the usual outcome when two people kiss like that, when a woman allows a man to touch her like that?" His eyes were dark with barely suppressed fury, and she sat mutely, having been unprepared for the degree his temper could reach. "You wanted me as much as I wanted you. Stop playing games. We've both been well aware that this would happen eventually. You're a grown woman. Stop behaving like an innocent young girl."

The remark scored, and the telltale flush crept to her cheeks before she could lower her lashes to conceal painful discomfort. Bret gaped at her, anger struggling with stunned disbelief. "Good heavens, you've never been with a man before, have you?"

Hillary shut her eyes in humiliation, and she remained stubbornly silent.

"How is that possible?" he asked in a voice tinged with reluctant amusement. "How does a woman reach the ripe old age of twenty-four with looks like yours and remain as pure as the driven snow?"

"It hasn't been all that difficult," she muttered, and looked anywhere in the room but at him. "I don't normally let things get so out of hand." She made a small, helpless shrug.

"You might let a man know of your innocence before things get out of hand," he advised caustically, crushing out his cigarette with undue force.

"Maybe I should paint a red V for virgin on my forehead—then there'd be no confusion." Hillary flared, lifting her chin in bold defiance.

"You know, you're gorgeous when you're angry." He spoke coolly, but the steel vibrated in his tone, casual elegance wrapped around a volatile force.

"Watch yourself, or I'll have another go at changing your status."

"I don't think you would ever stoop to forcing a woman," she retorted as he moved to pick up his jacket.

Pausing, he turned back to her, gray eyes narrowing into slits as he hauled her to her feet, possessing her again until her struggles had transformed into limp clinging.

"Don't count on it." His voice was deadly soft as he gave her a firm nudge back onto the couch. "I make a point of getting what I want." His eyes moved lazily over her slim body, pausing on the lips still soft from his. "Make no mistake," he went on as she began to tremble under his prolonged gaze. "I could have you here and now without forcing, but"—he moved to the door—"I can afford to wait."

Chapter 4

For the next few weeks shooting moved along with few complications. Larry was enthusiastic about the progress that was being made and brought Hillary a file of work prints so that she could view the fruits of their labor.

Studying the pictures with a professional objectivity, she admitted they were excellent, perhaps the best work Larry and she had done together or separately. There was a touch of genius in his choice of angles and lighting, using shadows and filters with a master hand. Added to this was Hillary's ability to assume varied roles. The pictures were already beginning to form a growing study of womanhood. They were nearly halfway through the planned shooting. If everything continued to go as well, they would be finished ahead of schedule. Bret was now planning a crash publication, which would put the issue on the stands in early spring.

Sessions would resume following the Thanksgiving weekend, while the art director and staff, with Bret's approval, began the selection of what would be printed in the final copy. Hillary was grateful for the time off, not only for the rest, but for the separation from the man who filled her thoughts and invaded her dreams.

She had expected some constraint between them when she returned to work after their evening together, but Bret had greeted her in his usual way, so casually, in fact, that she thought for a moment that she had imagined the feel of his lips on hers. There was no mention of their meal together or the scene that followed, while he slipped with apparent ease into the partly professional, partly mocking attitude he invariably directed toward her.

It was not as simple a task for Hillary to mirror his nonchalance after the emotions he had awakened in her—emotions that had laid sleeping within her until his touch had brought them to life—but outwardly she displayed a casualness at odds with her inner turmoil.

All in all, the remainder of the shooting time passed easily, and if Larry was forced to admonish her from time to time to relax and not to scowl, he was characteristically preoccupied and saw nothing amiss.

Hillary stood staring from the window of her apartment, her state of mind as bleak as the scene that greeted her. The late November sky was like lead, casting a depressing spell over the city, the buildings and skyscrapers taking on a dismal hue. Leaves had long since deserted the trees, leaving them naked and cheerless, and the grass, where sidewalks made room for it, had lost its healthy green tone, looking instead a sad, dreary yellow. The somberness of the day suited her mood precisely.

A sudden wave of homesickness washed over her, a strong desire for golden wheat fields. Moving to the stereo, she placed a Denver album on the turntable, halting in her movements when the image of Bret standing in the very spot she now occupied swept through her mind. The memory of the hardness of his body against hers and the intimacy briefly shared filled her with a painful longing, replacing homesickness. With a flash of insight, she realized that her attraction for him was more than physical. She switched on the player, filling the room with soft music.

Falling in love had not been in her plans, she reminded herself, and falling for Bret was out of the question, now or ever. That road would lead nowhere but to disaster and humiliation. But she could not quiet the voice that hammered in her brain telling her it was already too late. She sank down in a chair, confusion and depression settling over her like a fog.

It had grown late when Hillary let herself into her apartment after having joined Lisa and Mark for Thanksgiving dinner. The meal had been superb, but she had hidden her lack of appetite under the guise of keeping a careful watch on her figure. She had hidden her depression and concentrated on appearing normal and content. As she closed the door behind her, she breathed a sigh of relief, at last removing the frozen smile and relaxing. Before she could move to the closet to hang up her coat, the phone rang.

"Hello." Her voice reflected her weariness and annoyance.

"Hello, Hillary. Been out on the town?"

There was no need for the caller to identify himself. Hillary recognized Bret immediately, glad that the thumping of her heart was not audible over the wire.

"Hello, Mr. Bardoff." She schooled her voice to coolness. "Do you always call your employees so late?"

"Grouchy, aren't we?" He seemed unperturbed. The thrill of hearing his voice warred with irritation at his composure. "Did you have a nice day?"

"Lovely," she lied. "I'm just home from having dinner with a friend. And you?"

"Spectacular. I'm very fond of turkey."

"Did you call to compare menus or was there something on your mind?" Her voice grew sharp at the picture of Bret and Charlene enjoying a beautifully catered dinner in elegant surroundings.

"Oh, yes, I've something on my mind. To begin with, I had thought to share a holiday drink with you, if you still have that bottle of Scotch."

"Oh." Her voice cracked, panic-filled. Clearing her throat, she stumbled on. "No, I mean, yes, I have the Scotch, but it's late and…"

"Afraid?" he interrupted quietly.

"Certainly not," she snapped. "I'm just tired. I'm on my way to bed."

"Oh, really?" She could hear the amusement in his voice.

"Honestly." To her disgust, she felt herself blushing. "Must you continually make fun of me?"

"Sorry." His apology lacked conviction. "But you will insist on taking yourself seriously. Very well, I won't dip into your liquor supply." Pausing, he added, "Tonight. I'll see you Monday, Hillary, sleep well."

"Good night," she murmured, filled with regret as she replaced the receiver. Glancing around the room, she felt a swift desire to have him there, filling the emptiness with the excitement of his presence. She sighed and pushed at her hair, realizing she could hardly call him back and issue the invitation had she known where to reach him.

It's better this way, she rationalized, better to avoid him whenever possible. If I'm going to get over this infatuation, distance is my best medicine. He'll tire soon enough without encouragement. I'm sure he gets an ample supply of it from other quarters. Charlene is more his style, she went on, digging at the wound. I could never compete with her sophistication, I haven't the knack. She probably speaks French and knows about wines and can drink more than one glass of champagne before she starts to babble.

* * *

On Saturday Hillary met Lisa for lunch, hoping the short outing would boost her flagging spirits. The elegant restaurant was crowded. Spotting Lisa at a small table, Hillary waved and made her way through the room.

"Sorry, I know I'm late," Hillary apologized, picking up the menu set before her. "Traffic was dreadful, and I had a terrible time getting a cab. Winter's definitely on its way. It's freezing out there."

"Is it?" Lisa grinned. "It feels like spring to me."

"Love has apparently thrown you off balance. But," she added, "even if it's affected your brain, it's done wonders for the rest of you. I believe you could glow in the dark."

The blissful smile that lighted Lisa's face was a heart-catching sight, and Hillary's depression evaporated.

"I know my feet haven't touched the ground in weeks. I guess you're sick of watching me float around."

"Don't be silly. It's given me a tremendous lift watching you light up like a neon sign."

The two women ordered their meal, slipping into the easy camaraderie they enjoyed.

"I really should find a friend with warts and a hooked nose," Lisa commented.

Hillary's fork paused on its journey to her mouth. "Come again?"

"The most fascinating man just came in. I might as well be invisible for all the attention he paid me. He was too busy staring at you."

"He's probably just looking for someone he knows."

"He's got someone he knows hanging on to his arm like an appendage," Lisa declared, staring boldly at the couple across the room. "His attention, however, is riveted on you. No, don't turn around," she hissed as Hillary started to turn head. "Oh, good grief, he's coming over. Quick," she whispered desperately, "look natural."

"You're the one standing on her head, Lisa," Hillary returned calmly, amused by her friend's rapid capitulation.

"Well, Hillary, we just can't keep away from each other, can we?"

Hillary heard the deep voice and her wide eyes met Lisa's startled ones before she looked up to meet Bret's crooked smile. "Hello." Her voice was oddly breathless. Her glance took in the shapely redhead on his arm. "Hello, Miss Mason, nice to see you again," she said quietly.

Charlene merely nodded. From the expression in her frosty green eyes, it was apparent she couldn't have disagreed more. There was a short pause. Bret raised his brow in inquiry.

"Lisa MacDonald, Charlene Mason and Bret Bardoff," Hillary introduced quickly.

"Oh, you're *Mode* magazine," Lisa blurted out, her eyes shining with excitement. Hillary looked in vain for a hole to open up and swallow her.

"More or less."

Hillary watched, helpless, as Bret turned his most charming smile on Lisa.

"I'm a great fan of your magazine, Mr. Bardoff," Lisa bubbled. She appeared to be unaware of the darts shooting at her from Charlene's narrowed eyes. "I can barely wait for this big layout of Hillary's. It must be very exciting."

"It's been quite an experience so far." He turned to Hillary with an annoying grin. "Don't you agree, Hillary?"

"Quite an experience," she agreed carelessly, forcing her eyes to remain level.

"Bret," Charlene interrupted. "We really must get to our table and let these girls get on with their lunch." Her eyes swept both Hillary and Lisa, dismissing them as beneath notice.

"Nice to have met you, Lisa. See you later, Hillary." His lazy smile had Hillary's heart pounding in its now familiar way. But she managed to murmur goodbye. Nervously, she reached for her tea, hoping Lisa would not discuss the encounter.

Lisa stared at Bret's retreating back for several seconds. "Wow," she breathed, turning huge brown eyes on Hillary. "You didn't tell me he was so terrific! I was literally liquified when he smiled at me."

Dear heaven, Hillary thought wearily, does he affect all women that way? Aloud, she spoke with mock censure. "Shame on you—your heart's supposed to be taken."

"It is," Lisa affirmed. "But I'm still a woman." Looking at Hillary, she went on shrewdly, "Don't tell me he leaves you unmoved. We know each other too well."

A deep sigh escaped. "I'm not immune to Mr. Bardoff's devastating charm, but I'll have to develop some kind of antidote during the next couple of months."

"Don't you think the interest might be mutual? You're not without substantial charm yourself."

"You did notice the redhead clinging to him like ivy on a brick wall?"

"Couldn't miss her." Lisa grimaced. "I had the feeling

she expected me to rise and curtsy. Who is she, anyway? The Queen of Hearts?"

"Perfect match for the emperor," Hillary murmured.

"What?"

"Nothing. Are you done? Let's get out of here." Rising without waiting for an answer, Hillary gathered her purse and the two women left the restaurant.

The following Monday Hillary walked to work. She lifted her face to the first snow of the season. Cold flakes drifted to kiss her upturned face, and she felt a thrill of anticipation watching soft white swirl from the lead-colored sky. Snow brought memories of home, sleigh rides, and snow battles. Sluggish traffic was powerless against her mood of excitement, and Hillary arrived at Larry's studio as bright and exuberant as a child.

"Hi, old man. How was your holiday?" Wrapped in a calf-length coat, a matching fur hat pulled low over her head, and cheeks and eyes glowing with the combination of cold and excitement, she was outrageously beautiful.

Larry paused in his lighting adjustment to greet her with a smile. "Look what the first snow blew in. You're an ad for winter vacations."

"You're incorrigible." She slipped out of her outdoor

clothing and wrinkled her nose. "You see everything cropped and printed."

"Occupational hazard. June says my eye for a picture is fascinating," he added smugly.

"*June* says?" Delicate brows raised inquiringly.

"Well, yeah, I've, uh, been teaching her a little about photography."

"I see." The tone was ironic.

"She's, well, she's interested in cameras."

"Ah, her interest is limited to shutter speeds and wide-angle lenses," Hillary agreed with a wise nod.

"Come on, Hil," Larry muttered, and began to fiddle with dials.

Gliding over, she hugged him soundly. "Kiss me, you fox. I knew you had it in you somewhere."

"Come on, Hil," he repeated, disentangling himself. "What are you doing here so early? You've got half an hour."

"Amazing, you noticed the time." She batted her eyes, received a scowl, and subsided. "I thought I might look over the work prints."

"Over there." He indicated his overloaded desk in the back corner of the room. "Go on now and let me finish."

"Yes, master." She retreated to search out the file

filled with the prints of the layout. After a few moment's study, she drew out one of herself on the tennis court. "I want a copy of this," she called to him. "I look fiercely competitive." Receiving no response, she glanced over, seeing him once more totally involved and oblivious to her presence. "Certainly, Hillary, my dear," she answered for him. "Anything you want. Look at that stance," she continued with deep enthusiasm, glancing back at the picture in her hands. "The perfect form and intense concentration of a champion. Look out, Wimbledon, here I come. You'll tear them apart, Hil." She again assumed Larry's role. "Thanks, Larry. All that talent and beauty too. Please, Larry, you're embarrassing me."

"They lock people up for talking to themselves," a deep voice whispered in her ear. Hillary jumped. The picture dropped from her hands to the pile on the desk. "Nervous, too—that's a bad sign."

She whirled and found herself face to face with Bret—so close, in fact, she took an instinctive step in retreat. The action did not go unnoticed, and the corner of his mouth twitched into a disarmingly crooked smile.

"Don't creep up on me like that."

"Sorry, but you were so engrossed in your dialogue."

His shoulders moved eloquently, and he allowed his voice to trail away.

A reluctant smile hovered on Hillary's lips. "Sometimes Larry lets the conversation drag a mite, and I'm obliged to carry him." She gestured with a slender hand. "Just look at that. He doesn't even know you're here."

"Mmm, perhaps I should take advantage of his preoccupation." He tucked a silky strand of hair behind her ear. The warmth of his fingers shot through her as he made the disturbingly gentle gesture, and her pulse began to jump at an alarming rate.

"Oh, hi, Bret. When did you get in?"

At Larry's words, Hillary let out a sigh, unsure whether it was born of relief or frustration.

December was slipping slowly by. Progress on the layout was more advanced than expected, and it appeared that actual shooting would be completed before Christmas. Hillary's contract with Bret ran through March, and she speculated on what she would do when the shooting stage was over and she was no longer needed. It was possible that Bret would release her, though she admitted this was highly unlikely. He would hardly wish her to work for a competitor before his pet project was on the stands.

Maybe he'll find some other work for me through the next couple of months, she theorized during a short break in a session. Or maybe she could be idle for a time. Oddly, the latter prospect appealed to her, and this surprised her. She enjoyed her work, didn't she? Hard work, yes, but rarely boring. Of course she enjoyed her work. It was enough for her, and she intended to keep it first in her life for the next few years. After that, she could retire if she liked or take a long vacation, travel— whatever. Then, when everything was in order, there would be time for a serious romance. She'd find someone nice, someone safe, someone she could marry and settle down with. That was her plan, and it made perfect sense. Only now, when thought through, it sounded horribly cold and dull.

Larry's studio was more crowded than usual during the second week of December. This particular morning, voices and bodies mingled in the room in delightful chaos. In this shooting, Hillary was sharing the spotlight with an eight-month-old boy as she portrayed the young mother.

A small section of the room was set to resemble part of a living area. When Hillary emerged from the hairdresser's hands, Larry was busy double-checking his equipment. Bret worked with him, discussing ideas for the session, and she chided herself for staring at his strong, lean back.

Leaving the men to their duties, she went over to meet the young mother and the child who would be hers for a few minutes in front of the camera. She was both surprised and amused by the baby's resemblance to her. Andy, as his mother introduced him, had a tuft of hair as dark and shining as Hillary's, and his eyes, though not as deep as hers, were startlingly blue. She would be taken without question for his mother by any stranger.

"Do you know how hard it was to find a child with your looks?" Bret asked, approaching from across the room to where Hillary sat with Andy on her lap. Bret stopped in front of her as she laughed and bounced the baby on her knee, and both woman and child raised deep blue eyes. "A person could be struck blind by all that brilliance. Perhaps you two should turn down the wattage."

"Isn't he beautiful?" Her voice was warm as she rubbed her cheeks against the soft down of his hair.

"Spectacular," he agreed. "He could be yours."

A shadow clouded over dark blue, and Hillary lowered her lashes on the sudden longing his words aroused. "Yes, the resemblance is amazing. Are we ready?"

"Yes."

"Well, partner." She stood and rested Andy on her hip. "Let's get to work."

"Just play with him," Larry instructed. "Do what comes naturally. What we're looking for is spontaneity." He looked down at the round face, and Andy's eyes met his levelly. "I think he understands me."

"Of course," Hillary agreed with a toss of her head. "He's a very bright child."

"We'll keep the shots candid and hope he responds to you. We can only work with children a few minutes at a time."

And so they began, with the two dark heads bent near each other as they sat on the carpeted area with Hillary building alphabet blocks and Andy gleefully destroying her efforts. Soon both were absorbed in the game and each other, paying scant attention to Larry's movements or the soft click of camera. Hillary lay on her stomach, feet in the air, constructing yet another tower for ultimate demolition. The child reached out, diverted by a strand of silky hair. His stubby fingers curled around the softness, tugging on it and bringing it to his mouth wrapped in a small fist.

Rolling on her back, she lifted the child over her head, and he gurgled in delight at the new game. Setting him on her stomach, he soon became enchanted by the pearl buttons on her pale green blouse. She watched his concentration, tracing his features with her fingertip. Again, she felt the pull of sudden longing. She lifted the baby over her body, making the sounds of a plane as she swayed him over her. Andy squealed in delight and she stood him on her stomach, letting him bounce to his own music.

She stood with him, swinging him in a circle before hugging him against her. This is what I want, she realized suddenly, holding the child closer. A child of my own, tiny arms around my neck, a child with the man I love. She closed her eyes as she rubbed her cheek against Andy's round one. When she opened them again, she found herself staring up into Bret's intense gaze.

She held her eyes level a moment as it drifted over her quietly that this was the man she loved, the man whose child she wanted to feel in her arms. She had known the truth for some time, but had refused to acknowledge it. Now, there was no denying it.

Andy's none-too-gentle tug on her hair broke the spell, and Hillary turned away, shaken by what she had just been forced to admit to herself. This was not what she had planned. How could this happen? She needed time to think, time to sort things out. Right now she felt too confused.

She was profoundly relieved when Larry signaled the finish. With a supreme effort, Hillary kept her professional smile in place while inside she trembled at her new awareness.

"Outstanding," Larry declared. "You two work together like old friends."

Not work, Hillary corrected silently, a fantasy. She had been acting out a fantasy. Perhaps her entire career was a fantasy, perhaps her entire life. A hysterical giggle bubbled inside her, and she choked it back. She could not afford to make a fool of herself now. She could not allow herself to think about the feelings running through her or the questions buzzing inside her brain.

"It's going to take some time to break down and set up for the next segment, Hil." Larry consulted his watch. "Go grab a bite before you change. Give it an hour."

Hillary assented with a wave of relief at the prospect of some time alone.

"I'll go with you."

"Oh, no," she protested, picking up her coat and hurrying out. His brow lifted at her frantic tone. "I mean, don't bother. You must have work to do. You must have to get back to your office or something."

"Yes, my work never ceases," he acknowledged with a heavy dose of mockery. "But once in a while I have to eat."

He took her coat to help her with it. His hands rested on her shoulders, their warmth seeping through the material and burning her skin, causing her to stiffen defensively. His fingers tightened and he turned her to face him.

"It was not my intention to have *you* for lunch, Hillary." The words were soft, at odds with the temper darkening eyes. "Will you never cease to be suspicious of me?"

The streets were clear, but there was a light covering of white along the sidewalks and on the cars parked along the curb. Hillary felt trapped in the closed car sitting so close to the man who drove, long fingers closed over the steering wheel of the Mercedes. He skirted Central Park, and she endeavored to ease her tension and slow the incessant drumming of her heart.

"Look, it's beautiful, isn't it?" She indicated the trees, their bare branches now robed in white, glittering as if studded with diamonds. "I love the snow," she chattered on, unable to bear the silence. "Everything seems clean and fresh and friendly. It makes it seem more like…"

"Home?" he supplied.

"Yes," she said weakly, retreating from his penetrating gaze.

Home, she thought. Home could be anywhere with this man. But she must not reveal her weakness. He must never know the love that rushed through her, tossing her heart like the winds of a tornado that swept through Kansas in late spring.

Sitting in a small booth, Hillary babbled about whatever innocuous subject came to mind. Chattering to avoid a lull where he might glimpse the secret she held within her, securely locked like a treasure in a fortress.

"Are you O.K., Hillary?" Bret asked suddenly when she paused to take a breath. "You've been very jumpy lately." His eyes were sharp and probing, and for a terrifying moment Hillary feared they would penetrate her mind and read the secret written there.

"Sure, I am." Her voice was admirably calm. "I'm just excited about the layout." She grasped at the straw of an excuse. "We'll be finished soon, and the issue will be on the stands. I'm anxious about the reception."

"If it's only business that bothers you," he said abruptly, "I believe I'm qualified to predict the reaction will be tremendous." His eyes reached out and held hers.

"You'll be a sensation, Hillary. Offers will come pouring in—magazines, television, products for your endorsement. You'll be in a position to pick and choose."

"Oh." Was all that she could manage.

His brows knitted dangerously. "Doesn't it excite you? Isn't that what you've always wanted?" he asked brusquely.

"Of course it is," she stated with a great deal more enthusiasm than she was feeling. "I'd have to be demented not to be thrilled, and I'm grateful for the opportunity you gave me."

"Save your gratitude." He cut her off curtly. "This project has been a result of teamwork. Whatever you gain from it, you've earned." He drew out his wallet. "If you're finished, I'll drop you back before I return to the office."

She nodded mutely, unable to comprehend what she had said to arouse his anger.

The final phase of shooting was underway. Hillary changed in the small room off Larry's main studio. Catching sight of her reflection in the full-length mirror, she held her breath. She had thought the negligee lovely but uninspired when she had lifted it from its box, but now, as it swirled around her, she was awed by its beauty. White and filmy, it floated around her slim curves, falling in gentle folds to her ankles. It was low cut, but not extreme, the soft swell of her breasts merely hinted at above the neckline. Yes, Hillary decided as she moved, the drifting material following in a lovingly lazy manner, it's stunning.

Earlier that day, she had modeled an exquisite sable coat. She remembered the feel of the fur against her chin and sighed. Larry had captured the first expression of delight and desire as she had buried her face against the collar. But Hillary knew now that she would rather have this negligee than ten sables. There was something special about it, as though it had been created with her in mind.

She walked from the dressing room and stood watching as Larry completed his setup. He has outdone himself this time, she mused with admiration. The lighting was soft and gentle, like a room lit with candles, and he had set up backlighting, giving the illusion of moonlight streaming. The effect was both romantic and subtle.

"Ah, good, you're ready." Larry turned from his task, then, focusing on her directly, let out a low whistle. "You're gorgeous. Every man who sees your picture will be dying for love of you, and every woman will be putting herself in your place. Sometimes you still amaze me."

She laughed and moved to join him as the studio door opened. Turning, the gown drifting about her, she saw Bret enter the room with Charlene on his arm. Blue eyes locked with gray before his traveled slowly over her with the intensity of a physical caress.

He took his time in bringing his eyes back to her face. "You look extraordinary, Hillary."

"Thanks." She swallowed the huskiness of her voice and her gaze moved from his to encounter Charlene's icy stare. The shock was like a cold shower and Hillary wished with all her heart that Bret had not chosen to bring his shapely companion with him.

"We're just getting started." Larry's matter-of-fact tone shattered the spell, and three heads turned to him.

"Don't let us hold things up," Bret said easily. "Charlene wanted to see the project that's been keeping me so busy."

His implication that Charlene had a stake in his life caused Hillary's spirits to plummet. Shaking off encroaching depression, she reminded herself that what she felt for Bret was strictly one-sided.

"Stand here, Hil," Larry directed, and she drifted to the indicated spot.

Muted lighting lent a glow to her skin, as soft on her cheek as a lover's caress. Soft backlighting shone through the filmy material, enticingly silhouetting her curves.

"Good," Larry stared, and, switching on the wind machine, he added, "perfect."

The easy breeze from the machine lifted her hair and rippled her gown. Picking up his camera, Larry began to shoot. "That's good, now lift your hair. Good, good, you'll drive them crazy." His instructions came swiftly, and her expressions and stances changed in rapid succession. "Now, look right into the camera— it's the man you love. He's coming to take you into his arms." Her eyes flew to the back of the studio where Bret stood linked with Charlene. Her eyes met his and a tremor shook her body. "Come on, Hillary, I want passion, not panic. Come on now, baby, look at the camera."

She swallowed and obeyed. Slowly, she allowed her dreams to take command, allowed the camera to become Bret. A Bret looking at her not only with desire, but with love. He came to her with love and need. He was holding her close as she remembered him holding her. His hands moved gently over her as his lips claimed hers after he whispered the words she longed to hear.

"That does it, Hillary."

Lost in her own world, she blinked and stared at Larry without comprehension.

"That was great. I fell in love with you myself."

Letting out a deep breath, she shut her eyes a moment and sighed at her own imagination. "I suppose we could get married and breed little lenses," she murmured as she headed for the dressing room.

"Bret, that negligee is simply marvelous." Charlene's words halted Hillary's progress. "I really must have it, darling. You can get it for me, can't you?" Charlene's voice was low and seductive as she ran a well-manicured hand along Bret's arm.

"Hmm? Sure," he assented, his eyes on Hillary. "If you want it, Charlene."

Hillary's mouth fell open with astonishment. His casual gift to the woman at his side wounded her beyond belief. She stared at him for a few moments before fleeing to her dressing room.

In the privacy of the dressing room, she leaned against the wall battling the pain. How could he? she cried inwardly. The gown was special, it was hers, she belonged in it. She closed her eyes and stifled a sob. She had even imagined him holding her in it, loving her, and now…it would be Charlene's. He would look at Charlene, his eyes dark with desire. His hands would caress Charlene's body through the misty softness. Now a fierce anger began to replace the pain. If that was what he wanted, well, they were welcome to it—both of them. She stripped herself from frothy white folds and dressed.

When she left the dressing room, Bret was alone in the studio, sitting negligently behind Larry's desk. Summoning all her pride, Hillary marched to him and dropped the large box on its cluttered surface.

"For your friend. You'll want to have it laundered first."

She turned to make her exit with as much dignity as possible, but was outmaneuvered as his hand closed over her wrist.

"What's eating you, Hillary?" He stood, keeping his grip firm and towering over her.

"Eating me?" she repeated, glaring up at him. "Whatever do you mean?"

"Drop it, Hillary," he ordered, the familiar steel entering both voice and eyes. "You're upset, and I mean to know why."

"Upset?" She tugged fiercely at her arm. As her efforts for liberation proved fruitless, her anger increased. "If I'm upset, it's my own affair. It's not in my contract that I'm obliged to explain my emotions to you." Her free hand went to his in an attempt to pry herself free, but he merely transferred his hold to her shoulders and shook her briskly.

"Stop it! What's gotten into you?"

"I'll tell you what's gotten into me," she snapped as her hair tumbled around her face. "You walk in here with your redheaded girlfriend and just hand over that gown. She just bats her eyes and says the word, and you hand it over."

"Is that what all this is about?" he demanded, exasperated. "Good heavens, woman, if you want the damn thing, I'll get you one."

"Don't you patronize me," she raged at him. "You can't buy my good humor with your trinkets. Keep your generosity for someone who appreciates it and let me go."

"You're not going anywhere until you calm down and we get to the root of the problem."

Her eyes were suddenly filled with uncontrollable tears. "You don't understand." She sniffed as tears coursed down her cheeks. "You just don't understand anything."

"Stop it!" He began to brush her tears away with his hand. "Tears are my downfall. I can't handle them. Stop it, Hillary, don't cry like that."

"It's the only way I know how to cry," she said, weeping miserably.

He swore under his breath. "I don't know what this is all about. A nightgown can't be worth all this! Here, take it—it's obviously important to you." He picked up the box, holding it out to her. "Charlene has plenty." The last words, uttered in an attempt to lighten her mood, had precisely the reverse effect.

"I don't want it. I don't ever want to see it again," she shouted, her voice made harsh by tears. "I hope you and your lover thoroughly enjoy it." With this, she whirled, grabbed her coat, and ran from the studio with surprising speed.

Outside, she stood on the sidewalk, stomping her feet against the cold. Stupid! she accused herself. Stupid to get so attached to a piece of cloth. But no more stupid than getting attached to an arrogant, unfeeling man whose interests lay elsewhere. Spotting a cab, she stepped forward to flag it down when she was spun around to face the buttons on Bret's leather coat.

"I've had enough of your tantrums, Hillary, and I don't tolerate being walked out on." His voice was low and dangerous, but Hillary tilted back her head to meet his gaze boldly.

"We have nothing more to say."

"We have plenty more to say."

"I don't expect you to understand." She spoke with the exaggerated patience an adult uses when addressing a slow-witted child. "You're just a man."

She heard the sharp intake of his breath as he moved toward her.

"You're right about one thing, I am a man," she heard him whisper before he pulled her close, crushing her mouth in an angry kiss, forcing her lips to open to his demands. The world emptied but for his touch, and the two stood locked together, oblivious to the people who walked the sidewalk behind them.

When at last he freed her, she drew back from him, her breath coming quickly. "Now that you've proven your masculinity, I really must go."

"Come back upstairs. We'll finish our discussion."

"Our discussion is finished."

"Not quite." He began to drag her back toward the studio.

I can't be alone with him now, she thought wildly. Not now, when I'm already so vulnerable. He could see too much too easily.

"Really, Bret." She was proud of the calmness of her

voice. "I do hate to create a scene, but if you continue to play the caveman I shall be forced to scream. And I can scream very loud."

"No, you wouldn't."

"Yes," Hillary corrected, digging in her heels. "I would."

"Hillary." He turned, maintaining possession of her arm. "We have things to clear up."

"Bret, it's gotten blown out of proportion." She spoke sweetly, ignoring the weakness in her legs. "We've both had our outburst of temper—let's just leave it at that. The entire thing was silly anyway."

"It didn't seem silly to you upstairs."

The slender hold on her control was slipping rapidly, and she looked up at him in a last ditch attempt. "Please, Bret drop it. We're all temperamental sometimes."

"Very well," he agreed after a pause. "We'll drop it for the time being."

Hillary sighed tremulously. She felt that if she stayed any longer she ran the risk of agreeing to whatever he asked. Out of the corner of her eye she glimpsed a passing cab, and she put her fingers to her mouth to whistle it down.

Bret's mouth lifted in irrepressible amusement. "You never cease to surprise me."

Her answer was lost as she slammed the cab door behind her.

Chapter 5

Christmas was approaching, and the city was decorated in its best holiday garb. Hillary watched from her window as cars and people bustled through the brightly lit streets. The snow fell upon city sidewalks, the drifting white adding to her holiday mood. She watched the huge flakes float to earth like down from a giant pillow.

Shooting of the layout was complete, and she had seen little of Bret in the past few days. She would be seeing less of him, she realized, a shaft of gloom darkening her cheerful mood. Now that her part in the project was over, there would be no day-to-day contact, no chance meetings. She sighed and shook her head. I'm going home tomorrow, she reminded herself, home for Christmas.

That was what she needed, she told herself, closing her eyes on the image of Bret's handsome features. A complete change of scene. Ten days to help heal her heart, time to reevaluate all the plans she had laid out, which now seemed hopelessly dull and unsatisfying.

The knock on the door caused her to remove her face, which had been pressed against the glass. "Who is it?" she called as she placed her hand on the knob.

"Santa Claus."

"B-Bret?" she stammered, thrown off balance. "Is that you?"

"Just can't fool you, can I?" After a slight pause, he asked, "Are you going to let me in, or do we have to talk through the door?"

"Oh, sorry." She fumbled with the latch and opened the door, staring at his lean form, which leaned negligently against the frame.

"You're locking up these days." His eyes swept her pearl-colored velour housecoat before he brought them back to hers. "Are you going to let me in?"

"Oh, sure." Hillary stood back to let him enter, desperately searching for lost composure. "I, ah, I thought Santa came down the chimney."

"Not this one," he returned dryly, and removed his coat. "I could use some of your famous Scotch. It's freezing out there."

"Now I'm totally disillusioned. I thought Santa thrived on cookies and milk."

"If he's half the man I think he is, he's got a flask in that red suit."

"Cynic," she accused, and retreated to the kitchen. Finding the Scotch easily this time, she poured a measure into a glass.

"Very professional." Bret observed from the doorway. "Aren't you going to join me in some holiday cheer?"

"Oh, no." Hillary wrinkled her nose in disgust. "This stuff tastes like the soap I had my mouth washed out with once."

"You've got class, Hillary," he stated wryly, and took the glass from her hand. "I won't ask you what your mouth was washed out for."

"I wouldn't tell you anyway." She smiled, feeling at ease with the casual banter.

"Well, have something, I hate to drink alone."

She reached into the refrigerator and removed a pitcher of orange juice.

"You do live dangerously, don't you?" he commented as she poured. She raised the glass in toast and they returned to the living room.

"I heard you're off to Kansas in the morning," he said as she seated himself on the sofa. Hillary strategically made use of the chair facing him.

"That's right, I'll be home until the day after New Year's."

"Then I'll wish you both a Merry Christmas and a Happy New Year early." He lifted his glass to her. "I'll think of you when the clock strikes twelve."

"I'm sure you'll be too busy to think of me at the stroke of midnight," she retorted, and cursed herself for losing the calm, easy tone.

He smiled and sipped his Scotch. "I'm sure I'll find a minute to spare." Hillary frowned into her glass and refrained from a comment. "I've something for you, Hillary." He rose and, picking up his jacket, removed a small package from its pocket. Hillary stared at it dumbly, then raised her expressive eyes to his.

"Oh, but...I didn't think...that is...I don't have anything for you."

"Don't you?" he asked lazily, and color rushed to her cheeks.

"Really, Bret, I can't take it. I wouldn't feel right."

"Think of it as a gift from the emperor to one of his subjects." He took the glass from her hand and placed the package in its stead.

"You have a long memory." She smiled in spite of herself.

"Like an elephant," he said, then, with a touch of impatience: "Open it. You know you're dying to."

She stared at the package, conceding with a sigh. "I never could resist anything wrapped in Christmas paper." She tore the elegant foil away, then caught her breath as she opened the box and revealed its contents. Earrings of deep sapphire stones blinked up from their backing of velvet.

"They reminded me of your eyes, brilliantly blue and exquisite. It seemed a crime for them to belong to anyone else."

"They're beautiful, really very beautiful," she murmured when she found her voice. Turning her sapphire eyes to his, she added, "You really shouldn't have bought them for me, I—"

"I shouldn't have," he interrupted, "but you're glad I did."

She had to smile. "Yes, I am. It was a lovely thing to do. I don't know how to thank you."

"I do." He drew her from the chair, his arms slipping around her. "This will do nicely." His lips met hers and, after a moment's hesitation, she responded, telling herself she was only showing her gratitude for his thoughtfulness. As the kiss lingered, her gratitude was forgotten. He lifted his mouth, and dazedly she made to move from the warm circle of his arms. "There are two earrings, love." His mouth claimed possession again, now more demanding, and her lips parted beneath his insistence. Her body seemed to melt against his, her arms twining around his neck, fingers tangling in his hair. She was lost in the feel of him, all thought ceasing, her only reality his mouth on hers, and his hard body blending with her yielding softness.

When at last their lips separated, he looked down at her, his eyes darkened with emotion. "It's a pity you've only got two ears." His voice was husky, and his head lowered toward hers.

She dropped her forehead to his chest and attempted to catch her breath. "Please, Bret," she whispered, her hands slipping from his neck to his shoulders. "I can't think when you kiss me."

"Can't you now?" His mouth tarried a moment in her hair. "That's very interesting." He brought his hand under her chin and lifted her face, his eyes moving over her features slowly. "You know, Hillary, that's a very dangerous admission. I'm tempted to press my advantage." He paused, continuing to study the fragile, vulnerable face. "Not this time." He released her, and she checked the impulse to sway toward him. Walking to the table, he downed the remainder of his Scotch and lifted his coat. At the door, he turned, giving her his charming smile. "Merry Christmas, Hillary."

"Merry Christmas, Bret," she whispered at the door he closed behind him.

The air was brisk and cold, carrying the clean, pure scent that meant home, the sky brilliantly blue and naked of clouds. Hillary let herself into the rambling farmhouse and for a moment gave in to memories.

"Tom, what are you doing coming in all the way around the front?" Sarah Baxter bustled from the kitchen, wiping her hands on a full white apron. "Hillary." She stopped as she caught sight of the slim, dark woman in the center of the room. "Well, time's just gotten away from me."

Hillary ran and enveloped her mother in a fierce hug. "Oh, Mom, it's good to be home."

If her mother noticed the desperate tone of Hillary's words, she made no comment, but returned the embrace with equal affection. Standing back, she examined Hillary with a mother's practiced eye. "You could use a few pounds."

"Well, look what the wind blew in all the way from New York City." Tom Baxter entered through the swinging kitchen door and caught Hillary in a close embrace. She breathed deeply, reveling in the smell of fresh hay and horses that clung to him. "Let me look at you." He drew her away and repeated his wife's survey. "What a beautiful sight." He glanced over Hillary's head and smiled at his wife. "We grew a real prize here, didn't we, Sarah?"

Later, Hillary joined her mother in the large kitchen that served the farm. Pots were simmering on a well-used range, filling the air with an irresistible aroma. Hillary allowed her mother to ramble about her brothers and their families, fighting back the deep longing that welled inside her.

Her hand went unconsciously to the blue stones at her ears, and Bret's image flooded her mind, bringing him almost close enough to touch. She averted her face, hoping that the bright tears that sprung to her eyes would not be observed by her mother's sharp glance.

On Christmas morning, Hillary woke with the sun and snuggled lazily in her childhood bed. She had fallen into the bed late the night before, but, having slipped between the covers, had been unable to sleep. Tossing and turning, she had stared at a dark ceiling until the early hours. Bret had remained in her mind no matter how strenuously she had tried to block him out. His image broke through her defenses like a rock through plate glass. To her despair, she found herself aching to be close to him, the need an ache deep inside her.

In the morning, in the clear light of day, she once more stared at the ceiling. There's nothing I can do, she realized hopelessly. I love him. I love him and I hate him for not loving me back. Oh, he wants me all right—he's made no secret of that—but wanting's not loving. How did it happen? Where did all my defenses go? He's arrogant, she began, mentally ticking off faults in an effort to find an escape hatch in her solitary prison. He's short tempered, demanding, and entirely too self-assured. Why doesn't any of that matter? What's happened to my brain? Why can't I stop thinking about him for more than five minutes at a time?

It's Christmas, she reminded herself, shutting her eyes against his intrusion. I am not going to let Bret Bardoff spoil my day!

Rising, she threw back the quilt, slipped on a fleece robe, and hurried from the room.

The house was already stirring, the quiet morning hush vanishing into activity. For the next hour, the scene around the Christmas tree was filled with gaiety, exclamations for the gifts that were revealed, and the exchange of hugs and kisses.

Later Hillary slipped outside, the thin blanket of frost crunching under her boots as she pulled her father's worn work jacket tighter around her slimness. The air tasted of winter, and the quiet seemed to hang like a soft curtain. Joining her father in the barn, she automatically began to measure out grain, her movements natural, the routine coming back as if she had performed the tasks the day before.

"Just an old farm hand after all, aren't you?" Though the words had been spoken in jest, Hillary halted and looked at her father seriously.

"Yes, I think I am."

"Hillary." His tone softened as he noticed the clouding of her eyes. "What's wrong?"

"I don't know." She let out a deep sigh. "Sometimes New York seems so crowded. I feel closed in."

"We thought you were happy there."

"I was…I am," she amended, and smiled. "It's a very exciting place, busy and filled with so many different kinds of people." She forced back the image of clear gray eyes and strong features. "Sometimes I just miss the quiet, the openness, the peace. I'm being silly." She shook her head and scooped out more grain. "I've been a bit homesick lately, that's all. This layout I just finished was fascinating, but it took a lot out of me." Not the layout, she corrected silently, but the man.

"Hillary, if you're unhappy, if there's anything on your mind, I want to help you."

For a moment, she longed to lean on her father's shoulder and pour out her doubts and frustrations. But what good would it do to burden him? What could he do about the fact that she loved a man who saw her only as a temporary diversion, a marketable commodity for selling magazines? How could she explain that she was unhappy because she had met a man who had broken and captured her heart unknowingly and effortlessly? All these thoughts ran through her brain before she shook her head, giving her father another smile.

"It's nothing. I expect it's just a letdown from finishing the layout. Postphotography depression. I'll go feed the chickens."

The house was soon overflowing with people, echoing with mixed voices, laughter, and the sound of children. Familiar tasks and honest affection helped to erase the ache of emptiness that still haunted her….

When only the echoes of the holiday lingered, Hillary remained downstairs alone, unwilling to seek the comfort of her bed.

Curled in a chair, she stared at the festive lights of the tree, unable to prevent herself from speculating on how Bret had celebrated his holiday. A quiet day with Charlene, perhaps, or a party at the country club? Right now they were probably sitting in front of a roaring fire, and Charlene was snuggled in his arms draped in that beautiful negligee.

A pain shot through her, sharp as the point of an arrow, and she was enveloped by a tortuous combination of raging jealousy and hopeless despair. But the image would not fade.

* * *

The days at home went quickly. They were good days, following a soothing routine that Hillary dropped into gratefully. Kansas wind blew away a portion of her depression. She took long, quiet walks, gazing out at the rolling hills and acres of winter wheat.

People from the city would never understand, she mused. How could they comprehend this? Her arms were lifted wide as she spun in a circle. In their elegant apartments looking out at steel and concrete they could never feel the exuberation of being a part of the land. The land; she surveyed its infinity with wondering eyes. The land is indomitable; the land is forever. There had been Indians here, and plainsmen and pioneers and farmers. They came and went, lived and died, but the land lived on. And when she was gone, and another generation born, wheat would still wave in the bright summer sun. The land gave them what they needed, rich and fertile, generously giving birth to acres of wheat year after year, asking only for honest labor in return.

And I love it, she reflected, hugging herself tightly. I love the feel of it in my hands and under my bare feet in the summer. I love the rich, clean smell of it. I suppose, for all my acquired sophistication, I'm still just a farm girl. She retraced her steps toward the house. What am I going to do about it? I have a career; I have a place in New York as well. I'm twenty-four. I can't just throw in the towel and come back to live on the farm. No. She shook her head vigorously, sending her hair swirling in a black mist. I've got to go back and do what I'm qualified to do. Firmly, she ignored the small voice that asserted her decision was influenced by another resident of New York.

The phone jangled on the wall as she entered the house, and, slipping off her jacket, she lifted it.

"Hello."

"Hello, Hillary."

"Bret?" She had not known pain could come so swiftly at the sound of a voice.

"Very good." She heard the familiar mockery and pressed her forehead to the wall. "How are you?"

"Fine, I'm just fine." She groped for some small island of composure. "I…I didn't expect to hear from you. Is there a problem?"

"Problem?" he returned in a voice that mirrored his smile. "No permanent one in any case. I thought you might be needing a reminder of New York about now. We wouldn't want you to forget to come back."

"No, I haven't forgotten." Taking a deep breath, she made her voice lightly professional. "Have you something in mind for me?"

"In mind? You might say I had one or two things in mind." There was a slight pause before he continued. "Anxious to get back to work?"

"Uh, yes, yes, I am. I wouldn't want to get stale."

"I see."

You couldn't see through a chain-link fence, she thought with growing frustration.

"We'll see what we can do when you get back. It would be foolish not to put your talents to use." He spoke absently, as though his mind was already formulating a suitable project.

"I'm sure you'll think of something advantageous for both of us," she stated, trying to emulate his businesslike tone.

"Mmm, you'll be back at the end of the week?"

"Yes, on the second."

"I'll be in touch. Keep your calendar clear." The order was casual, confident, and brisk. "We'll get you in front of the camera again, if that's what you want."

"All right. I…well…thanks for calling."

"My pleasure. I'll see you when you get back."

"Yes. Bret…" She searched for something to say, wanting to cling to the small contact, perhaps just to hear him say her name one more time.

"Yes?"

"Nothing, nothing." Shutting her eyes, she cursed her lack of imagination. "I'll wait to hear from you."

"Fine." He paused a moment, and his voice softened. "Have a good time at home, Hillary."

Chapter 6

The first thing Hillary did upon returning to her New York apartment was to put a call through to Larry. When greeted by a feminine voice, she hesitated, then apologized.

"Sorry, I must have the wrong number…"

"Hillary?" the voice interrupted. "It's June."

"June?" she repeated, confused, then added quickly. "How are you? How were your holidays?"

"Terrific to both questions. Larry told me you went home. Did you have a good time?"

"Yes, I did. It's always good to get home again."

"Hang on a minute. I'll get Larry."

"Oh, well, no, I'll…"

Larry's voice broke into her protestations. She immediately launched into an apology, telling him she would call back.

"Don't be dumb, Hil, June's just helping me sort out my old photography magazines."

It occurred to Hillary that their relationship must be moving along at light speed for Larry to allow June to get her hands on his precious magazines. "I just wanted you to know I was back," she said aloud. "Just in case anything comes up."

"Mmm, well, I guess you really should get in touch with Bret." Larry considered. "You're still under contract. Why don't you give him a call?"

"I won't worry about it," she returned, striving to keep her tone casual. "I told him I'd be back after the first." Her voice dropped. "He knows where to find me."

Several days passed before Bret contacted Hillary. Much of the interim she spent at home because of the snow, which seemed to fall unceasingly over the city, alternating with a penetrating, bitter sleet. The confinement, coming on the heels of the open freedom she had experienced in Kansas, played havoc with her nerves, and she found herself staring down from her window at ice-covered sidewalks with increasing despair.

One evening, as the sky dropped the unwelcome gift of freezing rain, Lisa arranged to have dinner and spend a few hours in Hillary's company. Standing in the kitchen, Hillary was separating a small head of lettuce when the phone rang. Looking down at her wet, leaf-filled hands, she rubbed her nose on her shoulder and asked Lisa to answer the ring.

Lifting the receiver, Lisa spoke into it in her most formal voice. "Miss Hillary Baxter's residence, Lisa MacDonald speaking. Miss Baxter will be with you as soon as she gets her hands out of the lettuce."

"Lisa." Hillary laughed as she hurried into the room. "I just can't trust you to do anything."

"It's all right," she announced loudly, holding out the receiver. "It's only an incredibly sexy male voice."

"Thanks," Hillary returned with deep sincerity, and rescued the phone. "Go, you're banished back into the kitchen." Pulling a face, Lisa retreated, and Hillary gave her attention to her caller. "Hello, don't mind my friend, she's just crazy."

"On the contrary, that's the most interesting conversation I've had all day."

"Bret?" Until that moment, Hillary had not realized how much she needed to hear his voice.

"Right the first time." She could almost see the slow smile spread across his features. "Welcome back to the concrete jungle, Hillary. How was Kansas?"

"Fine," she stammered. "It was just fine."

"Mmm, how illuminating. Did you enjoy your Christmas?"

"Yes, very much." Struggling to regain the composure that had fled at the sound of his voice, she spoke quickly. "And you? Did you have a nice holiday?"

"Delightful, though I'm sure it was a great deal quieter than yours."

"Different anyway," Hillary rejoined, annoyed.

"Ah, well, that's behind us now. Actually, I'm calling about this weekend."

"Weekend?" Hillary repeated dumbly.

"Yes, a trip to the mountains."

"Mountains?"

"You sound like a parrot," he said shortly. "Do you have anything important scheduled from Friday through Sunday?"

"Well, I…ah…"

"Lord, what an astute conversationalist you are." His voice reflected growing annoyance.

Swallowing, she attempted to be more precise. "No. That is, nothing essential. I—"

"Good," he interrupted. "Ever been skiing?"

"In Kansas?" she retorted, regaining her balance. "I believe mountains are rather essential for skiing."

"So they are," he agreed absently. "Well, no matter. I had an idea for some pictures of a lovely lady frolicking in the snow. I've a lodge in the Adirondacks near Lake George. It'll make a nice setting. We can combine business with pleasure."

"We?" Hillary murmured weakly.

"No need for panic," he assured her, his words heavy with mockery. "I'm not abducting you to the wilderness to ravish you, although the idea does have some interesting angles." He paused, then laughed outright. "I can feel you blushing right through the phone."

"Very funny," she retorted, infuriated that he could read her so easily. "I'm beginning to recall an urgent engagement for the weekend, so—"

"Hold on, Hillary," he interrupted again, his words suddenly brooking no argument. "You're under contract.

My rights hold for a couple more months. You wanted to get back to work; I'm putting you back to work."

"Yes, but—"

"Read the fine print if you like, but keep this weekend clear. And relax," he continued as she remained silent. "You'll be well protected from my dishonorable advances. Larry and June will be coming with us. Bud Lewis, my assistant art director, will be joining us later."

"Oh," she replied inadequately, unsure whether she was relieved or disappointed.

"I—the magazine, that is—will provide you with suitable snow gear. I'll pick you up at seven thirty Friday morning. Be packed and ready."

"Yes, but—" Hillary stared at the dead receiver with a mixture of annoyance and trepidation. He had not given her the opportunity to ask questions or formulate a reasonable excuse to decline. Hanging up, she turned around, her face a study in bewilderment.

"What was all that? You look positively stunned." Lisa regarded her friend from the kitchen doorway.

"I'm going to the mountains for the weekend," she answered slowly, as if to herself.

"The mountains?" Lisa repeated. "With the owner of that fascinating voice?"

Hillary snapped back and attempted to sound casual. "It's just an assignment. That was Bret Bardoff. There'll be plenty of others along," she added.

Friday morning dawned clear and cloudless and cold. Hillary was packed and ready as instructed, sipping a second cup of tea, when the doorbell sounded.

"Good morning, Hillary," Bret said as she opened the door. "Ready to brave the uncharted wilderness?"

He looked quite capable of doing just that in a hip-length sheepskin jacket, heavy corded jeans, and sturdy boots. Now he appeared rugged, not the cool, calculating businessman to whom she had grown accustomed. Gripping the doorknob tightly, she maintained a cool exterior and invited him in.

Assuring him she was quite ready, she walked away to place the empty cup in the sink and fetch her coat. Slipping her coat over her sweater and jeans, she pulled a dark brown ski hat over her hair. Bret looked on silently.

"I'm ready." Suddenly aware of his intense regard, she moistened her lips nervously with her tongue. "Shall we go?"

Inclining his head, he bent to pick up the case she had waiting beside the sofa, his movements coinciding with hers. Straightening with a jerk, she flushed awkwardly.

His brow lifted with his smile as he captured her hand and led her to the door.

They soon left the city as Bret directed the Mercedes north. He drove quickly and skillfully along the Hudson, keeping up a light conversation. Hillary found herself relaxing in the warm interior, forgetting her usual inhibition at being in close contact with the man who stirred her senses. As they began to pass through small towns and villages, she could hardly believe they were still in New York, her experience with the state having been limited exclusively to Manhattan and the surrounding area. Ingenuously, she voiced her thoughts, pulling off her hat and shaking out her rich fall of hair.

"There's more in New York than skyscrapers," he informed her with a crooked smile. "Mountains, valleys, forests—it has a bit of everything. I suppose it's time we changed your impression."

"I've never thought of it except as a place to work," she admitted, shifting in her seat to face him more directly. "Noisy, busy, and undeniably exciting, but draining at times because it's always moving and never seems to sleep. It always makes the sound of the silence at home that much more precious."

"And Kansas is still home, isn't it?" He seemed to be

thinking of something else as he asked, his expression brooding on the road ahead. Hillary frowned at his change of mood, then gave her attention to the scenery without answering.

They continued northward, and she lost track of time, intoxicated by the newness and beauty of her surroundings. At her first glimpse of the Catskills, she let out a small cry of pleasure, spontaneously tugging on Bret's arm and pointing. "Oh, look—mountains!"

Turning her eyes from the view, she gave him her special smile. He returned the smile, and her heart did a series of acrobatics. She turned back to the scene out the window. "I suppose I must seem terribly foolish, but when you've only known acres of wheat and rolling hills, this is quite a revelation."

"Not foolish, Hillary." His voice was gentle, and she turned to face him, surprised at the unfamiliar tone. "I find you utterly charming."

Picking up her hand, he turned it upward and kissed her palm, sending shooting arrows of flame up her arm and down to her stomach. Dealing with his mockery and amusement was one thing, she pondered dizzily, she was quite used to that by now. But these occasional gentle moods turned her inside out, making her spark like a lighted match. This man was dangerous, she concluded, very dangerous. Somehow she must build up an impregnable defense against him. But how? How could she fight both him and the part of herself that wanted only to surrender?

"I could do with some coffee," Bret said suddenly, bringing Hillary back from her self interrogation. "How about you?" He turned to her and smiled. "Want some tea?"

"Sure," she answered casually.

The Mercedes rolled into the small village of Catskill and Bret parked in front of a cafe. He opened his door and stepped from the car, and she quickly followed suit before he circled the front and joined her on the curb. Her eyes were fixed on the overpowering encircling mountains.

"They look higher than they are," Bret commented. "Their bases are only a few hundred feet above sea level. I'd love to see the expression on that beautiful face of yours when you encounter the Rockies or the Alps."

Interlocking his hand with hers, he led her out of the cold and into the warmth of the cafe. When the small table was between them, Hillary shrugged out of the confines of her coat, concentrating on the view, attempting to erect a wall of defense between herself and Bret.

"Coffee for me and tea for the lady. Are you hungry, Hillary?"

"What? Oh, no…well, yes, actually a little." She grinned, remembering the lack of breakfast that morning.

"They serve an outstanding coffee cake here." He ordered two slices before Hillary could protest.

"I don't usually eat that kind of thing." She frowned, thinking of the half grapefruit she had had in mind.

"Hillary, darling," Bret broke in with exaggerated patience. "One slice of cake is hardly likely to affect your figure. In any case," he added with irritating bluntness, "a few pounds wouldn't hurt you."

"Really," she retorted, chin rising with indignation. "I haven't had any complaints so far."

"I'm sure you haven't, and you'll get none from me. I've become quite enchanted with tall, willowy women. Though," he continued, reaching over to brush a loose strand of hair from her face, "the air of frailty is sometimes disconcerting."

Hillary decided to ignore both gesture and remark. "I don't know when I've enjoyed a drive more," she said, determined to remain casual. "How much farther do we have to go?"

"We're at the halfway point." Bret added cream to his coffee. "We should arrive around noon."

"How is everyone else coming? I mean, are they driving together?"

"Larry and June are coming up together." He smiled and ate a forkful of cake. "I should say Larry and June are accompanying Larry's equipment. I'm amazed he allowed her to travel in the same car with his precious cameras and lenses."

"Are you?" Hillary questioned, grinning into her tea.

"I suppose I shouldn't be," he admitted wryly. "I have noticed our favorite photographer's increasing preoccupation with my secretary. He seemed inordinately pleased to have her company on the drive."

"When I phoned him the other day, he was actually allowing her to sort out his photography magazines." Hillary's voice was tinged with disbelief. "That's tantamount to a bethrothal." She gestured with her fork. "It might even be binding. I'm not sure of the law. I still can't believe it." She swallowed a piece of cake and looked at Bret in amazement. "Larry's actually serious about a flesh-and-blood woman."

"It happens to the best of us, love," Bret agreed gently.

But would it ever to Bret? She could not meet his eyes.

* * *

On the road once more, Hillary contented herself with the scenery as Bret kept up a general conversation. The warmth of the Mercedes' interior and its smooth, steady ride had lulled her into a state of deep relaxation, and leaning back, she closed her suddenly heavy lids as they crossed the Mohawk River. Bret's deep voice increased her peaceful mood, and she murmured absently in response until she heard no more.

Hillary stirred restlessly as the change in road surface disturbed her slumber. Her eyes blinked open, and after a moment's blankness, reality returned. Her head was nestled against his shoulder, and, sitting up quickly, she turned sleep flushed face and heavy dark eyes to him.

"Oh, I'm sorry. Did I fall asleep?"

"You might say that," he said, glancing over as she pushed at tumbled hair. "You've been unconscious for an hour."

"Hour?" she repeated, attempting to clear the cobwebs. "Where are we?" she mumbled, gazing around her. "What did I miss?"

"Everything from Schenectady on, and we're on the road that leads to my lodge."

"Oh, it's beautiful." She came quickly awake as she focused on her surroundings.

The narrow road they traveled was flanked with snow-covered trees and rugged outcroppings of rock. Snow draped the green needles of pine, and what would have been dark, empty branches glistened with icicles and pure, sparkling white. Dense and thick, they seemed to be everywhere, rising majestically from a brilliant virgin blanket.

"They're so many." She scooted in her seat to experiment with the view from Bret's window, her knees brushing his thigh.

"The forest is full of them."

"Don't make fun." She punched his shoulder and continued to stare. "This is all new to me."

"I'm not making fun," he said, rubbing his shoulder with exaggerated care. "I'm delighted with your enthusiasm."

The car halted, and Hillary turned from Bret to look out the front window of the car. With a cry of pleasure, she spotted the large A-frame dwelling nestled in a small clearing so much a part of the surroundings it might have grown there. Picture windows gleamed and glistened in the filtered sunlight.

"Come get a closer look," Bret invited, stepping from

the car. He held his hand out to her, and she slipped hers into his grasp as they began to crunch through the un-touched snow. An ice-crusted stream tumbled swiftly on the far side of the house and, like a child wishing to share a new toy, Hillary pulled Bret toward it.

"How marvelous, how absolutely marvelous," she proclaimed, watching water force its way over rocks, its harsh whisper the only disturbance of peace. "What a fabulous place." She made a slow circle. "It's so wild and powerful, so wonderfully untouched and primitive."

Bret's eyes followed her survey before staring off through a dense outcropping of trees. "Sometimes I escape here, when my office begins to close in on me. There's such blessed peace—no urgent meetings, no deadlines, no responsibilities."

Hillary regarded him in open amazement. She had never imagined his needing to escape from anything or seeking deliberate solitude in a place so far from the city and its comforts and pleasures. To her, Bret Bardoff had represented the epitome of the efficient businessman, with employees rushing to do his bidding at the snap of his imperious finger. Now, she began to see another aspect of his nature, and she found the knowledge brought her a swift rush of pleasure.

He turned and encountered her stare, locking her eyes to his with a force that captured her breath. "It's also quite isolated," he added, in such a swift change of mood it took her a moment to react.

Blue eyes deepened and widened and she looked away, staring at the trees and rocks. She was here in the middle of nowhere, she realized, unconsciously chewing on her lip. He had told her the others were coming, but there was only his word. She had not thought to check with Larry. What if he had made the whole thing up? She would be trapped with him, completely alone. What would she do if…

"Keep calm, Hillary." Bret laughed wryly. "I haven't kidnapped you, the others will be along to protect you." He had deliberately provoked her reaction, and Hillary whirled to tell him what she thought of him, but he went on before she could speak. "That is, if they can find the place," he muttered, his brow creasing before his features settled in a wide smile. "It would be a shame if my directions were inadequate, wouldn't it?" Taking her hand once more, he led a confused and uneasy Hillary toward the lodge.

The interior was spacious, with wide, full windows bringing the mountains inside. The high ceiling with exposed beams added to the openness. Rough wooden stairs led to a balcony that ran the length of the living room. A stone fireplace commanded an entire wall, with furniture arranged strategically around it. Oval braid rugs graced the dark pine floor, their bright colors the perfect accent for the rustic, wood-dominated room.

"It's charming," Hillary said with delight as she gazed about her. She walked over to the huge expanse of glass, "You can stand here and be inside and out at the same time."

"I've often felt that way myself," Bret agreed, moving to join her and slipping her coat from her shoulders. "What is that scent you wear?" he murmured, his fingers massaging the back of her neck, their strength throbbing through her. "It's always the same, very delicate and appealing."

"It's, ah, it's apple blossom." She swallowed and kept her eyes glued to the window.

"Mmm, you mustn't change it, it suits you…. I'm starving," he announced suddenly, turning her to face him. "How about opening a can or something, and I'll start the fire? The kitchen's well stocked. You should be able to find something to ward off starvation."

"All right," she agreed, smiling. "We wouldn't want you to fade away. Where's the kitchen?" He pointed, and leaving him still standing by the window, she set off in the direction he indicated.

The kitchen was full of old-fashioned charm, with a small brick fireplace of its own and copper-bottomed pots hanging along the wall. The stove itself Hillary regarded doubtfully, thinking it resembled something her grandmother might have slaved over, until she observed that it had been adapted for modern use. The large pantry was well stocked, and she located enough cans for an adequate midday meal. Not precisely a gourmet feast, she reflected as she opened a can of soup, but it will have to do. She was spooning soup into a pan when she heard Bret's footsteps behind her.

"That was quick!" she exclaimed. "You must have been a terrific boy scout."

"It's a habit of mine to set the fire before I leave," he explained, standing behind her as she worked. "That way all I have to do is open the flu and light a match."

"How disgustingly organized," Hillary observed with a sniff, and switched the flame under the soup.

"Ah, ambrosia," he proclaimed, slipping his arms around her waist. "Are you a good cook, Hillary?"

The hard body pressed into her back was very distracting. She struggled to remain cool. "Anyone can open a can of soup." The last word caught in her throat as his hand reached up to part the dark curtain of her hair, his lips warm as they brushed the back of her neck. "I'd better make some coffee." She attempted to slip away, but his arms maintained possession, his mouth roaming over her vulnerable skin. "I thought you were hungry." The words came out in a babbling rush as her knees melted, and she leaned back against him helplessly for support.

"Oh, I am," he whispered, his teeth nibbling at her ear. "Ravenous."

He buried his face in the curve of her neck, and the room swayed as his hands slid upward under her sweater.

"Bret, don't," she moaned as a rush of desire swept over her, and she struggled to escape before she was lost.

He muttered savagely and spun her around, roughly crushing her lips under his.

Though he had kissed her before, demanding, arousing kisses, there had always been a measure of control in his lovemaking. Now it was as if the wildness of their surroundings had entered him. Like a man whose control has been too tightly bound, he assaulted her mouth, parting hers and taking possession. His hands pressed her hips against him, molding them together into one form. She was drowning in his explosion of passion, clinging to him as his hands roamed over her, seeking, demanding, receiving. The fire of his need ignited hers, and she gave herself without reservation, straining against him, wanting only to plunge deeper into the heat.

The sound of a car pulling up outside brought a muffled curse from Bret. Lifting his mouth from hers, he rested his chin on top of her head and sighed.

"They found us, Hillary. Better open another can."

Chapter 7

Voices drifted through the building, June's laughter and Larry's raised tones in some shared joke. Bret moved off to greet them, leaving Hillary battling to regain some small thread of composure. The urgent demand of Bret's lovemaking had awakened a wild, primitive response in her. She was acutely aware that, had they been left undisturbed, he would not have held back, and she would not have protested. The need had been too vital, too consuming. The swift beginning and sudden end of the contact left her trembling and unsteady. Pressing hands to burning cheeks, she went back to the stove, to attend to soup and coffee, hoping the simple mechanical tasks would restore her equilibrium.

"So, he's got you slaving away already." June entered the kitchen, arms ladened with a large paper bag. "Isn't that just like a man?"

"Hi." Hillary turned around, showing a fairly normal countenance. "It appears we've both been put in our places. What's in the bag?"

"Supplies for the long, snowbound weekend." Unpacking the bag, June revealed milk, cheese, and other fresh goods.

"Always efficient," Hillary stated, and, feeling the tension melt away, flashed her smile.

"It is difficult being perfect," June agreed with a sigh. "But some of us are simply born that way."

Meal preparations complete, they carried bowls and plates into the adjoining room to a large, rectangular wooden table with long benches running along each side. The group devoured the simple meal as though months had passed since they had seen a crust of bread. Mirroring Bret's now casual manner was at first difficult, but, summoning all her pride, Hillary joined in the table talk, meeting his occasional comments with an easy smile.

She retreated with June upstairs as the men launched into a technical discussion on the type of pictures required, and found the room they would share as charmingly rustic as the remainder of the house. The light, airy room with a breathtaking view of forest and mountains held two twin beds covered in patchwork quilts. Again wood predominated, the high sloping ceiling adding to the space. Brass lamps ensured soft lighting once the sun had descended behind the peaks outside.

Hillary busied herself with the case containing her wardrobe for the photo session as June threw herself heavily on a bed.

"Isn't this place fantastic?" Stretching her arms to the ceiling, June heaved a deep sigh of contentment. "Far from the maddening crowd and typewriters and telephones. Maybe it'll snow like crazy, and we'll be here until spring."

"We'd only be able to stick it out if Larry brought enough film for a couple of months. Otherwise, he'd go into withdrawal," Hillary commented. Removing a red parka and bibbed ski pants from the case, she studied them with a professional eye. "Well, this should stand out in the snow."

"If we painted your nose yellow, you'd look like a very large cardinal," June commented, clasping her hands behind her head. "That color will look marvelous on you. With your hair and complexion, and the snow as a backdrop, you'll be smashing. The boss never makes a mistake."

The sound of a car caught their attention, and they moved to the window looking down as Bud Lewis assisted Charlene from the vehicle. "Well"—June sighed and grimaced at Hillary—"Maybe one."

Stunned, Hillary stared at the top of Charlene's glossy red head. "I didn't…Bret didn't tell me Charlene was coming." Infuriated by the intrusion on her weekend, Hillary turned from the window and busied her hands with unpacking.

"Unless I'm very much mistaken, he didn't know." Scowling, June turned and leaned against the window-sill. "Maybe he'll toss her out in the snow."

"Maybe," Hillary countered, relieving some of her frustration by slamming the top of her suitcase, "he'll be glad to see her."

"Well, we won't find out anything standing around up here." June started toward the door, grabbing Hillary's arm along the way. "Come on, let's go see."

Charlene's voice drifted to Hillary as she descended the stairs. "You really don't mind that I came to keep you company, do you, Bret? I thought it would be such a lovely surprise."

Hillary entered the room in time to see Bret's shrug. He was seated on a love seat in front of the blazing fire, Charlene's arm tucked possessively through his. "I didn't think the mountains were your style, Charlene." He gave her a mild smile. "If you'd wanted to come, you should have asked instead of spinning a tale to Bud about my wanting him to drive you up."

"Oh, but, darling, it was just a little fib." Tilting her head, she fluttered darkened lashes. "A little intrigue is so amusing."

"Let's hope your 'little intrigue' doesn't lead you to 'a lot of boredom.' We're a long way from Manhattan."

"I'm never bored with you."

Soft and coaxing, the voice grated on Hillary's nerves. Perhaps she made some small sound of annoyance for Bret's eyes shifted to where she stood with June in the doorway. Charlene followed his gaze, her lips tightening for a moment before settling into a vague smile.

There followed an unenthusiastic exchange of greetings. Opting for distance, Hillary seated herself across the room with Bud as Charlene again gave Bret her full attention.

"I thought we'd never get here," Charlene complained with a petulant pout. "Why you would own a place in this godforsaken wilderness is beyond me, darling." She glanced up at Bret with cool green eyes. "All this snow, and nothing but trees and rocks, and so cold." With a delicate shiver, she huddled against him. "Whatever do you find to do up here all alone?"

"I manage to find diversions," Bret drawled, and lit a cigarette. "And I'm never alone—the mountains are teeming with life." He gestured toward the window. "There are squirrels, chipmunks, rabbits, foxes—all manner of small animal life."

"That's not precisely what I meant by company," Charlene murmured, using her most seductive voice. Bret granted her a faint smile.

"Perhaps not, but I find them entertaining and undemanding. I've often seen deer pass by as I stood by that window, and bear."

"Bears?" Charlene exclaimed, and tightened her hold on his arm. "How dreadful."

"Real bears?" Hillary demanded, eyes bright with adventure. "Oh, what kind? Those huge grizzlies?"

"Black bear, Hillary," he corrected, smiling at her reaction. "But big enough just the same. And safely in hibernation at the moment," he added with a glance at Charlene.

"Thank heaven," she breathed with genuine feeling.

"Hillary's quite taken to the mountains, haven't you?"

"They're fabulous," she agreed with enthusiasm. "So wild and untamed. All this must look nearly the same as it did a century ago, unspoiled by buildings and housing developments. Nothing but undisturbed nature for miles and miles."

"My, my, you are enthusiastic," Charlene observed.

Hillary shot her a deadly glance.

"Hillary grew up on a farm in Kansas," Bret explained, observing danger signals in dark blue eyes. "She'd never seen mountains before."

"How quaint," Charlene murmured, lips curving in a smile. "They grow wheat or something there, don't they? I would imagine you're quite accustomed to primitive conditions coming from a little farm."

The superior tone had Hillary bristling with anger, her rising temper reflected in her voice. "The farm is hardly little or primitive, Miss Mason. Impossible, I suppose, for one of your background to visualize the eternity of wheat, the miles of gently rolling hills. Not as sophisticated as New York, perhaps, but hardly prehistoric. We even manage to have hot and cold running water right inside the house most of the time. There are those who appreciate the land and respect it in all forms."

"You must be quite the outdoor girl," Charlene said in a bored voice. "I happen to prefer the comforts and culture of the city."

"I think I'll take a walk before it gets dark." Hillary rose quickly, needing to put some distance between herself and the other woman before her temper was irrevocably lost.

"I'll go with you." Bud stood, moving to join her as she slipped on her outdoor clothing. "I've been cooped up with that woman all day," he whispered with a conspirator's smile. "I think the fresh air will do me a world of good."

Hillary's laughter floated through the room as she strolled through the door, arm in arm with Bud. She was oblivious of the frown that darkened the gray eyes that followed her.

Once outside, the two breathed deeply, then giggled like children at their private joke. By mutual consent, they headed for the stream, following its tumbling progress downstream as they ambled deeper into the forest. Sunlight winked sporadically through the trees, glistening on the velvet snow. Bud's easy conversation soothed Hillary's ruffled spirits.

They stopped and rested on a mound of rock for a moment of companionable silence.

"This is nice," Bud said simply, and Hillary made a small sound signifying both pleasure and agreement. "I begin to feel human again," he added with a wink. "That woman is hard to take. I can't imagine what the boss sees in her."

Hillary grinned. "Isn't it strange that I agree with you?"

They walked home in the subtle change of light that signified encroaching dusk. Again, they followed the stream, easily retracing the footsteps they had left in the pure, white snow. They were laughing companionably as they entered the A-frame.

"Don't either of you have more sense than to wander about the mountains after dark?" Bret asked them, scowling.

"Dark? Don't be silly." Hillary hopped on one foot as she pried off a boot. "We only followed the stream a little way, and it's barely dusk." Losing her balance, she collided with Bud, who slipped an arm around her waist to right her, keeping it there while she struggled with her other boot.

"We left a trail in the snow," Bud stated with a grin. "Better than bread crumbs."

"Dusk turns to dark quickly, and there's no moon tonight," Bret said. "It's a simple matter to get lost."

"Well, we're back, and we didn't," Hillary told him. "No need for a search party or a flask of brandy. Where's June?"

"In the kitchen, starting dinner."

"I better go help then, hadn't I?" She gave him a radiant smile and brushed past them, leaving Bud to deal with his boss's temper.

"A woman's work is never done," Hillary observed with a sigh as she entered the kitchen.

"Tell that to Miss Nose-in-the-Air." June wrinkled her own as she unwrapped the steaks. "She was so fatigued from the arduous drive"—June placed a dramatic hand to her forehead—"she simply had to lie down before dinner."

"That's a blessing. Anyway," Hillary went on as she joined in the meal preparation, "who voted us in charge of kitchen duty? I'm quite sure it's not in my contract."

"I did."

"Voluntarily?"

"It's like this," June explained, searching through cupboards. "I've had a small example of Larry's talents, culinary talents, and I don't want another bout of ptomaine. The boss even makes lousy coffee. And as for Bud—well, he might be Chef Boy-Ar-Dee as far as I know, but I was unwilling to take the chance."

"I see what you mean."

In easy companionship they prepared the meal. The kitchen came to life with the clatter of dishes and sizzling of meat. Larry materialized in the doorway, breathing deeply.

"Ah, exquisite torture. I'm starving," he announced. "How much longer?"

"Here." June thrust a stack of dishes in his hands. "Go set the table—it'll keep your mind off your stomach."

"I knew I should have stayed out of here." Grumbling, he vanished into the adjoining room.

"I guess it's the mountain air," Hillary commented between bites as the group sat around the long table. "I'm absolutely ravenous."

The slow smile that drifted across Bret's face brought

back the memory of the earlier scene in the kitchen, and warm color seeped into her cheeks. Picking up her glass containing a red wine Bret had produced from some mysterious place, she took a deep, impulsive swallow and firmly gave her attention to the meal.

The clearing up was confused and disorganized as the men, through design or innocence, served only to get in the way, causing June to throw up her hands and order them away.

"I'm the boss," Bret reminded her. "I'm supposed to give the orders."

"Not until Monday," June returned, giving him a firm shove. She watched with a raised brow as Charlene floated with him.

"Just as well," she observed, turning back to Hillary. "I probably couldn't have prevented myself from drowning her in the sink."

The party later spread out with lazy contentment in the living room. Refusing Bret's offer of brandy, Hillary settled herself on a low stool near the fire. She watched the dancing flames, caught up in their images, unaware of the picture she created, cheeks and hair glowing with flickering light, eyes soft and dreamy. Her mind floated, only a small portion of it registering the quiet hum of conversation, the occasional clink of glass. Elbows on knees, head on palms, she drifted with the fire's magic away from conscious thought.

"Are you hypnotized by the flames, Hillary?" Bret's lean form eased down beside her as he stretched out on the hearth rug. Tossed suddenly into reality, she started at his voice, then smiled as she brushed at her hair.

"Yes, I am. There're pictures there if you look for them," she answered, inclining her head toward the blaze, "There's a castle there with turrets all around, and there's a horse with his mane lifted in the wind."

"There's an old man sitting in a rocker," Bret said softly, and she turned to stare at him, surprised that he had seen the image too. He returned her look, with the intensity of an embrace, and she rose, flustered by the weakness his gaze could evoke.

"It's been a long day," she announced, avoiding his eyes. "I think I'll go up to bed. I don't want Larry to complain that I look washed out in the morning."

Calling her good nights, she went swiftly from the room without giving Bret the opportunity to comment.

The room was dim in early morning light when she awoke. She stretched her arms to the ceiling and sat up, knowing sleep was finished. When she had slipped under the blankets the night before, her emotions had been in turmoil, and she had been convinced the hours would be spent tossing and turning. She was amazed that she had slept not only immediately but deeply, and the mood with which she greeted the new day was cheerful.

June was still huddled under her quilt, the steady rhythm of her breathing the only sound in the absolute silence. Easing from the bed, Hillary began to dress quietly. She tugged a heavy sweater in muted greens over her head, mating it with forest green cords that fit with slim assurance. Foregoing makeup, she donned the snowsuit Bret had provided, pulling the matching ski cap over her hair.

Creeping down the stairs, she listened for the sounds of morning stirring, but the house remained heavy in slumber. Pulling on boots and gloves, Hillary stepped outside into the cold, clear sunlight.

The woods were silent, and she looked about her at the solitude. It was as if time had stopped—the mountains were a magic fairyland without human habitation. Her companions were the majestic pines, robed in glistening ermine, their tangy scent permeating the air.

"I'm alone," she said aloud, flinging out her arms.

"There's not another soul in the entire world." She raced through the snow, drunk with power and liberation. "I'm free!" She tossed snow high above her head, whirling in dizzying circles before flinging herself into the cold snow.

Once more, she contemplated the white-topped mountains and dense trees, realizing her heart had expanded and made room for a new love. She was in love with the mountains as she was with the free-flowing wheat fields. The new and old love filled her with jubilation. Scrambling up, she sped once more through the snow, kicking up mists of white before she stopped and fell on her back, the soft surface yielding beneath her. She lay, spread-eagle, staring up at the sky until a face moved into her view, gray eyes laughing down at her.

"What are you doing, Hillary?"

"Making an angel," she informed him, returning his smile. "You see, you fall down, and then you move your arms and legs like this." She demonstrated, and her smile faded. "The trick is to get up without making a mess of it. It requires tremendous ability and perfect balance." Sitting up carefully, she put her weight on her feet and started to stand, teetering on her heels. "Give me a hand," she demanded. "I'm out of practice." Grabbing his arm, she jumped clear, then turned back to regard her handi-work. "You see," she stated with arrogant pride, "an angel."

"Beautiful," he agreed. "You're very talented."

"Yes, I know. I didn't think anyone else was up," she added, brushing snow from her bottom.

"I saw you dancing in the snow from my window. What game were you playing?"

"That I was alone in all this." She whirled in circles, arms extended.

"You're never alone up here. Look." He pointed into the woods, and her eyes widened at the large buck that stared back at her, his rack adorning his head like a crown.

"He's magnificent." As if conscious of her admiration, the stag lifted his head before he melted into the cover of the woods. "Oh, I'm in love!" she exclaimed, racing across the snow. "I'm absolutely madly in love with this place. Who needs a man when you've got all this?"

"Oh, really?" A snow ball thudded against the back of her head, and she turned to stare at him narrowly.

"You know, of course, this means war."

She scooped up a handful of snow, balling it swiftly and hurling it back at him. They exchanged fire, snow landing on target as often as it missed, until he closed the gap between them, and she engaged in a strategic retreat. Her flight was interrupted as he caught her, tossing her down and rolling on top of her. Her cheeks glowed with the cold, her eyes sparkled with laughter, as she tried to catch her breath.

"All right, you win, you win."

"Yes, I did," he agreed. "And to the victor go the spoils." He touched her mouth with his, his lips moving with light sensuality, stilling her laughter. "I always win sooner or later," he murmured, kissing her eyes closed. "We don't do this nearly often enough," he muttered against her mouth, deepening the kiss until her senses whirled. "You've snow all over your face." His mouth roamed to her cheek, his tongue gently removing flakes, instilling her with exquisite terror. "Oh, Hillary, what a delectable creature you are." Lifting his face, he stared into her wide, anxious eyes. He let out a deep breath and brushed the remaining snow from her cheeks with his hand. "The others should be stirring about now. Let's go have some breakfast."

"Stand over there, Hil." Hillary was once more out in the snow, but this time it was Larry and his camera joining her.

He had been taking pictures for what seemed to Hillary hours. Fervently, she wished the session would end, her mind lingering on the thought of steaming chocolate in front of the fire.

"All right, Hillary, come back to earth. You're supposed to be having fun, not floating in a daze."

"I hope your lenses freeze." She sent him a brilliant smile.

"Aw, cut it out, Hil," he mumbled, continuing to crouch around her.

"That'll do," he announced at last, and she fell over backwards in a mock faint. Larry leaned over her, taking still another picture. Shutting her eyes in amusement, she laughed up at him.

"Are the sessions getting longer, Larry, or is it just me?"

"It's you," he answered, shaking his head, allowing the camera to dangle by its strap. "You're over the hill, past your prime. It's all downhill from here."

"I'll show you who's over the hill." Hillary scrambled up, grabbing a handful of snow.

"No, Hil." Placing a protective hand over his camera, Larry backed away. "Remember my camera, don't lose control." Turning, he ran through the snow toward the lodge.

"Past my prime, am I?" The snowball hit him full on the back as Hillary gave chase. Catching him, she leaped on his back, beating him playfully on the top of the head.

"Go ahead," he told her, carrying her without effort. "Strangle me, give me a concussion—just don't touch my camera."

"Hello, Larry." Bret strolled over as they approached the house. "All finished?"

Hillary noted with some satisfaction that, with the advantage of being perched on Larry's back, she could meet Bret's eyes on level.

"I shall have to speak to you, Mr. Bardoff, about a new photographer. This one has just inferred that I am over the hill."

"I can't help it if your career's shot," Larry protested. "I've been carrying you figuratively for months, and now that I've carried you literally, I think you're putting on weight."

"That does it," Hillary decided. "Now I have no choice—I have to kill him."

"Put it off for a while, would you?" June requested, joining them by the door. "He doesn't know it yet, but I'm dragging him off for a walk in the woods."

"Very well," Hillary agreed. "That should give me time to consider. Put me down, Larry—you've been reprieved."

"Cold?" Bret asked as Hillary began to strip off her outdoor clothing.

"Frozen. There are those among us who have developing fluid rather than blood in their veins."

"Modeling is not all glamour and smiles, it is?" he commented as she shook snow from her hair. "Are you content with it?" he asked suddenly, capturing her chin with his hand, his eyes narrowed and serious. "Is there nothing else you want?"

"It's what I do," she countered. "It's what I'm able to do."

"Is it what you *want* to do?" he persisted. "Is it *all* you want to do?"

"All?" she repeated, and, battling the urgent longing, she shrugged. "It's enough, isn't it?"

He continued to stare down at her before he mirrored her shrug and walked away. He moved, even in jeans, with a rather detached elegance. Puzzled, Hillary watched him disappear down the hall.

The afternoon passed in vague complacency. Hillary sipped the hot chocolate of her dreams and dozed in a chair by the fire. She watched Bret and Bud play a long game of chess, the three of them unconcerned by Larry's occasional, irrepressible intrusions with his camera.

Charlene remained stubbornly by Bret's side, following the contest with ill-concealed boredom. When the match was over, she insisted that he show her through the forest. It was apparent to Hillary that her mind was not on trees and squirrels.

The day drifted away into darkness. Charlene, looking disgruntled after her walk, complained about the cold, then stated regally that she would soak in a hot tub for the next hour.

Dinner consisted of beef stew, which left the redhead aghast. She compensated by consuming an overabundance of wine. Her complaints were genially ignored, and the meal passed with the casual intimacy characteristic of people who have grown used to each other's company.

Again accepting kitchen detail, Hillary and June worked in the small room, the latter stating she felt she was due for a raise. The job was near completion when Charlene strolled in, yet another glass of wine in her hand.

"Almost done with your womanly duties?" she demanded with heavy sarcasm.

"Yes. Your assistance was greatly appreciated," June answered, stacking plates in a cupboard.

"I should like to have a word with Hillary, if you don't mind."

"No, I don't mind," June returned, and continued to clatter dishes.

Charlene turned to where Hillary was now wiping the surface of the stove. "I will not tolerate your behavior any longer."

"Well, all right—if you'd rather do it yourself." Hillary offered the dishcloth with a smile.

"I saw you this morning," Charlene flung out viciously, "throwing yourself at Bret."

"Did you?" Hillary shrugged, turning back to give the stove her attention. "Actually, I was throwing snowballs. I thought you were asleep."

"Bret woke me when he got out of bed." The voice was soft, the implication all too clear.

Pain throbbed through Hillary. How could he have left one woman's arms and come so easily into hers? How could he degrade and humiliate her that way? She shut her eyes, feeling the color drain from her face. The simple fun and precious intimacy they had shared that morning now seemed cheap. Holding on to her pride desperately, she turned to face Charlene, meeting triumphant green eyes with blue ice. "Everyone's entitled to his own taste." She shrugged indifferently, tossing the cloth on the stove.

Charlene's color rose dramatically. With a furious oath, she threw the contents of her glass, splattering the red liquid over Hillary's sweater.

"That's going too far!" June exploded, full of righteous anger on Hillary's behalf. "You're not going to get away with this one."

"I'll have your job for speaking to me that way."

"Just try it, when the boss sees what you—"

"No more," Hillary broke in, halting her avenger. "I don't want any more scenes, June."

"But, Hillary."

"No, please, just forget it." She was torn between the need to crawl away and lick her wounds and the urge to pull out handfuls of red hair. "I mean it. There's no need to bring Bret into this. I've had it."

"All right, Hillary," June agreed, casting Charlene a disgusted look. "For your sake."

Hillary moved quickly from the room, wanting only to reach the sanctuary of her bedroom. Before she reached the stairs, however, she met Bret.

"Been to war, Hillary?" he asked, glancing at the red splatters on her sweater. "Looks like you lost."

"I never had anything to lose," she mumbled, and started to walk by him.

"Hey." He halted her, taking her arms and holding her in front of him. "What's wrong?"

"Nothing," she retorted, feeling her precious control slipping with each passing moment.

"Don't hand me that—look at you." His hand reached out to tilt her chin, but she jerked back. "Don't do that," he commanded. His fingers gripped her face and held her still. "What's wrong with you anyway?"

"Nothing is the matter with me," she returned, retreating behind a sheet of ice. "I'm simply a bit weary of being pawed."

She watched, his eyes darkening to a thunderous gray. His fingers tightened painfully on her flesh. "You're darned lucky there're other people in the house, or I'd give you a fine example of what it's really like to be pawed. It's a pity I had a respect for fragile innocence. I shall certainly keep my hands off you in the future."

He relaxed his grip, and with chin and arm aching from the pressure, she pushed by him and calmly mounted the stairs.

Chapter 8

February had drifted into March. The weather had been as cold and dreary as Hillary's spirits. Since the fateful weekend in the Adirondacks, she had received no word from Bret, nor did she expect to.

The issue of *Mode* with Hillary's layout was released, but she could build up no enthusiasm as she studied the tall, slim woman covering the pages. The smiling face on the glossy cover seemed to belong to someone else, a stranger Hillary could neither recognize nor relate to. The layout was, nevertheless, a huge success, with the magazines selling as quickly as they were placed on the stands. She was besieged by offers as the weeks went by, but none of them excited her. She found the pursuit of her career of supreme indifference.

A call from June brought an end to her listlessness. The call brought a summons from the emperor. She debated refusing the order, then, deciding she would rather face Bret in his office than to have him seek her out at home, she obeyed.

She dressed carefully for the meeting, choosing a discreetly elegant pale yellow suit. She piled her hair up from her neck, covering it with a wide-brimmed hat. After a thorough study, she was well pleased with the calm, sophisticated woman reflected in her mirror.

During the elevator ride to Bret's office, Hillary schooled herself to remain aloof and detached, setting her expression into coolly polite lines. He would not see the pain, she determined. Her vulnerability would be well concealed. Her ability to portray what the camera demanded would be her defense. Her years of experience would not betray her.

June greeted her with a cheery smile. "Go right on in." She pushed the button on her phone. "He's expecting you."

Swallowing fear, Hillary fixed a relaxed smile on her face and entered the lion's den.

"Good afternoon, Hillary," Bret greeted her, leaning back in his chair but not rising. "Come sit down."

"Hello, Bret." Her voice matched the polite tone of his. Her smile remained in place though her stomach had begun to constrict at the first contact with his eyes.

"You're looking well," he commented.

"Thank you, so are you." She thought giddily, What absurd nonsense!

"I've just been looking over the layout again. It's certainly been every bit as successful as we had hoped."

"Yes, I'm glad it worked out so well for everyone."

"Which of these is you, Hillary?" he muttered absently, frowning over the pictures. "Free-spirited tomboy, elegant socialite, dedicated career woman, loving wife, adoring mother, exotic temptress?" He raised his eyes suddenly, boring into hers, the power almost shattering her frail barrier.

She shrugged carelessly. "I'm just a face and body doing what I'm told, projecting the image that's required. That's why you hired me in the first place, isn't it?"

"So, like a chameleon, you change from one color to the next on command."

"That's what I'm paid to do," she answered, feeling slightly ill.

"I've heard you've received quite a number of offers." Once more leaning back in his chair, Bret laced his fingers and studied her through half-closed eyes. "You must be very busy."

"Yes," she began, feigning enthusiasm. "It's been very exciting. I haven't decided which ones to accept. I've been told I should hire a manager to sort things out. There's an offer from a perfume manufacturer"— she named a well-known company—"that involves a long-term contract—three years endorsing on TV and, of course, magazines. It's by far the most interesting, I think." It was at the moment the only one she could clearly remember.

"I see. I'd heard you'd been approached by one of the networks."

"Oh, yes." She made a dismissive gesture, wracking her brains for the details. "But that involves acting. I have to give that a great deal of thought." I'd win an Oscar for this performance, she added silently. "I doubt if it would be wise to jump into something like that."

He stood and turned his back, staring out at the steel and glass. She studied him without speaking, wondering what was going on in his mind, noting irrelevantly how the sunlight combed his thick blond hair.

"Your contract with me is finished, Hillary, and though I'm quite prepared to make you an offer, it would hardly be as lucrative as a television contract."

An offer, Hillary thought, her mind whirling, and she was grateful his back was to her so that he could not observe her expression. At least she knew why he had wanted to see her—to offer her another contract, another piece of paper. She would have to refuse, even though she had no intention of accepting any of the other contracts. She could never endure continuous contact with this man. Even after this brief meeting, her emotions were torn.

She rose before answering. "I appreciate your offer, Bret, but I must consider my career. I'm more than grateful to you for the opportunity you gave me, but,"— her voice was calm, even professional—

"I told you before, I don't want your gratitude!" He spun to face her, the all-too-familiar temper darkening his eyes. "I'm not interested in perfunctory expressions of gratitude and appreciation. Whatever you receive as a result of this"—he picked up the magazine with Hillary's face on the cover—"you earned yourself. Take that hat off so I can look at you." He whipped the hat from her head and thrust it into her hands.

Hillary resisted the need to swallow. She met his angry, searching gaze without flinching.

"Your success, Hillary, is of your own making. I'm not responsible for it, nor do I want to be." He seemed to struggle for a measure of control and went on in calm, precise tones. "I don't expect you to accept an offer from me. However, if you change your mind, I'd be willing to negotiate. Whatever you decide, I wish you luck—I should like to think you're happy."

"Thank you." With a light smile, she turned and headed for the door.

"Hillary."

Hand on knob, she shut her eyes a moment and willed herself the strength to face him again. "Yes?"

He stared at her, giving her the sensation that he was filing each of her features separately in his brain. "Goodbye."

"Goodbye," she returned, and turning the knob, she escaped.

Shaken, she leaned her back against the smooth other side of the door. June glanced up from her work.

"Are you all right, Hillary? What's the matter?'"

Hillary stared without comprehension, then shook

her head. "Nothing," she whispered. "Oh, everything." With a muffled sob, she streaked from the room.

Hillary hailed a cab a few nights later with little enthusiasm. She had allowed herself to be persuaded by Larry and June to attend a party across town in Bud Lewis's penthouse apartment. She must not wallow in self-pity, cut off from friends and social activities, she had decided. It was time, she told herself, pulling her shawl closer against the early April breeze, to give some thought to the future. Sitting alone and brooding would not do the job.

As a result of her self-lecturing, she arrived at the already well-moving party determined to enjoy herself. Bud swung a friendly arm over her shoulders and, leading her to the well-stocked bar, inquired what was her pleasure. She started to request her usual well-diluted drink when a punch bowl filled with a sparkling rose pink liquid caught her eye.

"Oh, that looks nice—what is it?"

"Planter's punch," he informed her, already filling a glass.

Sounds safe enough, she decided as Bud was diverted by another of his guests. With a tentative sip,

Hillary thought it remarkably good. She began to mingle with the crowd.

She greeted old and new faces, pausing occasionally to talk or laugh. She glided from group to group, faintly amazed at how light and content was her mood. Depression and unhappiness dissolved like a summer's mist. This is what she needed all along, she concluded—some people, some music, a new attitude.

She was well into her third glass, having a marvelous time, flirting with a tall, dark man who introduced himself as Paul, when a familiar voice spoke from behind her.

"Hello, Hillary, fancy running into you here."

Turning, Hillary was only somewhat surprised to see Bret. She had only agreed to attend the party when June had assured her Bret had other plans. She smiled at him vaguely, wondering momentarily why he was slightly out of focus.

"Hello, Bret, joining the peasants tonight?"

His eyes roamed over her flushed cheeks and absent smile before traveling down the length of her slim form. He lifted his gaze back to her face, one brow lifting slightly as he answered. "I slum it now and then—it's good for the image."

"Mmm." She nodded, draining the remainder of her glass and tossing back an errant lock of hair. "We're both good with images, aren't we?" She turned to the other man at her side with a brilliant smile that left him slightly dazed. "Paul, be a darling and fetch me another of these. It's the punch over there"—she gestured largely—"in that bowl."

"How many have you had, Hillary?" Bret inquired, tilting her chin with his finger as Paul melted into the crowd. "I thought two was your limit."

"No limit tonight." She tossed her head, sending raven locks trembling about her neck and shoulders. "I am celebrating a rebirth. Besides, it's just fruit punch."

"Remarkably strong fruit I'd say from the looks of you," he returned, unable to prevent a grin. "Perhaps you should consider the benefits of coffee after all."

"Don't be stuffy," she ordered, running a finger down the buttons of his shirt. "Silk," she proclaimed and flashed another smile up at him. "I've always had a weakness for silk. Larry's here, you know, and," she added with dramatic emphasis, "he doesn't have his camera. I almost didn't recognize him."

"It won't be long before you have difficulty recognizing your own mother," he commented.

"No, my mother only takes Polaroid shots on odd occasions," she informed him as Paul returned with her drink. Taking a long sip, she captured Paul's arm. "Dance with me. I really love to dance. Here"—she handed her glass to Bret—"hang on to this for me."

She felt light and free as she moved to the music and marveled how she had ever let Bret Bardoff disturb her. The room spun in time to the music, drifting with her in a newfound sense of euphoria. Paul murmured something in her ear she could not quite understand, and she gave an indefinite sigh in response.

When the music halted briefly, a hand touched her arm, and she turned to find Bret standing beside her.

"Cutting in?" she asked, pushing back tumbled hair.

"Cutting out is more what I had in mind," he corrected, pulling her along with him. "And so are you."

"But I'm not ready to leave." She tugged at his arm. "It's early, and I'm having fun."

"I can see that." He continued to drag her after him, not bothering to turn around. "But we're going anyway."

"You don't have to take me home. I can call a cab, or maybe Paul will take me."

"Like hell he will," Bret muttered, pulling her purposefully through the crowd.

"I want to dance some more." She did a quick spin and collided full in his chest. "You want to dance with me?"

"Not tonight, Hillary." Sighing, he looked down at her. "I guess we do this the hard way."

In one swift movement, he had her slung over his shoulder and began weaving his way through the amused crowd. Instead of suffering from indignation, Hillary began to giggle.

"Oh, what fun, my father used to carry me like this."

"Terrific."

"Here, boss." June stood by the door holding Hillary's bag and wrap. "Got everything under control?"

"I will have." He shifted his burden and strode down the hall.

Hillary was carried from the building and dumped without ceremony into Bret's waiting car. "Here." He thrust her shawl into her hands. "Put this on."

"I'm not cold." She tossed it carelessly into the back seat. "I feel marvelous."

"I'm sure you do." Sliding in beside her, he gave her one despairing glance before the engine sprang to life. "You've enough alcohol in your system to heat a two-story building."

"Fruit punch," Hillary corrected, and snuggled back

against the cushion. "Oh, look at the moon." She sprang up to lean on the dash, staring at the ghostly white circle. "I love a full moon. Let's go for a walk."

He pulled up at a stoplight, turned to her, and spoke distinctly. "No."

Tilting her head, she narrowed her eyes as if to gain a new perspective. "I had no idea you were such a wet tire."

"Blanket," he corrected, merging with the traffic.

"I told you, I'm not cold." Sinking back into the seat, she began to sing.

Bret parked the car in the garage that serviced Hillary's building, turning to her with reluctant amusement. "All right, Hillary, can you walk or do I carry you?"

"Of course I can walk. I've been walking for years and years." Fumbling with the door handle, she got out to prove her ability. Funny, she thought, I don't remember this floor being tilted. "See?" she said aloud, weaving dangerously. "Perfect balance."

"Sure, Hillary, you're a regular tightrope walker." Gripping her arm to prevent a spill, he swept her up, cradled against his chest. She lay back contented as he carried her to the elevator, twining her arms around his neck.

"I like this much better," she announced as the

elevator began its slow climb. "Do you know what I've always wanted to do?"

"What?" His answer was absent, not bothering to turn his head. She nuzzled his ear with her lips. "Hillary," he began, but she cut him off.

"You have the most fascinating mouth." The tip of her finger traced it with careful concentration.

"Hillary, stop it."

She continued as if he had not spoken. "A nicely shaped face too." Her finger began a slow trip around it. "And I've positively been swallowed up by those eyes." Her mouth began to roam his neck, and he let out a long breath as the elevator doors opened. "Mmm, you smell good."

He struggled to locate her keys, hampered with the bundle in his arms and the soft mouth on his ear lobe.

"Hillary, stop it," he ordered. "You're going to make me forget the game has rules."

At last completing the complicated process of opening the door, he leaned against it a moment, drawing in a deep breath.

"I thought men liked to be seduced," she murmured, brushing her cheek against his.

"Listen, Hillary." Turning his face, he found his mouth captured.

"I just love kissing you." She yawned and cradled her head against his neck.

"Hillary…for heaven's sake!"

He staggered for the bedroom while Hillary continued to murmur soft, incoherent words in his ear.

He tried to drop her down on the spread, but her arms remained around his neck, pulling him off balance and down on top of her. Tightening her hold, she once more pressed her lips to his.

He swore breathlessly as he struggled to untangle himself. "You don't know what you're doing." With a drowsy moan, she shut her eyes. "Have you got anything on under that dress?" he demanded as he removed her shoes.

"Mmm, a shimmy."

"What's that?"

She gave him a misty smile and murmured. Taking a deep breath, he shifted her over, released the zipper at the back of her dress, pulled the material over smooth shoulders, and continued down the length of the slimly curved body.

"You're going to pay for this," he warned. His cursing became more eloquent as he forced himself to ignore the honey skin against the brief piece of silk. He drew the spread over the inert form on the bed. Hillary sighed and snuggled into the pillow.

Moving to the door, he leaned wearily on the frame, allowing his eyes to roam over Hillary as she lay in blissful slumber. "I don't believe this. I must be out of my mind." His eyes narrowed as he listened to her deep breathing. "I'm going to hate myself in the morning." Taking a long, deep breath, he went to search out Hillary's hoard of Scotch.

Chapter 9

Hillary awoke to bright invading sunlight. She blinked in bewilderment attempting to focus on familiar objects. She sat up and groaned. Her head ached and her mouth felt full of grit. Placing her feet on the floor, she attempted to stand, only to sink back moaning, as the room revolved around her like a carousel. She gripped her head with her hands to keep it stationary.

What did I drink last night? she wondered, squeezing eyes tight to jar her memory. What kind of punch was that? She staggered unsteadily to her closet to secure a robe.

Her dress was tossed on the foot of the bed, and she

stared at it in confusion. I don't remember undressing, she thought. Shaking her head in bemusement, she pressed a hand against her pounding temple. Aspirin, juice, and a cold shower, she decided. With slow, careful steps, she walked toward the kitchen. She stopped abruptly and leaned against the wall for support as a pair of men's shoes and a jacket stared at her in accusation from her living room sofa.

"Good heavens," she whispered as a partial memory floated back. Bret had brought her home, and she had... She shuddered as she remembered her conduct on the elevator. But what happened? She could only recall bits and pieces, like a jig-saw puzzle dumped on the floor— and the thought of putting them together was thoroughly upsetting.

"Morning, darling."

She turned slowly, her already pale face losing all color as Bret smiled at her, clad only in slacks, a shirt carelessly draped over his shoulder. The dampness of his hair attested to the fact that he had just stepped from the shower. My shower. Hillary's brain pounded out as she stared at him.

"I could use some coffee, darling." He kissed her lightly on the cheek in a casual intimate manner that tightened her stomach. He strode past her into the kitchen, and she followed, terrified. After placing the kettle to boil, he turned and wrapped his arms around her waist. "You were terrific." His lips brushed her brow, and she knew a moment's terror that she would faint dead away. "Did you enjoy yourself as much as I did?"

"Well, I-I guess, I don't…I don't remember… exactly."

"Don't remember?" He stared in disbelief. "How could you forget? You were amazing."

"I was…Oh." She covered her face with her hands. "My head."

"Hung over?" he asked, full of solicitude. "I'll fix you up." Moving away, he rummaged in the refrigerator.

"Hung over?" she repeated, supporting herself in the doorway. "I only had some punch."

"And three kinds of rum."

"Rum?" she echoed, screwing up her eyes and trying to think. "I didn't have anything but—"

"Planter's punch." He was busily involved in his remedy, keeping his back toward her. "Which consists, for the most part, of rum—amber, white, and dark."

"I didn't know what it was." She leaned more heavily on the doorway. "I had too much to drink. I'm not used to it. You-you took advantage of me."

"I took advantage?" Glass in hand, he regarded her in

astonishment. "Darling, I couldn't hold you off." He lifted his brow and grinned. "You're a real tiger when you get going."

"What a dreadful thing to say," she exploded, then moaned as her head hammered ruthlessly.

"Here, drink." He offered the concoction, and she regarded it with doubtful eyes.

"What's in it?"

"Don't ask," he advised. "Just drink."

Hillary swallowed in one gulp, then shivered as the liquid poured down her throat. "Ugh."

"Price you pay, love," he said piously, "for getting drunk."

"I wasn't drunk exactly," she protested. "I was just a little…a little muddled. And you"—she glared at him—"you took advantage of me."

"I would swear it was the other way around."

"I didn't know what I was doing."

"You certainly seemed to know what you were doing—and very well too." His smile prompted a groan from Hillary.

"I can't remember. I just can't remember."

"Relax, Hillary," he said as she began to sniffle. "There's nothing to remember."

"What do you mean?" She sniffed again and wiped her eyes with the back of her hand.

"I mean, I didn't touch you. I left you pure and unsullied in your virginal bed and slept on that remarkably uncomfortable couch."

"You didn't…we didn't…"

"No to both." He turned in response to the shrilling kettle and poured boiling water into a mug.

The first flood of relief changed into irritation. "Why not? What's wrong with me?"

He turned back to stare at her in amazement, then roared with laughter. "Oh, Hillary, what a contradiction you are! One minute you're desperate because you think I've stolen your honor and the next you're insulted because I didn't."

"I don't find it very funny," she retorted. "You deliberately led me to believe that I, that we—"

"Slept together," Bret offered, casually sipping his coffee. "You deserved it. You drove me crazy all the way from the elevator to the bedroom." His smile widened at her rapid change of color. "You remember that well enough. Now remember this. Most men wouldn't have left a tempting morsel like you and slept on that miserable couch, so take care with your fruit punch from now on."

"I'm never going to take another drink as long as I

live," Hillary vowed, rubbing her hands over her eyes. "I'm never going to look at a piece of fruit again. I need some tea or some of that horrible coffee, *something*." The sound of the doorbell shrilled through her head, and she swore with unaccustomed relish.

"I'll fix you some tea," Bret offered, grinning at her fumbling search for obscenities. "Go answer the door."

She answered the summons wearily, opening the door to find Charlene standing at the threshold, taking in her disheveled appearance with glacial eyes.

"Do come right in," Hillary said, shutting the door behind Charlene with a force that only added to her throbbing discomfort.

"I heard you made quite a spectacle of yourself last night."

"Good news travels fast, Charlene—I'm flattered you were so concerned."

"You don't concern me in the least." She brushed invisible lint from her vivid green jacket. "Bret does, however. You seem to make a habit of throwing yourself at him, and I have no intention of allowing it to continue."

This is too much for anyone to take in my condition, Hillary decided, feeling anger rising. Feigning a yawn, she assumed a bored expression. "Is that all?"

"If you think I'm going to have a little nobody like you marring the reputation of the man I'm going to marry, you're very much mistaken."

For an instant, anger's heat was frozen in agony. The struggle to keep her face passive caused her head to pound with new intensity. "My congratulations to you, my condolences to Bret."

"I'll ruin you," Charlene began. "I'll see to it that your face is never photographed again."

"Hello, Charlene," Bret said casually as he entered the room, his shirt now more conventionally in place.

The redhead whirled, staring first at him, then at his jacket thrown carelessly over the back of the sofa. "What…what…are you doing here?"

"I should think that's fairly obvious," he answered, dropping to the sofa and slipping on his shoes. "If you didn't want to know, you shouldn't have taken it upon yourself to check up on me."

He's using me again, Hillary thought, banking down on shivering hurt and anger. Just using me to make her jealous.

Charlene turned on her, her bosom heaving with emotion. "You won't hold him! You're only a cheap one-night stand! He'll be bored with you within the week! He'll soon come back to me," she raved.

"Terrific," Hillary retorted, feeling her grip on her temper slipping. "You're welcome to him, I'm sure. I've had enough of both of you. Why don't you both leave? Now, at once!" She made a wild gesture at the door. "Out, out, out!"

"Just a minute," Bret broke in, buttoning up the last button of his shirt.

"You keep out of this," Hillary snapped, glaring at him. She turned back to Charlene. "I've had it up to the ears with you, but I'm in no mood for fighting at the moment. If you want to come back later, we'll see about it."

"I see no reason to speak to you again," Charlene announced with a toss of her head. "You're no problem to me. After all, what could Bret possibly see in a cheap little tramp like you?"

"Tramp," Hillary repeated in an ominously low voice. "Tramp?" she repeated, advancing.

"Hold on, Hillary." Bret jumped up, grabbing her around the waist. "Calm down."

"You really are a little savage, aren't you?" shot Charlene.

"Savage? I'll show you savage." Hillary struggled furiously against Bret.

"Be quiet, Charlene," he warned softly, "or I'll turn her loose on you."

He held the struggling Hillary until her struggles lost their force.

"Let me go. I won't touch her," she finally agreed. "Just get her out of here." She whirled on Bret. "And you get out, too! I've had it with the pair of you. I won't be used this way. If you want to make her jealous, find someone else to dangle in front of her! I want you out— out of my life, out of my mind." She lifted her chin, heedless of the dampness that covered her cheeks. "I never want to see either of you again."

"Now you listen to me." Bret gripped her shoulders more firmly and gave her a brief but vigorous shake.

"No." She wrenched herself out of his grip. "I'm through listening to you. Through, finished—do you understand? Just get out of here, take your friend with you, and both of you leave me alone."

Picking up his jacket, Bret stared for a moment at flushed cheeks and swimming eyes. "All right, Hillary, I'll take her away. I'll give you a chance to pull yourself together, then I'll be back. We haven't nearly finished yet."

She stared at the door he closed behind him through

a mist of angry tears. He could come back all right, she decided, brushing away drops of weakness. But she wouldn't be here.

Rushing into the bedroom, she pulled out her cases, throwing clothes into them in heaps. I've had enough! she thought wildly, enough of New York, enough of Charlene Mason, and especially enough of Bret Bardoff. I'm going home.

In short order, she rapped on Lisa's door. Her friend's smile of greeting faded at the sight of Hillary's obvious distress.

"What in the world—" she began, but Hillary cut her off.

"I don't have time to explain, but I'm leaving. Here's my key." She thrust it into Lisa's hand. "There's food in the fridge and cupboards. You take it, and anything else you like. I won't be coming back."

"But, Hillary—"

"I'll make whatever arrangements have to be made about the furniture and the lease later. I'll write and explain as soon as I can."

"But, Hillary," Lisa called after her, "Where are you going?"

"Home," she answered without turning back. "Home where I belong."

* * *

If Hillary's unexpected arrival surprised her parents, they asked no questions and made no demands. Soon she fell into the old, familiar pattern of days on the farm. A week drifted by, quiet and undemanding.

During this time it became Hillary's habit to spend quiet times on the open porch of the farmhouse. The interlude between dusk and sleep was the gentlest. It was the time that separated the busy hours of the day from the reflective hours of the night.

The porch swing creaked gently, disturbing the pure stillness of the evening, and she watched the easy movement of the moon, enjoying the scent of her father's pipe as he sat beside her.

"It's time we talked, Hillary," he said, draping his arm around her. "Why did you come back so suddenly?"

With a deep sigh, she rested her head against him. "A lot of reasons. Mostly because I was tired."

"Tired?"

"Yes, tired of being framed and glossed. Tired of seeing my own face. Tired of having to pull emotions and expressions out of my hat like a second-rate magician, tired of the noise, tired of the crowds." She made a helpless movement with her shoulders. "Just plain tired."

"We always thought you had what you wanted."

"I was wrong. It wasn't what I wanted. It wasn't all I wanted." She stood and leaned over the porch rail, staring into the curtain of night. "Now I don't know if I've accomplished anything."

"You accomplished a great deal. You worked hard and made a successful career on your own, and one that you can be proud of. We're all proud of you."

"I know I worked for what I got. I know I was good at my job." She moved away and perched on the porch rail. "When I left home, I wanted to see what I could do for myself by myself. I knew exactly what I wanted, where I was going. Everything was catalogued in neat little piles. First A, then B, and down the line. Now I've got something most women in my position would jump at, and I don't want it. I thought I did, but now, when all I have to do is reach out and take it, I don't want it. I'm tired of putting on the faces."

"All right, then it's time to stop. But I think there's more to your decision to come home than you're saying. Is there a man mixed up in all this?"

"That's all finished," Hillary said with a shrug. "I got in over my head, out of my class."

"Hillary Baxter, I'm ashamed to hear you talk that way."

"It's true." She managed a smile. "I never really fit into his world. He's rich and sophisticated, and I keep forgetting to be glamorous and do the most ridiculous things. Do you know, I still whistle for cabs? You just can't change what you are. No matter how many images you can slip on and off, you're still the same underneath." Shrugging again, she stared into space. "There was never really anything between us—at least not on his side."

"Then he must not have too many brains," her father commented, scowling at his pipe.

"Some might claim you're just a little prejudiced." Hillary gave him a quick hug. "I just needed to come home, I'm going up now. With the rest of the family coming over tomorrow, we'll have a lot to do."

The air was pure and sweet when Hillary mounted her buckskin gelding and set off on an early morning ride. She felt light and free, the wind blowing wildly through her hair, streaming it away from her face in a thick black carpet. In the joy of wind and speed, she forgot time and pain, and the clinging feeling of failure was lost. Reining in the horse, she contemplated the huge expanse of growing wheat.

It was endless, stretching into eternity—a golden ocean rippling under an impossibly blue sky. Somewhere a meadowlark heralded life. Hillary sighed with contentment. Lifting her face, she enjoyed the caressing fingers of sun on her skin, the surging scent of land bursting into life after its winter sleep.

Kansas in the spring, she mused. All the colors so real and vivid, the air so fresh and full of peace. Why did I ever leave? What was I looking for? She closed her eyes and let out a long breath. I was looking for Hillary Baxter, she thought, and now that I've found her, I don't know what to do with her.

"Time's what I need now, Cochise," she told her four-legged companion, and leaned forward to stroke his strong neck. "Just a little time to find all the scattered pieces and put them back together."

Turning the horse toward home, she set off in an easy, gentle lope, content with the soothing rhythm and the spring-softened landscape. As the farm and outbuildings came into view, however, Cochise pawed the ground, straining at the bit.

"All right, you devil." She tossed back her head and laughed, and with a touch of her heels sent the eager horse racing. The air vibrated with the sound of hooves on hard dirt. Hillary let her spirits fly as she gave the gelding his head. They cleared an old wooden jump in a fluid leap, touched earth, and streaked on, sending a flock of contented birds into a flurry of protesting activity.

As they drew nearer the house, her eyes narrowed as she spotted a man leaning on the paddock fence. She pulled back sharply on the reins, causing Cochise to rear in insult.

"Easy," she soothed, stroking his neck and murmuring soft words as he snorted in indignation. Her eyes were focused on the man. It appeared half a continent had not been big enough for a clean escape.

Chapter 10

"Quite a performance." Bret straightened his lean form and strode toward them. "I couldn't tell where the horse let off and the woman began."

"What are you doing here?" she demanded.

"Just passing by—thought I'd drop in." He stroked the horse's muzzle.

Gritting her teeth, Hillary slipped to the ground.

"How did you know where to find me?" She stared up at him, wishing she had kept her advantage astride the horse.

"Lisa heard me pounding on your door. She told me

you'd gone home." He spoke absently, appearing more interested in making the gelding's acquaintance than enlightening her. "This is a fine horse, Hillary." He turned his attention from horse to woman, gray eyes sweeping over windblown hair and flushed cheeks. "You certainly know how to ride him."

"He needs to be cooled off and rubbed down." She felt unreasonably annoyed that her horse seemed so taken with the long fingers caressing his neck. She turned to lead him away.

"Does your friend have a name?" He fell into step beside her.

"Cochise." Her answer was short. She barely suppressed the urge to slam the barn door in his face as Bret entered beside her.

"I wonder if you're aware how perfectly his coloring suits you." He made himself comfortable against the stall opening. Hillary began to groom the gelding with fierce dedication.

"I'd hardly choose a horse for such an impractical reason." She kept her attention centered on the buckskin's coat, her back firmly toward the man.

"How long have you had him?"

This is ridiculous, she fumed, wanting desperately to throw the curry comb at him. "I raised him from a foal."

"I suppose that explains why the two of you suit so well."

He began to poke idly about the barn while she completed her grooming. While her hands were busy, her mind whirled with dozens of questions she could not find the courage to form into words. The silence grew deep until she felt buried in it. Finally she was unable to prolong the gelding's brushing. She turned to abandon the barn.

"Why did you run away?" he asked as they were struck with the white flash of sunlight outside.

Her mind jumped like a startled rabbit. "I didn't run away." She improvised rapidly. "I wanted time to think over the offers I've had—it wouldn't do to make the wrong decision at this point in my career."

"I see."

Unsure whether the mockery in his voice was real or a figment of her imagination, she spoke dismissively. "I've got work to do. My mother needs me in the kitchen."

The fates, however, seemed to be against her as her mother opened the back door and stepped out to meet them.

"Why don't you show Bret around, Hillary? Everything's under control here."

"The pies." Hillary sent out rapid distress signals.

Ignoring the silent plea, Sarah merely patted her head. "There's plenty of time yet. I'm sure Bret would like a look around before supper."

"Your mother was kind enough to ask me to stay, Hillary." He smiled at her open astonishment before turning to her mother. "I'm looking forward to it, Sarah."

Fuming at the pleasant first-name exchange, Hillary spun around and muttered without enthusiasm, "Well, come on then." Halting a short distance away, she looked up at him with a honey-drenched smile. "Well, what would you care to see first? The chicken coop or the pig sty?"

"I'll leave that to you," he answered genially, her sarcasm floating over him.

Frowning, Hillary began their tour.

Instead of appearing bored as she had expected, Bret appeared uncommonly interested in the workings of the farm, from her mother's vegetable garden to her father's gigantic machinery.

He stopped her suddenly with a hand on her shoulder and gazed out at the fields of wheat. "I see what you meant, Hillary," he murmured at length. "They're magnificent. A golden ocean."

She made no response.

Turning to head back, his hand captured hers before she could protest.

"Ever seen a tornado?"

"You don't live in Kansas for twenty years and not see one," Hillary said briefly.

"Must be quite an experience."

"It is," she agreed. "I remember when I was about seven, we knew one was coming. Everyone was rushing around, securing animals and getting ready. I was standing right about here." She stopped, gazing into the distance at memory. "I watched it coming, this enormous black funnel, blowing closer and closer. Everything was so incredibly still, you could feel the air weighing down on you. I was fascinated. My father picked me up, tossed me over his shoulder, and hauled me to the storm cellar. It was so quiet, almost like the world had died, then it was like a hundred planes thundering right over our heads.

He smiled down at her, and she felt the familiar tug at her heart. "Hillary." He lifted her hand to his lips briefly. "How incredibly sweet you are."

She began walking again, stuffing her hands strategically in her pockets. In silence, they rounded the side of the farmhouse, while she searched for the courage to ask him why he had come.

"You, ah, you have business in Kansas?"

"Business is one way to put it." His answer was hardly illuminating, and she attempted to match his easy manner.

"Why didn't you send one of your minions to do whatever you had in mind?"

"There are certain areas that I find more rewarding to deal with personally." His grin was mocking and obviously intended to annoy. Hillary shrugged as if she were indifferent to the entire conversation.

Hillary's parents seemed to take a liking to Bret, and Hillary found herself irritated that Bret fit into the scene so effortlessly. Seated next to her father, on a firm first-name basis, he chatted away like a long-lost friend. The numerous members of her family might have intimidated anyone else. However, Bret seemed undaunted. Within thirty minutes, he had charmed her two sisters-in-law, gained the respect of her two brothers, and the adoration of her younger sister. Muttering about pies, Hillary retreated to the kitchen.

A few minutes later, she heard: "Such domesticity."

Whirling around, she observed Bret's entrance into the room.

"You've flour on your nose." He wiped it away with his finger. Jerking away, she resumed her action with the rolling pin. "Pies, huh? What kind?" He leaned against the counter as though settling for a comfortable visit.

"Lemon meringue," she said shortly, giving him no encouragement.

"Ah, I'm rather partial to lemon meringue—tart and sweet at the same time." He paused and grinned at her averted face. "Reminds me of you." She cast him a withering glance that left him undaunted. "You do that very well," he observed as she began rolling out a second crust.

"I work better alone."

"Where's that famous country hospitality I've heard so much about?"

"You got yourself invited to dinner, didn't you?" She rolled the wooden pin over the dough as if it were the enemy. "Why did you come?" she demanded. "Did you want to get a look at my little farm? Make fun of my family and give Charlene a good laugh when you got back?"

"Stop it." He straightened from the counter and took her by the shoulders. "Do you think so little of those people out there that you can say that?" Her expression altered from anger to astonishment, and his fingers relaxed on her arms. "This farm is very impressive, and your family is full of warm, real people. I'm half in love with your mother already."

"I'm sorry," she murmured, turning back to her work. "That was a stupid thing to say."

He thrust his hands in the pockets of slim-fitting jeans and strolled to the screen door. "It appears baseball's in season."

The door slammed behind him, and Hillary walked over and looked out, watching as Bret was tossed a glove and greeted with open enthusiasm by various members of her family. The sound of shouting and laughter carried by the breeze floated to her. Hillary turned from the door and went back to work.

Her mother came into the kitchen and Hillary responded to her chattering with occasional murmurs. She felt annoyingly distracted by the activity outside.

"Better call them in to wash up." Sarah interrupted her thoughts, and Hillary moved automatically to the door, opening it and whistling shrilly. Her fingers retreated from her mouth in shock, and she cursed herself for again playing the fool in front of Bret. Stomping back into the kitchen, she slammed the screen behind her. Hillary found herself seated beside Bret at dinner, and ignoring the bats waging war in her stomach, she gave herself over to the table chaos, unwilling for him or her family to see she was disturbed in any way.

As the family gravitated to the living room, Hillary saw Bret once more in discussion with her father, and pointedly gave her attention to her nephew, involving herself with his game of trucks on the floor. His small brother wandered over and climbed into Bret's lap, and she watched under the cover of her lashes as he bounced the boy idly on his knee.

"Do you live with Aunt Hillary in New York?" the child asked suddenly, and a small truck dropped from Hillary's hand with a clatter.

"Not exactly." He smiled slowly at Hillary's rising color. "But I do live in New York."

"Aunt Hillary's going to take me to the top of the Empire State Building," he announced with great pride. "I'm going to spit from a million feet in the air. You can come with us," he invited with childlike magnanimity.

"I can't think of anything I'd rather do." Lean fingers ruffled dark hair. "You'll have to let me know when you're going."

"We can't go on a windy day," the boy explained, meeting grey eyes with six-year-old wisdom. "Aunt Hillary says if you spit into the wind you get your face wet."

Laughter echoed through the room, and Hillary rose and picked up the boy bodily, marching toward the kitchen. "I think there's a piece of pie left. Let's go fill your mouth."

The light was muted and soft with dusk when Hillary's brothers and their families made their departure. A few traces of pink bleeding from the sinking sun traced the horizon. She remained alone on the porch for a time, watching twilight drifting toward darkness, the first stars blinking into life, the first crickets disturbing the silence.

Returning inside, the house seemed strangely quiet. Only the steady ticking of the old grandfather clock disturbed the hush. Curling into a chair, Hillary watched the progress of a chess game between Bret and her father. In spite of herself, she found herself enchanted by the movements of his long fingers over the carved pieces.

"Checkmate." She started at Bret's words, so complete had been her absorption.

Tom frowned at the board a moment, then stroked his

chin. "I'll be darned, so it is." He grinned over at Bret and lit his pipe. "You play a fine game of chess, son. I enjoyed that."

"So did I." Bret leaned back in his chair, flicking his lighter at the end of a cigarette. "I hope we'll be able to play often. We should find the opportunity, since I intend to marry your daughter."

The statement was matter-of-factly given. As the words passed from Hillary's ear to brain, her mouth opened, but no sound emerged.

"As head of the family," Bret went on, not even glancing in her direction, "I should assure you that financially Hillary will be well cared for. The pursuit of her career is, of course, her choice, but she need only work for her own satisfaction."

Tom puffed on his pipe and nodded.

"I've thought this through very carefully," Bret continued, blowing out a lazy stream of smoke. "A man reaches a time when he requires a wife and wants children." His voice was low and serious, and Tom met laughing gray eyes equally. "Hillary suits my purposes quite nicely. She is undoubtedly stunning, and what man doesn't enjoy beauty? She's fairly intelligent, adequately strong, and is apparently not averse to children.

She is a bit on the skinny side," he added with some regret, and Tom, who had been nodding in agreement to Hillary's virtues, looked apologetic.

"We've never been able to fatten her up any."

"There is also the matter of her temper," Bret deliberated, weighing pros and cons. "But," he concluded with a casual gesture of his hand. "I like a bit of spirit in a woman."

Hillary sprang to her feet, unable for several attempts to form a coherent sentence. "How dare you?" she managed at length. "How dare you sit there and discuss me as if I were a-a brood mare! And you," she chastised her father, "you just go along like you were pawning off the runt of the litter. My own father."

"I did mention her temper, didn't I?" Bret asked Tom, and he nodded sagely.

"You arrogant, conceited, son of a—"

"Careful, Hillary," Bret cautioned, stubbing out his cigarette and raising his brows. "You'll get your mouth washed out with soap again."

"If you think for one minute that I'm going to marry you, you're crazy! I wouldn't have you on a platter! So go back to New York, and…and print your magazines," she finished in a rush, and stormed from the house.

After her departure, Bret turned to Sarah. "I'm sure Hillary would want to have the wedding here. Any close friends can fly in easily enough, but since Hillary's family is here, perhaps I should leave the arrangements to you."

"All right, Bret. Did you have a date in mind?"

"Next weekend."

Sarah's eyes opened wide for a moment as she imagined the furor of arrangements, then tranquilly returned to her knitting. "Leave it to me."

He rose and grinned down at Tom. "She should have cooled off a bit now. I'll go look for her."

"In the barn," Tom informed him, tapping his pipe. "She always goes there when she's in a temper." Bret nodded and strode from the house. "Well, Sarah." With a light chuckle, Tom resumed puffing on his pipe. "Looks like Hillary has met her match."

The barn was dimly lit, and Hillary stomped around the shadows, enraged at both Bret and her father. The two of them! she fumed. I'm surprised he didn't ask to examine my teeth.

With a groan, the barn door swung open, and she spun around as Bret sauntered into the building.

"Hello, Hillary, ready to discuss wedding plans?"

"I'll never be ready to discuss anything with you!" Her angry voice vibrated in the large building.

Bret smiled into her mutinous face unconcernedly. The lack of reaction incensed her further and she began to shout, storming around the floor. "I'll never marry you—never, never, never. I'd rather marry a three-headed midget with warts."

"But you will marry me, Hillary," he returned with easy confidence. "If I have to drag you kicking and screaming all the way to the altar, you'll marry me."

"I said I won't." She halted her confused pacing in front of him. "You can't make me."

He grabbed her arms and surveyed her with laconic arrogance. "Oh, can't I?"

Pulling her close, he captured her mouth.

"You let go of me," she hissed, pulling away. "You let go of my arms."

"Sure." Obligingly, he relinquished his hold, sending her sprawling on her back in a pile of hay.

"You—bully!" she flung at him, and attempted to scramble to her feet, but his body neatly pinned her back into the sweet-smelling hay.

"I only did what I was told. Besides," he added with a crooked smile, "I always did prefer you horizontal."

She pushed against him, averting her face as his mouth descended. He contented himself with the soft skin of her neck.

"You can't do this." Her struggles began to lose their force as his lips found new areas of exploration.

"Yes, I can," he murmured, finding her mouth at last. Slow and deep, the kiss battered at her senses until her lips softened and parted beneath his, her arms circled his neck. He drew back, rubbing her nose with his.

"Wretch!" she whispered, pulling him close until their lips merged again.

"Now are you going to marry me?" He smiled down at her, brushing hair from her cheek.

"I can't think," she murmured and shut her eyes. "I can't ever think when you kiss me."

"I don't want you to think." He busied his fingers loosening her buttons. "I just want you to say it." His hand took possession of her breast and gently caressed it. "Just say it, Hillary," he ordered, his mouth moving down from her throat, seeking her vulnerability. "Say it, and I'll give you time to think."

"All right," she moaned. "You win, I'll marry you."

"Good," he said simply, bringing his lips back to hers for a brief kiss.

She fought the fog of longing clouding her senses and attempted to escape. "You used unfair tactics."

He shrugged, holding her beneath him easily. "All's fair in love and war, my love." His eyes lost their laughter as he stared down at her. "I love you, Hillary. You're in every part of my mind. I can't get you out. I love every crazy, beautiful inch of you." His mouth crushed hers, and she felt the world slip from her grasp.

"Oh, Bret." She began kissing his face with wild abandon. "I love you so much. I love you so much I can't bear it. All this time I thought… When Charlene told me you'd been with her that night in the mountains, I—"

"Wait a minute." He halted her rapid kisses, cupping her face with his hands. "I want you to listen to me. First of all, what was between Charlene and me was over before I met you. She just wouldn't let go." He smiled and brushed her mouth with his. "I haven't been able to think of another woman since the first day I met you, and I was half in love with you even before that."

"How?"

"Your picture—your face haunted me."

"I never thought you were serious about me." Her fingers began to tangle in his hair.

"I thought at first it was just physical. I knew I wanted you as I'd never wanted another woman. That night in your apartment, when I found out you were innocent, that threw me a bit." He shook his head in wonder and buried his face in the lushness of her hair. "It didn't take long for me to realize what I felt for you was much more than a physical need."

"But you never indicated anything else."

"You seemed to shy away from relationships—you panicked everytime I got too close—and I didn't want to scare you away. You needed time. I tried to give it to you. Hanging on in New York was difficult enough." He traced the hollow of her cheek with a finger. "But that day in my lodge, my control slipped. If Larry and June hadn't come when they did, things would have progressed differently. When you turned on me, telling me you were sick of being pawed, I nearly strangled you."

"Bret, I'm sorry, I didn't mean it. I thought—"

"I know what you thought," he interrupted. "I'm only sorry I didn't know then. I didn't know what Charlene had said to you. Then I began to think you wanted only your career, that you didn't want to make room in your life for anything or anyone else. In my office that day, you were so cool and detached, ticking off your choices, I wanted to toss you out the window."

"They were all lies," she whispered, rubbing her cheek against his. "I never wanted any of it, only you."

"When June finally told me about the scene with Charlene at the lodge, and I remembered your reaction, I began to put things together. I came looking for you at Bud's party." He pulled up his head and grinned. "I intended to talk things out, but you were hardly in any condition for declarations of love by the time I got there. I don't know how I stayed out of your bed that night, you were so soft and beautiful…and so smashed! You nearly drove me over the edge."

He lowered his head and kissed her, his control ebbing as his mouth conquered her. His hands began to mold her curves with an urgent hunger, and she clutched him closer, drowning in the pool of his desire.

"Good God, Hillary, we can't wait much longer." He removed his weight from her, rolling over on his back, but she went with him, closing her mouth over his. Drawing her firmly away, he let out a deep breath. "I don't think your father would think kindly of me taking his daughter in a pile of hay in his own barn."

He pushed her on her back, slipping his arm around

her, cradling her head against his shoulder. "I can't give you Kansas, Hillary," he said quietly. She turned her head to look at him. "We can't live here—at least not now. I've obligations in New York that I simply can't deal with from here."

"Oh, Bret," she began, but he pulled her closer and continued.

"There's upper New York or Connecticut. There are plenty of places where commuting would be no problem. You can have a house in the country if that's what you want. A garden, horses, chickens, half a dozen kids. We'll come back here as often as we can, and go up to the lodge for long weekends, just the two of us." He looked down, alarmed at the tears spilling from wide eyes and over smooth cheeks. "Hillary, don't do that. I don't want you to be unhappy. I know this is home to you." He began to brush the drops from her face.

"Oh, Bret, I love you." She pulled his cheek against hers. "I'm not unhappy. I'm wonderfully, crazily happy that you care so much. Don't you know it doesn't matter where we are? Anyplace I can be with you is home."

He drew her away and regarded her with a frown. "Are you sure, love?"

She smiled and lifted her mouth, letting her kiss give him the answer.

* * * * *

Song of the West

Chapter 1

The land in southeast Wyoming is a magnificent paradox. Spreading plains and rolling hills coexist with rocky mountains and thick velvet pines. From the kitchen window, the view was astounding, and Samantha Evans halted in her duties for a moment to drink it in.

The Rockies dominated the vast curtain of sky, their peaks laced with snow, though it was late March.

Samantha wondered if she would still be in Wyoming the following winter. She dreamed of long walks with the air biting and sharp on her cheeks, or wild rides on a spirited mount with hooves kicking up a flurry of white. But none of that could happen until her sister was well enough to be left alone.

A frown creased her smooth brow. Sabrina was her reason for being in Wyoming, with its majestic mountains and quiet plains, rather than in the more familiar surroundings of Philadelphia's tall buildings and traffic-choked streets.

The two sisters had always been close, with that special, magical intimacy that twins share. They were not identical. Though they were the same in height and build, Samantha's eyes were a dark cornflower blue, widely set, with thick, spiky lashes, while Sabrina's eyes were a light gray. Both faces were oval set with small, straight noses and well-shaped mouths, but while Samantha's rich brown hair, with its highlights of gold, was shoulder length with a fringe of bangs, Sabrina's ash blonde was short, framing her face with delicate curls. The bond between them was strong and enduring. Even when Sabrina had married Dan Lomax and moved so many miles away to settle on his ranch in the Laramie Basin, their devotion had remained constant and unwavering.

They kept in touch by phone and letter, which helped to mitigate Samantha's aching loneliness. And she was happy in her sister's delight in the coming baby. The two women had laughed and planned together over the phone. But that was before Dan's call. Samantha had been aroused from a deep predawn sleep by the shrill ringing of the phone. She reached groggily for it, but was instantly alerted by the anxious tone of her brother-in-law's voice. "Sam," he said without any preamble, "Bree's been very ill. We did manage to save the baby, but she has to be very careful for a while now. She will have to stay in bed and have constant round-the-clock care. We are trying to find someone to—"

Samantha had only one thought—her sister, the person she loved best in the world. "Don't worry, Dan, I will come immediately."

She was on the plane to Wyoming less than twenty-four hours later....

The whistle of the kettle brought Samantha back to the present. She began to brew the herbal tea, placing delicate floral cups on a silver tray.

"Teatime," she called as she entered the living room. Sabrina was propped up with pillows and comforters on the long wood-edged sofa. Though her smile was warm, her cheeks still retained a delicate pallor.

"Just like the movies," Sabrina commented as her sister set a tray on the pine table. "But the role of Camille is getting to be a bore."

"I imagine so." Samantha poured the fragrant tea into cups. "But you may as well get used to it, Bree, you've got the part for a month's run." She transferred a large gray striped cat from Sabrina's lap to her own, offered Sabrina a steaming cup and sat on the rug. "Has Shylock been keeping you company?"

"He's a terrible snob." With a wry smile, Sabrina sipped at her tea. "He did graciously allow me to scratch his ears. I have to admit, I'm glad you brought him with you, he's my biggest entertainment." She sighed and lay back against the pillows, regarding her sister seriously. "I'm ashamed to be lying here feeling sorry for myself. I'm lucky." She rested her hand on her stomach in a protective gesture. "I shall have my baby, and I sit here moaning about your waiting on me."

"You're entitled to moan a bit, Bree," said Samantha, immediately sympathetic. "You're used to being active and busy."

"I've no right to complain. You gave up your job and left home to come out here and take care of me." Another deep sigh escaped, and her gray eyes were dangerously moist. "If Dan had told me what you were planning to do, I would never have allowed it."

"You couldn't have stopped me." Samantha attempted to lighten the mood. "That's what older sisters are for."

"You never forget those seven minutes, do you?" Sabrina's eyes cleared, and a reluctant smile curved her generous mouth.

"Nope, it gives me seniority."

"But your job, Sam."

"Don't worry." Samantha made another dismissive gesture. "I'll get another job in the fall. There's more than one high school in the country, and they all have gym teachers. Besides, I needed a vacation."

"Vacation!" Sabrina exclaimed. "Cleaning, cooking, caring for an invalid. You call that a vacation?"

"My dear Sabrina, have you ever tried to teach an overweight, totally uncoordinated teenager the intricacies of the parallel bars? Well, the stories I could tell you about vacations."

"Sam, what a pair we are. You with your teenagers and me with my preadolescent Mozarts. Lord knows how many times I cleaned peanut butter off the keys of that old Wurlitzer before Dan came along and took me away from scales and infant prodigies. Do you think Mom expected us to come to this when she dragged us to all those lessons?"

"Ah, but we're well-rounded." Samantha's grin was faintly wicked. "Aren't you grateful? She always told us we'd be grateful one day for the ballet and the piano lessons."

"The voice lessons and the riding lessons," Sabrina continued, ticking them off on her fingers.

"Gymnastics and swimming lessons," Sabrina concluded with a giggle.

"Poor Mom." Samantha shifted Shylock to a more comfortable position. "I think she expected one of us to marry the president, and she wanted us to be prepared."

"We shouldn't make fun." Sabrina wiped her eyes with a tissue. "The lessons did give us our living."

"True. And I can still whip up a mean spinach soufflé.

"Ugh." Sabrina grimaced, and Samantha lifted her brows.

"Exactly."

"You have your medals," Sabrina reminded her. Her smile warmed with pride and a trace of awe.

"Yes, I have the medals and the memories. Sometimes, it feels like yesterday instead of nearly ten years ago."

Sabrina smiled. "I can still remember my terrified excitement when you first swung onto the uneven bars. Even though I'd watched the routine countless times, I couldn't quite believe it was you. When they put that first Olympic medal around your neck, it was one of the happiest moments of my life."

"I remember thinking just before that competition, after I'd botched the balance beam so badly, that I couldn't do it. My legs felt like petroleum jelly, and I was mortally afraid I was going to be sick and disgrace myself. Then I saw Mom in the stands, and it ran through my mind how much she'd sacrificed. Not the money. The bending of those rather strange values of hers to allow me those years of training and those few heady moments of competition. I had to prove it was justified, I had to pay her back with something, even though I knew she'd never be able to say she was proud of me."

"You proved it was justified." Sabrina gave her twin a soft smile. "Even if you hadn't won on the bars and the floor exercises, you'd proved it by just being there. And she was proud of you, even if she didn't say it."

"You've always understood. So get over the idea I'm doing you a favor coming here. I want to be here. I *belong* here."

"Sam." Sabrina held out a hand. "I don't know what I'd do without you. I don't know what I *ever* would have done without you."

"You'd manage," Samantha returned, giving the frail hand a squeeze. "You have Dan."

"Yeah, I do." The smile became soft. "This is the time of day that I miss him most. He should be home soon." Her gaze wandered to the glass-domed anniversary clock on the mantel above the fire.

"He said something about checking fences today. I can't quite get away from the image of him chasing rustlers or fighting off renegade Indians."

With a light laugh, Sabrina settled back among the cushions. "City slicker. You know, Sam, sometimes I can't even remember what Philadelphia looks like. Jake Tanner was riding along with Dan today to make sure the boundary fences were in good repair."

"Jake Tanner?" Samantha's question was idle.

"Oh, that's right, you haven't met him yet. The northwest corner of the ranch borders his. Of course, the Lazy L would fit into one corner of his ranch. He owns half the county."

"Ah, a land baron," Samantha concluded.

"A very apt description," Sabrina agreed. "The Double T, his ranch, is the most impressive I've seen. He runs it like clockwork, super efficient. Dan says he's not only an incredible rancher, but a very crafty businessman."

"Sounds like a bore," Samantha commented, wrinkling her nose. "Steel-gray hair around a leathered face, a handlebar mustache drooping over his mouth and a generous belly hanging over his belt…"

Sabrina's laughter rang out, high and sweet.

"You're about as far off the mark as you can get. Jake Tanner is anything but a bore, and speaking from the safety of marital bliss, he's a fascinating man to look at. And, being rich, successful and unattached, all the females under forty buzz around him like bees around honey."

"Sounds like a good catch," Samantha said dryly. "Mom would love him."

"Absolutely," Sabrina agreed. "But Jake has eluded capture so far. Though from what Dan says, he does enjoy the chase."

"Now he sounds like a conceited bore." Samantha tickled Shylock's smooth belly.

"You can hardly blame him for taking what's offered." Sabrina defended the absent Jake Tanner with a vague movement of her shoulders. "I imagine he'll settle down soon. Lesley Marshall—her father's ranch borders the other side of the Double T—has her sights set on him. She's a very determined woman, as well as being more than a little spoiled, and dreadfully rich."

"Sounds like a perfect match."

"Mmm, maybe," Sabrina murmured. Her face creased in a small frown. "Lesley's nice enough when it suits her, and it's about time Jake had a wife and family. I'm fond of Jake. I'd like to see him set up with someone with more warmth."

"Listen to the old married woman." Samantha addressed a dozing and unconcerned Shylock. "A year of nuptial bliss, and she can't stand to see anyone unattached."

"True. I'm going to start on you next."

"Thanks for the warning."

"Wyoming's full of good-looking cowboys and handsome ranchers." Sabrina continued to smile as her sister grimaced. "You could find a worse place to settle down."

"I have no objection to settling here, Bree. I've become quite attached to the wide open spaces. But—" she paused significantly "—cowboys and ranchers are not among my immediate plans for the future." She rose from the floor in a fluid motion. "I've got to check on that roast. Here." She handed her sister the novel that rested on the table. "Read your love stories, you incurable romantic."

"You won't be so cynical when you fall in love," Sabrina predicted with the wisdom of experience.

"Sure." Samantha's grin was indulgent.

"There'll be bells ringing and fireworks shooting and trumpets blaring." She patted her sister's hand and strolled from the room, calling over her shoulder. "Angels singing, flames leaping…"

"Just you wait," Sabrina shouted after her.

Samantha busied herself preparing vegetables for the evening meal, clucking her tongue at her sister's nonsense. *Love,* she sniffed derisively. Her only experience with that complex emotion had been fending off unwanted attentions from eager males. Not once had any man lit an answering spark in her. But whatever this love was, it worked for Bree. The younger twin had always been more delicate, softer and more dependent. And though Sabrina was trying to be brave and strong, her sister knew the fear of miscarriage still lurked in the back of her mind. She needed Dan's support and love, and right now, she needed to feel his arms around her.

Like the answer to a prayer, Samantha spotted two figures on horseback approaching from the lower pasture. Grabbing her heavy jacket from the hook by the back door, she scurried out of the kitchen and into the cold March air.

As Dan and his companion drew closer, Samantha greeted him with a smile and a wave. She had noticed, even at a distance, Dan's expression of concern. But a smile relaxed his features when he spotted Samantha.

"Sabrina's all right?" he asked as he reined in next to her.

"She's fine," Samantha assured him. "Just a trifle restless, and tremendously lonely for her husband."

"Did she eat better today?"

Samantha's smile warmed, lighting her face with a quick flash of astonishing beauty.

"Her appetite was much better. She's trying very hard." Samantha lifted a hand to stroke the smooth flank of the gelding he rode. "What she needs now is you."

"I'll be in as soon as I stable my horse."

"Oh, Dan, for heaven's sake. Let your hand do it, or I'll do it myself. Bree needs you."

"But…"

"'S all right, boss," the other horseman interrupted, and Samantha spared him a brief glance. "I'll tend to your horse. You go on and see the missus."

Dan flashed his companion a wide grin and dismounted. "Thanks," he said simply as he handed over the reins and turned to Samantha. "Coming in?"

"No." She shook her head and hunched her shoulders

in the confines of her jacket. "You two could use some time alone, and I'd like some air."

"Thanks, Sam." He pinched her cheek with brotherly affection and moved off toward the house.

Waiting until the door closed behind him, Samantha walked over and dropped wearily onto the stump used for splitting wood. Resting her back against the fence, she breathed deeply, devouring the brisk, cold air. The strain of caring for her sister in addition to running the house and cooking the meals, including, over his objection, Dan's predawn breakfast, had taken its toll.

"A few more days," she whipered as she closed her eyes. "A few more days and I'll have adjusted to the routine and feel more like myself." The heavy corded jacket insulated her from the bite of the cold, and she tilted back her head, allowing the air to play on her cheeks as her mind drifted on the edge of exhaustion.

"Funny place to take a nap."

Samantha sat up with a jerk, confused and disoriented by sleep. Her eyes traveled up to the speaker's face. It was a lean face, skin bronzed by the sun and stretched tightly over cheekbones, all lines and shadows, hollows and angles. The eyes were arresting, deep-set and heavily lashed. But it was their color, a deep, pure jade that caught and held her attention. His dusky gold hair curled from under a well-battered Stetson.

"Evening, ma'am." Though he touched the brim of his hat with due respect, his extraordinary eyes were faintly mocking.

"Good evening," she returned, struggling for dignity.

"Person could catch a bad chill sitting out too long after the sun's low. Wind's picking up, too." His speech was slow and thickly drawled. His weight was distributed evenly on both legs, hands deep in pockets. "Oughtn't to be out without a hat." His comment was accompanied by a fractional movement of his head toward her unadorned one. "Hat helps keep the heat in."

"I'm not cold." She feared for a moment her teeth would chatter and betray her. "I was…I was just getting some air."

"Yes, ma'am." He nodded in agreement, glancing behind her at the last, dying brilliance of sun as it slipped behind circling peaks. "Fine evening for setting out and watching the sunset."

Her eyes flashed at the teasing. She was embarrassed to have been caught sleeping. He smiled a slow, careless smile that crept unhurried across his face. The movement of his lips caused the hollows to deepen, the shadows to shift. Unable to resist, Samantha's lips curved in response.

"All right, I confess. You caught me napping. I don't suppose you'd believe I was just resting my eyes."

"No, ma'am." His answer was grave, with just a hint of apology.

"Well." She rose from her seat and was dismayed at how far she still had to look up to meet his eyes. "If you keep quiet about it, I'll see to it that you get a piece of the apple pie I baked for dinner."

"That's a mighty tempting offer." He considered it with a long-fingered hand reaching up to stroke his chin. "I'm partial to apple pie. Only one or two things I'm more partial to." His eyes roamed over her in a thorough and intense study that caused her heart to pound with unaccustomed speed.

There was something different about this man, she thought swiftly, something unique, a vitality at odds with lazy words and careless smiles. He pushed his hat back farther on his head, revealing more disorderly curls. "You've got yourself a deal." He held out his hand to confirm the agreement, and she placed her small hand in his.

"Thanks." The single word was breathless, as she

found her speech hampered by the currents running up her arm. Abruptly, she pulled her hand away, wondering what it was about him which disturbed her equilibrium. "I'm sorry if I was short before, about Dan's horse." She spoke now in a rush, to conceal a reaction she could not understand.

"No need to apologize," he assured her, and the new soft texture in his tone both warmed and unnerved her. "We're all fond of Mrs. Lomax."

"Yes, well, I…" she stammered, suddenly needing to put a safe distance between herself and this slow-talking man. "I'd better go inside. Dan must be hungry." She looked past him and spotted his horse, still saddled, waiting patiently. "You didn't stable your horse. Aren't you finished for the day?" Hearing the concern in her own voice, she marveled at it. Really, she thought, annoyed, why should I care?

"Oh, yes, ma'am, I'm finished." There was laughter in his voice now, but Samantha failed to notice. She began to study the mount with care.

It was a magnificent animal, dark, gleaming chestnut, at least sixteen hands, she estimated, classic lines, fully flowing mane and proud, dished face. Arabian. Samantha knew horses and she recognized a full-blooded Arabian stallion when she saw one. What in the world…? "Than's an Arabian." Her words interrupted her thoughts.

"Yes, ma'am," he agreed easily, entirely too easily. Her eyes narrowed with suspicion as she turned to him.

"No ranch hand is going to be riding around on a horse that's worth six months' pay." She stared at him and he returned the steady survey with a bland, poker face. "Who are you?"

"Jake Tanner, ma'am." The slow grin appeared again, widening, deepening, then settling as he lifted the brim of his hat at the introduction. "Pleased to meet you."

The land baron with the women at his feet, Samantha's brain flashed. Anger darkened her eyes.

"Why didn't you say so?"

"Just did," he pointed out.

"Oh." She tossed back her thick fall of hair. "You know very well what I mean. I thought you were one of Dan's men."

"Yes, ma'am." He nodded.

"Stop *ma'aming* me," she commanded. "What a mean trick! All you had to do was open your mouth and say who you were. I would have stabled Dan's horse myself."

"I didn't mind." His expression became annoyingly agreeable. "It wasn't any trouble, and you had a nice rest."

"Well, Mr. Tanner, you had a fine laugh at my expense. I hope you enjoyed it," she said coldly.

"Yes, ma'am." The grin widened without seeming to move at all. "I did."

"I told you to stop…" She halted, biting her lip with frustration. "Oh, forget it." Tossing her head, she took a few steps toward the house, then turned back crossly. "I notice your accent has modified quite a bit, Mr. Tanner."

He did not reply, but continued to stand negligently, his hands in his pockets, his face darkened by the late-afternoon shadows. Samantha spun back around and stomped toward the house.

"Hey," he called out, and she turned toward him before she could halt the reflex. "Do I still get that pie?"

She answered his question with a glare. His laughter, deep and rich, followed her into the house.

Chapter 2

The sound of the slamming door reverberated through the ranch house as Samantha struggled out of her jacket and marched into the living room. At the sight of her sister's face Sabrina slipped down into the pillows, picked up the novel lying on her lap and buried her nose in its pages. Dan, however, did not recognize the storm warning in his sister-in-law's blue eyes and flushed cheeks. He greeted her with a friendly, ingenuous smile.

"Where's Jake?" His gaze slid past her. "Don't tell me he went home without a cup of coffee?"

"He can go straight to the devil without his coffee."

"I expect he wanted to get home before dark," Dan concluded. His nod was sober, but his eyes were brilliant with merriment.

"Don't play innocent with me, Dan Lomax." Samantha advanced on him. "That was a rotten trick, letting me think he was one of your hands, and…" A giggle escaped from behind the paperback. "I'm glad you think it's amusing that your sister's been made a fool of."

"Oh, Sam, I'm sorry." Warily, Sabrina lowered the book. "It's just hard to believe anyone could mistake Jake Tanner for a ranch hand." She burst out laughing, and Samantha was torn between the pleasure of seeing her sister laugh and irritation at being the brunt of the joke.

"Well, really, what makes him so special?" she demanded. "He dresses like every other cowboy I've seen around here, and that hat of his has certainly seen better days." But, she remembered, there *had* been something special about him that she had not quite been able to define. She firmly dismissed this disquieting thought. "The nerve of him." She rounded on Don again. "Calling you boss, and ma'aming me in that exaggerated drawl."

"Reckon he was just being polite," Dan suggested. His

smile was amiable and pure. Samantha sent him the look that terrified her students.

"Men." Raising her eyes, she searched the ceiling in hopes of finding the answer there. "You're all alike, and you all stick together." She bent and scooped up the sleeping Shylock and marched into the kitchen.

Time at the ranch passed quickly. Though her days were full and busy, Samantha fretted for some of the physical outlet that had so long been part of her life. At times, the confinement of the house was suffocating. Years of training and discipline had left her with an inherent need for activity.

Unconsciously, she separated her life into three categories: the pre-Olympic years, the Olympic years and the post-Olympic years.

The pre-Olympic years were a blur of lessons, piano teachers, dance instructors, her mother's gentle but inescapable admonishments to "be a lady." Then, the first time she had gripped the lower bar of the unevens, the new chapter had begun.

By the time she was twelve years old, she had remarkable promise. The gymnastics instructor had informed her mother, who was more distressed than pleased at the praise. Though her mother had objected to more intense training, Samantha had ultimately prevailed.

The hours of training became months, county meets became state meets, and national competitions became international competitions. When Samantha was picked for the Olympic team, it was just another step down a road she was determined to follow. Weariness and aching muscles were accepted without hesitation.

Then it was over, and at fifteen she had found it necessary to alter what had become a way of life. College had to be considered, and earning a living. The years passed into the post-Olympic period, and she remembered her days of athletic competitions as a dream. Now her life was shifting again, though she was unsure as to the direction. The mountains and plains were calling to her, inviting her to explore, but she buried her desires, remaining indoors to see to her sister's needs. Dan is a busy man, she thought as she prepared lunch, and Bree needs someone within calling distance during this critical period. When she's better, there will be plenty of time to see the country.

She arched her back and rubbed a small spot of tension at the base of her neck. The kitchen door opened and Dan burst in, accompanied by Jake Tanner.

Samantha met the amused green eyes levelly, though once more she felt treacherously at a disadvantage.

Her hair had been carelessly scooped on the top of her head that morning, and now, with their usual abandonment, stray locks were beginning to escape confinement. She was dressed in a black ribbed sweater that had seen too many washings and ancient jeans, splattered, faded, patched and too tight. She resisted the urge to raise her hand to her tumbling hair, forced a smile and turned to her brother-in-law.

"Hello, Dan. What are you doing home this time of day?" Purposefully, she ignored the tall figure beside him.

"Wasn't too far out," Dan explained. Slipping off his jacket and hat, he tossed both over the hooks provided. "Jake was giving me a hand, so I figured it was only neighborly to bring him back for lunch."

"Hope I'm not imposing, ma'am." The slow smile spread, once more rearranging the angles of his face.

"No imposition, Mr. Tanner. But you'll have to settle for potluck."

"My favorite dish—" he paused, giving her a cheeky wink "—next to apple pie."

Samantha sent him a withering glance and turned away to warm the previous evening's stew.

"I'll just go tell Sabrina I'm home," Dan announced to the room in general, and strode away. Samantha did her best to ignore Jake's disturbing presence. She stirred the stew busily.

"Smells good." Jake moved over to the stove and lounged against it. Samantha went to the cupboard to get the bowls.

When she turned back to place them on the round kitchen table, she noticed that he had shed his outdoor clothing. The slim-fitting jeans, snug and low on narrow hips, accentuated his leanness. His flannel shirt fitted over his broad shoulders and hard chest before tapering down to a narrow waist. The athlete in her immediately responded to the firm, well-proportioned body; there was not an ounce of spare flesh on him.

"Don't talk much, do you?" The drawl was there again, the exaggerated twang of the previous evening. Samantha turned her head, prepared to freeze him with her eyes.

His face was barely inches from hers as he slouched by the stove. For a moment, her mind ceased to function.

"I really have nothing to say to you, Mr. Tanner." She struggled to keep her voice cold and detached, but she could feel the blood rush to her face.

"Well, now, we'll have to see if we can change that."

He spoke with easy confidence as he straightened to his full height. "We're not much on formalities around here. Just make it Jake." Though his words were spoken with his usual lazy delivery, there was an undertone of command. Samantha's chin rose in defense.

"Maybe I prefer to keep things formal between us, Mr. Tanner."

His lips were curved in his careless smile, but in his eyes she now recognized that special something that separated him from an ordinary ranch hand. *Power.* She wondered how she had missed it at their first meeting.

"I don't think there's much chance of that." He paused and tugged at a loose lock of his hair before adding with irritating emphasis, "Ma'am. Nope, I don't think there's much chance of that at all."

Samantha was saved from coming up with a suitable rebuttal by Dan's reappearance. She began to spoon the stew into ceramic bowls, noting to her dismay that her hands were not altogether steady. This man was infuriating her with his arrogantly lazy confidence. I have never met a more irritating male, she thought. He thinks he can switch on that rugged cowboy charm and women will drop in droves at his feet. Well, maybe some do, but not this one.

"Okay, Sam?" Dan's voice shattered the electric silence.

"What? I'm sorry, I wasn't listening."

"You'll keep Jake company over lunch, won't you? I'll have mine in the living room with Sabrina."

She swore silently. "Of course," she answered with an impersonal smile.

Within a short time, Samantha found herself sitting across from the man she wanted most to avoid.

"You've a fine hand with dumplings, Sam." Her brows rose involuntarily at his easy use of her nickname, but she kept her voice even.

"Thank you, Mr. Tanner. It's just one of my many talents."

"I'm sure it is," he agreed with an inclination of his head.

"You haven't changed much from the girl in the picture in Sabrina's parlor." Samantha was astonished.

"You'd have been about fifteen," he continued. "A bit skinnier than you are now, but your hair was the same, not quite willing to stay bundled on top of your head." Samantha's blank expression had turned to a frown at the word skinnier. She remembered the photo clearly.

"You'd just finished winning your second medal."

She had indeed been fifteen. The picture had been snapped at the moment she had completed her floor routine. It had captured the look of stunned triumph, for she had known in that instant that a medal was hers.

"Sabrina's just about as proud of you as you are worried about her." Samantha said nothing, only staring into the lean, handsome features. His brows rose ever so slightly, a movement that would have gone unnoticed had she not been so intent on his face. For a moment, she forgot the thread of the conversation, caught up suddenly in a series of small, irrelevant details: the curling gold which spilled over his brow, the tiny white scar on his jawline, the thickness of his long lashes. Confused, she dropped her eyes to her bowl and struggled to bring her thoughts to order.

"I'd forgotten Bree had that picture," she said. "It was a long time ago."

"So now you teach. You don't look like any gym teacher I ever knew."

"Oh, really?"

"No, ma'am." He shook his head slowly and considered her through another mouthful of stew. "Don't look strong enough or old enough."

"I assure you, Jake, I'm both strong enough and old enough for my profession."

"What made you become a gym teacher?" His sudden question caught her off balance, and she stared at him.

"Well, I…" Her shoulders moved restlessly. "Our mother was a fanatic on lessons when Bree and I were growing up." She smiled in spite of herself. "We took lessons in everything, Mom's theory on being well-rounded. Anyway, Bree found her talent in music and I developed a knack for the physical. For a while, I focused on gymnastics, then, when the time came to work, it seemed natural. Bree taught little people to play the classics, and I teach bigger people to tumble."

"Do you like your work? Are you happy with it?"

"As a matter of fact, I do," she retorted. "I like the activity, I like being involved in a physical type of work. It can be frustrating at times, of course. Some of the girls I teach would rather be flirting with their boyfriends than learning gymnastics, I suspect."

"And you yourself are more interested in calisthenics than men?" The question was delivered with a broad masculine smile.

"That's hardly relevant," she snapped, annoyed that she had lowered her guard.

"You don't think so?"

Samantha scraped back her chair and moved to the stove. "Coffee?"

"Yes, ma'am, black." It was unnecessary to turn around; she felt the slow grin crease his face as clearly as if she had witnessed it with her eyes. She set the cup down on the table with a bang. Before she could spin back to pour her own, her hand was captured in a firm grip. There was nothing soft about the hand. It was hard and masculine.

Completely outmatched in the short battle that ensued, Samantha discovered that under the lean, lanky exterior lay an amazing strength. Deciding that it was undignified to grapple in her sister's kitchen, she allowed her hand to rest quietly in his, meeting his laughing eyes with a resentful glare. Her heart began to pound uncomfortably against her ribs.

"What do you want?" Her voice came out in a husky whisper. His eyes left hers to travel slowly down to the generous curve of her mouth, lingering until she could taste the heat on her lips, as real as a kiss. Taking his time, he moved his gaze back to her eyes.

"You're jumpy." His observation was laconic, as if none of the heat had touched him, though she herself was beginning to suffocate. "Powerful strong for such a little bit of a thing."

"I'm not little," she retorted. "You're just so big." She

began to tug at her hand again, feeling a near desperate urgency to shake off the contact that was infusing her with an unexplained weakness around the knees.

"Your eyes are fabulous when you're angry, Sam." His tone was conversational. "Temper agrees with you. You grow beautiful with it." He laughed and pulled her closer.

"You're insufferable," she said, still struggling to escape his grasp.

"For telling you you're beautiful? I was just stating the obvious. I'm sure it's been mentioned to you once for twice before."

"You men are all the same." She ceased her struggles long enough to aim a lethal glare. "Always grabbing and groping."

"I don't grope, Samantha." His drawl was feather-soft. For an instant, the cocky cowboy vanished, and she glimpsed the man, shrewd and ruthless, beneath. Here was a man who not only expected to have his own way, but would. "And the next time I grab you, it won't only be to hold your hand." Releasing her, he leaned back in his chair. "You have been warned."

Later, as Sabrina napped and the house grew still around her, Samantha found herself staring blankly at the pages of a novel. Scowling, she tossed it aside and rose from the sofa to pace to the window. What an infuriating man. Obviously, he considers himself irresistible. She began to wander the room, attempting to block out the effect his blatant virility had had on her.

It was too bad, she decided on her fourth circle, that all those good looks, all that strength and appeal, had to belong to such a rude, arrogant man.

Deciding that a brisk walk was just what she needed to get Jake Tanner out of her mind, she stopped her pacing and grabbed a warm jacket. Moments later she was out the door, gazing around her in delight at the beauty of the starlit Wyoming night. Her breath puffed out in thin white mists as she moved. The air, tinged with frost, carried the aroma of pine, and she drank it in greedily, enjoying the mixed scent of hay and horses and aged wood. She could hear the lonely sound of a coyote calling to the full silver moon. And suddenly she realized that she had fallen in love with Wyoming. The spell of the mountains and plains was on her, and she was inexplicably glad she had come.

"Goodness, you were out a long time," her sister commented as Samantha plopped down in a wing-backed chair in front of the fire a few minutes later. "You must be frozen."

"No." Samantha stretched out her legs and sighed. "I love it out there. It's fantastic! I never realized how big the sky was before, and I don't think I'll ever get used to the space, the openness."

She turned her attention to the powerfully built man sitting next to her sister on her sofa. "I wonder if you appreciate it, Dan, living here all of your life. Even your letters, Bree, didn't do justice to that world out there." Running her fingers through her hair, she made a small sound of pleasure. "To someone used to traffic-choked streets and huge buildings, all this…" Her hands moved in an inadequate gesture.

"You haven't had much of a chance to see anything since you've been here," Dan observed. "You've been with us a month and you haven't gone a quarter mile away from the house. And that's been mostly to fetch the mail in the mornings."

"I'll have plenty of time to explore later. I'll be around through the summer."

"Just the same, we're not having you tied to the house while you're here, Sam," Dan announced, and sat back against the cushions. "Even the most devoted sister is entitled to a day off."

"Don't be silly. You make it sound as though I were slaving from dawn to dusk. Half the time I'm not doing anything."

"We know how hard you're working, Sam," Sabrina said quietly, glancing up at Dan before returning her gaze to her twin. "And I know the lack of activity is harder on you than the work. I also know how you disrupted your life to come out here and take care of me."

"Oh, Bree, for heaven's sake," Samantha began, shifting uncomfortably. "I never would have found out how much I love Wyoming if I hadn't come."

"Don't try to shrug if off, Sam." Dan grinned at the embarrassed motion of her shoulders. "We're grateful, and you'll just have to get used to us telling you so. But tomorrow, we're going to show we're grateful instead of just talking about it. We're kicking you out for the day."

"Huh?" Blankly, Sam blinked at the bland smile before shifting her gaze to Sabrina's serene one.

"That's right." His grin widened as she drew her brows together. "Tomorrow's Sunday, and I'm staying home with my wife. And you…" He pointed a warning finger at his sister-in-law. "You're going to have your pick of the horses and take off."

272   *Song of the West*

Samantha sprung up from her slouched position. "Do you mean it?" Her face was glowing with pleasure, and Dan's smile warmed with affection.

"Yes, little sister, I mean it. It should be more."

"The dapple-gray gelding," she began in a rush, ignoring the last part of his comment. "Can I take him?"

"Already inspected the stock, and it appears you know your horses." Dan chuckled and shook his head. "Spook's a good mount. A little frisky, but from what Sabrina's told me, you can handle him."

"Oh, I can, and I promise I'll be careful with him." She sprang from her chair and crossed the room, flinging her arms around his neck. "Thanks, Dan. You are absolutely my favorite brother-in-law, bar none."

"I think she likes the idea, Sabrina," Dan commented as he met his wife's eyes over Samantha's head. "In fact, I'd say she's downright pleased about it."

"And I thought I hid my emotions so effectively." She gave his cheek a loud, smacking kiss.

"You be ready to start out about nine." He patted Samantha's slim shoulder. "Jake'll be around, then."

"Jake?" Samantha repeated. Her smile froze.

"Yeah, he'll be riding out with you. Actually," Dan continued, "he suggested the idea this afternoon. He thought it would do you good to get out of the house for a while." He sighed and scratched his dark head, managing to appear sheepish, for all his size. "I'm ashamed I didn't think of it first. I guess I've been a bit preoccupied and didn't notice you were looking a littled tired and hemmed in."

"I'm not tired," she denied automatically.

"Hemmed in?" Sabrina offered with a knowing smile.

"A little, maybe, but I'm hardly in the last stages of cabin fever. I'm sure it's very kind of Mr. Tanner to be so concerned about my welfare." She managed to say his name in a normal voice. "But there's certainly no need for him to go with me. I know he has hundreds of more important things to do with his Sunday."

"Well, now, he didn't seem to think so," Dan said. "It was his suggestion, and he seemed keen on the idea, too."

"I don't know why he would be," she muttered. "Besides, I don't want to impose on him. We're practically strangers. I can just go by myself."

"Nonsense." Dan's refusal was good-natured but firm. "I couldn't possibly let you ride out by yourself just yet, no matter how good you are on a horse. You don't know the country, and it's easy to get lost. There's always the possibility of an accident. Besides," he added, and his grin was expansive, "you're part of the family, and I grew up with Jake, so you're not strangers. If anyone knows his way around this part of Wyoming, he does." He shrugged and rested his back against the cushions. "He owns half of it, anyway." Samantha glanced at her sister for help. Sabrina, however, appeared to be engrossed in her needlepoint.

Frowning at the lack of support, Samantha stewed over her predicament. If she refused Jake's company, she would not only forfeit the opportunity to ride the Wyoming countryside, but she would spoil Sabrina's and Dan's plans for a day alone together. She shrugged in resignation and offered a smile.

"I'll be ready at nine." She added to herself, If Jake Tanner can stand a day in my company, I guess I can stand a day in his.

Chapter 3

Sunday dawned with a sky as cold and clear as sapphire. The sun offered thin light and little warmth. To her annoyance, Samantha had overslept. Hurriedly, she showered and dressed in forest-green cords and a chunky beige pullover.

Her riding boots clattered on the parquet floor as she hurried from her room and down the hall to the kitchen. She frowned as she reached the doorway. Jake was sitting at the table, enjoying a cup of coffee with the air of one very much at home.

He was, she noted with illogical irritation, every bit as attractive as she remembered.

"Oh, you're here." Her greeting was hardly welcoming, but he returned it with his slow smile.

"Morning, ma'am."

"Don't start ma'aming me again," she said.

He remained silent as she clattered the cups in the cupboard and filled one with the steaming liquid from the pot on the stove.

"Sorry." She popped a piece of bread in the toaster and turned to offer a peace-offering smile. "My! I overslept. I hope you haven't been waiting long."

"I've got all day," he answered, leaning back in his chair as if to emphasize his words.

She drew a slab of bacon and a carton of eggs from the refrigerator. "Have you eaten?" she asked in invitation.

"Yeah, thanks." He rose, poured himself another cup of coffee and resumed his position at the table. "Dan's already seen to breakfast for himself and Sabrina. They're having it in their room."

"Oh." She replaced the items and pulled out the butter.

"Aren't you going to eat?"

"Toast and coffee. I'm not much on breakfast."

"If you always eat like that," he observed over the

rim of his cup, "it's no wonder you never grew any bigger."

"For goodness' sake." She whirled around, brandishing the butter knife. "I'm hardly a midget. I'm five-four, that's tall enough for anybody."

He held up his hands in mock surrender. "I never argue with an armed woman."

"Ready?" He rose when she had finished both the toast and another cup of coffee.

When she mumbled her assent, he plucked her jacket from its hook, holding it out so that she had no choice but to allow him to help her into it. She stiffened as his hands touched her shoulders and turned her to face him. Her pulses responded immediately. As if he were aware of her reaction, he began to do up her leather buttons with slow care. She jerked back, but his hold on the front of her coat prevented her from a clean escape.

"You're a pretty little thing," he drawled, completing his task with his eyes directly on hers. "Can't have you catching cold." He reached out and plucked Sabrina's dark wide-brimmed hat from a peg and placed it neatly on her head. "This'll keep your head warm."

"Thanks." She pushed the hat firmly in place.

"Anytime, Sam." His face was unperturbed as he

pulled his own sheepskin jacket over his flannel shirt and jeans.

On the way to the stables, Samantha increased her pace to a trot to keep up with Jake's long, careless stride. Despite herself, she admired the confident, loose-limbed grace of his movement. He took his time, she noted, deciding he probably did nothing quickly, and more than likely still finished ahead of everyone else.

The dapple gray had been saddled and led outside by a smiling ranch hand.

"Howdy, ma'am. Dan said to have Spook ready for you."

"Thanks." She returned his friendly smile and patted the gelding's neck. "But I could have done it. I don't like to give you extra work."

"No trouble, ma'am. Dan said you weren't to do a lick of work today. You just go and have yourself a good time, and I'll rub old Spook down when you get back."

Samantha vaulted easily onto the horse's back, happy to feel a mount beneath her again. Riding was an old pleasure, to be enjoyed only when finances allowed.

"Now, you take good care of Miss Evans, Jake," the cowboy admonished with a conspirator's wink Samantha failed to catch. "Dan sets great store by this little lady."

Little again, Samantha thought.

"Don't you worry about Miss Evans, Lon." Jake mounted his stallion with a fluid motion. Again Samantha noticed that he wasted no time on superfluous movement. "I intend to keep a close eye on her."

Samantha acknowledged Jake's statement with a wrinkled nose, then, following the direction his hand indicated, set off in a brisk canter.

As the neat cluster of ranch buildings was left behind, her irritation vanished. The rushing air was exciting, filling her lungs and whipping roses into her cheeks. She had almost forgotten the sense of liberation riding gave her. It was the same sensation that she had experienced many times when flying from top to bottom or springing high in a double twist.

They rode in silence for a quarter of an hour. Jake allowed her to fill her being with the thrill of movement and the beauty of the countryside. Wild peaks jutted arrogantly into the sky. The rolling plains below were yellow-green with winter. They rode by Herefords, white-faced and sleek, who noted their passing with a lazy turn of the head before resuming their grazing.

A shape darted across an open field, and Samantha slowed her horse to a walk and pointed. "What's that?"

"Antelope," Jake answered, narrowing his eyes against the sun.

"Oh!" She halted her mount and watched the animal's graceful, bounding progress until it streaked over a hill and out of her view. "It must be marvelous to run like that, graceful and free." She turned her unguarded face to the man beside her and found him regarding her intently. His eyes held an expression she did not understand. A strange tingling raced along her spine, like warm fingers on cold skin. The tingling increased, the sensation spreading to settle somewhere in her stomach. Suddenly, his expression changed. The shadows of his face shifted as his lips moved into a smile.

"Someday you will be caught, little antelope."

She blinked at him, totally disoriented, trying to remember what they had been talking about. His grin increased. He pointed to a large, bare-limbed tree a quarter of a mile away.

"Race you." There was challenge under the lazy dare.

Her eyes brightened with excitement. "Fine chance I'd have against a horse like that. What handicap do I get?"

Jake pushed his hat back as if to view her more completely. "From the look of you, I'd say you've got a good fifty-pound advantage. That should balance the odds some."

"No head start?"

"No, ma'am."

She pouted for a moment, then grinned. "All right, Jake Tanner, I'll give you a run for your money."

"Whenever you say, Sam." He pulled the brim of his hat low over his forehead.

"Now!"

She met the gelding's sides with her heels and spurted forward in a gallop. The quiet morning air vibrated with the thunder of hooves. Samantha, her hair flowing behind her, gave herself over to the thrill of the race. She reached the finish just ahead of her competitor and reined in, filling the morning with dusty, breathless laughter.

"Oh, that was wonderful, absolutely wonderful."

"Any time you want to give up teaching, Sam, you can work for me. I can use a hand who rides like you."

"I'll keep that in mind, even though I know you let me beat you."

"Now what makes you think that?" He leaned his arm on the horn of his saddle and watched her thoughtfully.

"I'm not stupid." Her grin was good-natured and

friendly. "I couldn't beat that Arabian in a million years. You, maybe," she added with a touch of arrogance, "but not that horse."

"Pretty sharp, aren't you?" he returned, answering her grin.

"As a tack," she agreed. "And," she continued, brushing her hair from her shoulders, "I am not a weak female who needs to be placated. With my background, I know how to compete, I know how to lose, and—" she grinned and lifted her brows "—I know how to win."

"Point taken." He tilted his head as if to view her from a different angle. "From now on, Sam, we play head-to-head." He smiled, and she was no longer sure they were talking about the same thing. "I know how to win, too," he added slowly. They continued at a leisurely pace for a time, crossing a narrow branch of the Medicine Bow River. They paused there for the horses to quench their thirst in the icy water that forced its way over shining rocks with hisses and whispers. At Samantha's request, Jake began to identify the surrounding mountains.

Pointing to the long fingers of peaks at the south, the Laramie Range, he told her they extended from eastern Colorado. The middle section was the Medicine Bow

Range, and the Sierra Madre loomed to the west. The vast ranges were separated by broad tongues of the Wyoming Basin. Silver-blue, they gleamed in the sunlight, lacings of snow trembling from their summits.

She had reined in without being aware of her action. "I can never look at them long enough. I suppose you're used to them."

"No." There was no laughter or mockery in his tone. "You never get used to them."

She smiled a bit uncertainly, not at all sure she could deal with this side of him.

"Are there bears up there?" she asked.

He glanced up at the mountains, smiled, then looked back at her. "Black bear and grizzly," he informed her. "Elk, coyotes, mountain lions…"

"Mountain lions?" she repeated, a little nervously.

"You're not likely to run into one down here," he returned with an indulgent smile.

She ignored the mockery in his voice and looked around her, again awed by the miles of open space. "I wonder if this looked the same a century ago."

"Some of it. Those don't change much." He indicated the Rockies with an inclination of his head. "The Indians are gone," he continued, as if thinking aloud. "There were Arapaho, Sioux, Cheyenne, Crow, Shoshone, all roaming free over the state before the first white man set foot here. Then trappers came, trading with Indians, dressing like them, living like them, and the beaver was nearly driven into extinction." He turned back to her, as if suddenly remembering she was there. "You're the teacher." His smile appeared. "You should be telling me."

Samantha shook her head in mock despair. "My knowledge of Wyoming's history is limited to late-night westerns." They were walking their horses slowly, side by side. She had completely forgotten her aversion to the man beside her. "It's impossible to believe the killing and cruelty that must have gone on here. It's so serene, and so vast. It seems there would have been room enough for everyone."

This time it was Jake who shook his head. "In 1841 more than a hundred and fifty thousand people crossed the South Pass going west, and a few years later, fifty thousand more came through on their way to California looking for gold. This was Indian land, had been Indian land for generations. Game disappeared, and when people get hungry, they fight. Treaties were signed, promises made by both sides, broken by both sides." He shrugged.

"In the 1860s, they tried to open the Bozeman Pass

from Fort Laramie to Montana, and open war broke out. The trail ran through the Sioux hunting ground. The fighting was of the worst kind, massacres, indiscriminate killing of women and children, butcheries by both white and Indian. More treaties were signed, more misunderstandings, more killing, until the whites outnumbered the Indians, drove them away or put them on reservations."

"It doesn't seem fair," Samantha whispered, feeling a wave of sadness wash over her.

"No, it doesn't." He heard the wistful note in her voice and turned to regard her. "Life isn't always fair, though, is it, Samantha?"

"I suppose not." She sighed. "You seem to know quite a bit about what happened here. You must have had a good history teacher."

"I did." He held her curious look with a teasing half-smile on his lips. "My great-grandmother lived to be ninety-eight. She was Sioux."

Samantha lifted her brows in surprised interest. "Oh, I'd love to have met her. The things she must have seen, the changes in nearly a century of living."

"She was quite a woman." His smile faded a moment. "She taught me a lot. Among other things, she told me that the land goes on no matter who walks on it, that life moves on whether you fight against it or flow with it, that when you want something, you go after it until it's yours."

Suddenly, she felt he was leading her out of her depth, reaching for something she was not sure she possessed. She turned from the directness of his eyes to search the land.

"I'd like to have seen all this before there were any fences, before there was any fighting."

Jake pointed skyward. Glancing up, Samantha watched the graceful flight of an eagle. For a timeless moment, he soared overhead, the undisputed sovereign of the skies. They moved off again, in companionable silence. "I hope you're getting some fun out of this trip, some compensation for taking care of your sister," Jake said at last.

"I don't need any compensation for taking care of Bree, she's my sister, my…"

"Responsibility?"

"Well…yes. I've always looked out for Bree, she's more delicate, more…dependent than I am." She shrugged and felt uncomfortable without knowing why. "Dad always joked that I took my share of strength and half of Bree's while we were still in the womb. She needs me," she added, feeling compelled to defend what she had always taken for granted.

"She has Dan," Jake reminded her. "And she's a grown woman now—just as you are. Did it ever occur to you that you have your own life to lead now that Sabrina has a husband to care for her?"

"I'm not trying to take over for Dan," she said quickly. "Perhaps you can figure out how he could see to her needs and tend to the house and the ranch all at the same time, but I can't." She glared at him, half in anger, half in exasperation. "What do you expect me to do? Sit up in Philadelphia teaching kids to jump on a tramp while my sister needs help?"

"No, Samantha." He met her eyes with a quiet patience that was more disturbing than angry words and shouts. "What you're doing is very kind and unselfish."

"There's nothing kind or unselfish about it," she interrupted, shrugging the words away. "We're sisters. More than that, we're twins. We shared life from its beginning. You can't understand the kind of bond that creates. I'd give up a hundred jobs to help Bree if she needed me."

"No one's condemning your loyalty, Samantha. It's an admirable trait." He gave her a long, level look. "Just a word of advice. Don't become so involved that you forget who Samantha Evans is, and that she just might have the right to her own woman's life."

Samantha drew herself up to her full height in the saddle. "I hardly need your advice on how to run my life. I've been managing nicely for some time now."

His face creased in a lazy smile. "Yes, ma'am, I'm sure you have."

Chapter 4

Samantha had been riding the dapple gray in stubborn silence for nearly thirty minutes when she noticed more cattle. Her guide seemed unperturbed by her silence and slowed his Arabian's gait to the gelding's meandering walk. She would never have admitted to the man at her side that his words had disturbed her peace of mind.

What business was it of his how she chose to run her life? What gave Jake Tanner the right to question her relationship with Sabrina? No one asked him for his advice. And why in heaven's name should anything he said matter in the first place?

They were approaching a large ranch house. A redwood porch skirted the building's front, graced by evergreen shrubs. A gray wisp of smoke rose in a welcoming spire from the chimney. Ranch buildings sat neat and unobtrusive in the background.

"Welcome to the Double T, ma'am."

Jake drew her eyes with the uncharacteristic formality in his tone. She turned to see him smile and touch the brim of his well-worn Stetson.

"Thank you, Mr. Tanner. I can honestly say your ranch is spectacular. But what, may I ask, are we doing here?"

"Well, now…" Jake shifted in the saddle to face her directly. "I don't know about you, but nearly three hours in the saddle gives me a powerful appetite. I figured here we might do a bit better than beef jerky."

"Three hours?" Samantha repeated, and pushed Sabrina's hat from her head so it lay against her back. "Has it really been that long?"

The angles of his face moved slowly with his grin, and she found herself once more intrigued by the process. "I'll take that to mean you were so delighted with my company, time stood still."

She answered with a toss of her head. "I hate to tread on your ego, Jake, but the credit goes to Wyoming."

"Close enough for now." Reaching over, he plopped the brimmed hat back in place on Samantha's head and urged his mount into a canter.

Samantha stared after him in exasperation, watching the confidence with which he rode the Arabian. They moved like one form rather than horse and man. Scowling, she pressed her heels to the gelding's side and raced forward to join him.

As she reached his side, he skirted the ranch house and rode toward the buildings in the rear, following the left fork on a long, hard-packed road. A large, sleepy-eyed Saint Bernard rose from his siesta and romped forward to greet them. A deep, hoarse bark emitted from his throat. Jake halted in front of the stables. He slid off the Arabian's back, running his hand through the dog's thick fur as he hit the ground.

"Wolfgang's harmless." He acknowledged the loving, wet kisses with another brief caress and moved to the gelding's side. "He's just a puppy."

"A puppy," Samantha repeated. "You don't see many hundred-and-fifty-pound puppies." Tilting her head, she gave the overgrown baby a thorough examination before she brought her leg over the saddle to dismount.

Jake gripped her waist as she made her descent,

holding her off the ground a moment as if she were weightless. As her boots touched earth, she was turned around and drawn against a hard chest. She tilted her head to inform him that his assistance was unnecessary, but saw only a brief blur of his face before his lips captured hers.

Her mind whirled with the touch and scent of him. She felt as though she were falling into a deep well and her heart began to beat a mad tempo against her ribs. She clutched at his jacket in defense. Perhaps the kiss was brief. It could have lasted no more than a portion of a minute, but it felt like forever. She knew his mouth was warm and sure on hers while decades flew into centuries.

The strange sensations of timelessness and loss of control frightened her. She stiffened and began to struggle against his grasp. He released her immediately, staring down at her clouded blue eyes with a satisfied smile. The smile transformed terror into fury.

"How dare you?"

"Just testing, ma'am." His answer was complacent, as though the kiss had been no more than that, a traditional touching of lips.

"Testing?" she repeated, running an agitated hand through her hair. "Testing what?"

"I've always wanted to kiss a teacher." Grinning, he gave her a friendly pat on the cheek. "I think there're some holes in your education."

"I'll show you holes, you conceited, high-handed—" her mind searched for something appropriately derogatory and settled on a generality "—*man*. If I didn't consider that kiss so insignificant, you'd be lying on your back checking out the sky."

He surveyed her as she trembled with a mixture of fury and wounded pride. He rubbed his chin thoughtfully. "You know, Sam, I almost believe you could do it."

"You can bank on it," she confirmed with an arrogant toss of her head. "And the next time you…" Feeling her arm sharply pulled, she glanced down to see the sleeve of her jacket captured in the awesome jaws of the Saint Bernard. "What'd you do, teach him to eat unwilling females?"

"He just wants to make your acquaintance," Jake laughed, as he led the horses to the stable to turn them over to one of his men.

Samantha was not normally timid, and her pride refused to allow her to call Jake to untangle her from the teeth of his puppy. She swallowed and spoke to her canine captor.

"Hello…Wolfgang, wasn't it?" she muttered. "I'm

Sam. You, ah, wouldn't consider letting go of my jacket, would you?" The dog continued to stare with droopy, innocent eyes. "Well, that's all right," she said, trying out magnanimity. "It's just an old one, anyway. I'm very fond of dogs, you know." Tentatively, she brought her free hand up to touch the fur on his huge head. "Well, actually, I have a cat," she admitted in apology, "but I have absolutely no prejudices."

Though his expression did not alter, she decided it was prudent to give him time for consideration. Her patience was rewarded when he released her sleeve and bathed her hand with his enormous tongue.

"Well, I see you two have made friends," Jake drawled, coming up behind her.

"No thanks to you," she said. "He might have eaten me alive."

"Not you, Sam," Jake disagreed, taking her hand and striding toward the house. "Too tough for Wolfgang's taste."

Jake led her to the back entrance through a paneled, tiled-floor mudroom and into the kitchen. A large square room, it was bright and cheery with tangerine curtains framing the wide windows. The pleasant-looking woman who stood by the sink smiled at Samantha.

"Jake, you scoundrel, have you had this poor little lady out in the cold all this time?" Samantha met the warm brown eyes with a returning smile.

Jake grinned, unabashed. "Samantha Evans, meet Annie Holloway, my cook, housekeeper and best girl."

"Don't you try soft soaping me, you young devil." She brushed off his words with indulgent affection, but pleased color rose to her pudgy cheeks. "Thinks he can get around me with sweet talk. Pleased to meet you, Miss Evans." Samantha found her hand enclosed in a firm grip.

"Hello, Miss Holloway, I hope I'm not putting you out."

"Putting me out?" Annie let out a rich, full laugh, her ample bust heaving with the sound. "Isn't she the sweet one? Don't you be silly, now, and you just call me Annie like everyone else."

"Thank you, Annie." Samantha's smile warmed. "Everyone calls me Sam."

"Now that's a pretty thing," Annie commented, peering candidly into Samantha's face. "Yes, sir, a right pretty thing. You two run along," she commanded with an attempt at sternness. "Out of my kitchen. Lunch will be along, and I'll bring you in some tea to warm you up.

Not you," she said with a scowl as Jake grimaced. "For the little lady. You don't need any warming up."

"Annie runs things," Jake explained as he led Samantha down a wide hall into the living room.

"I can see she does, even when she's securely wrapped around your little finger."

For a moment, his smile was so boyish and full of mischief, she nearly gave in to the urge to brush the curls from his forehead.

The paneling in the living room was light. The expanse of wood was broken by a large stone fireplace and wide windows framed with cinnamon-colored sheers. The dark gleaming furniture had been upholstered in gold, burnt sienna and rich browns. There was a comfortable hodgepodge of Hepplewhites and Chippendales with piecrust tilt-top tables and Pembrokes, ladder-back chairs and candlestands. In the center of the hardwood floor lay a wide rug of Indian design, so obviously old and handworked, that Samantha wondered if it had been his great-grandmother's fingers that had hooked it perhaps nearly a century ago. The room reflected a quiet, understated wealth, a wealth she somehow did not associate with the rangy, brash cowboy side of Jake.

A Charles Russell painting caught her eye. She turned

to study it, attempting to sort out her new impressions of this complex man. Turning back, she found him watching her reaction with unconcealed amusement.

"I have a feeling you were expecting bearskins and oilcloth."

Samantha focused her attention on the inviting fire. "I never know what to expect from you," she muttered.

"No?" He dropped his lanky form into a wing-backed chair and pulled out a long, thin cigar. "I thought you were pretty bright."

Samantha seated herself in the chair across from him, keeping the warmth and hiss of the fire between them. "This is a lovely room, very appealing and very warm."

"I'm glad you like it." If he noticed her blatant change of subject, he gave no sign. Lighting his cigar, he stretched out his legs and looked totally relaxed and content.

"I have a weakness for antiques," she continued, deciding the topic was safe and impersonal.

He smiled, the smoke curling lazily above his head. "There's a piece in one of the bedrooms you might like to see. A blanket chest in walnut that was brought over from the East in the 1860s."

"I'd like that very much." She returned his smile and

settled back as Annie wheeled a small tea cart into the room.

"I brought you coffee," she said to Jake, and passed him a cup. "I know you won't take tea unless you douse it with bourbon. Something not quite decent about doing that to a good cup of tea."

"Tea is an old ladies' drink," he stated, ignoring her rapidly clucking tongue.

"How do you think Sabrina looks?" Samantha asked him when Annie had bustled back to the kitchen.

"I think you worry too much about her."

She bristled instinctively before replying. "Perhaps you're right," she surprised herself by admitting. "Our mother always said Bree and I were mirror images, meaning, I discovered after a while, opposites."

"Right down to Sabrina being right-handed, and you being left."

"Why, yes." She looked at him in faint surprise. "You don't miss much, do you?" He merely shook his head and gave her an enigmatic smile. "Well," she plunged on, not sure she liked his expression, a bit like a cat who already had the mouse between his paws. "I suppose the summary of my discrepancies was that I could never keep the hem in my white organdy party dress. You'd have to know my mother to understand that. She would have Bree and me all decked out in these frilly white organdy dresses and send us off to a party. Bree would come back spotless, pure and angelic. I'd come back with dirt on my frills, bloody knees and a trailing hem."

During her story, Jake's smile had widened. The coffee in his cup cooled, unattended as he watched her. "There're doers and there're watchers, Samantha. I imagine you had fun scraping up your knees."

As ridiculous as it seemed, she felt she'd just been complimented, and was both pleased and faintly embarrassed.

"I suppose you're a doer, too." She dropped her eyes. "You couldn't run a ranch like this and not be. Cattle ranching sounds romantic, but I imagine it's long hours, hot summers and cold winters. I don't suppose it's really all that different from the way it used to be a hundred years ago."

"The range isn't open anymore," he corrected. "You don't find cowboys going off to Texas to punch cattle with a ten-dollar horse and a forty-dollar saddle." He shrugged and set his empty cup on the table beside him. "But some change slow, and I'm one who likes to take my time."

She was frowning into his smile when Annie announced lunch. It was not until they were settled in the dining room that she spoke directly to him again, pressing him for more details on how the ranch was run.

He explained how roundups, which had once been accomplished on the vast open range with only men and horses, were now aided by fences and technology. But it was still men and ponies who moved the cattle into corrals. Over a few states there were still strongholds of riders and ropers, men who cultivated the old technique and blended it with the new. On the Double T, Jake employed the best of both.

"If roundups aren't what they once were, they still accomplish the same end. Getting the cattle together and branding them."

"Branding?" Samantha interrupted, and shuddered.

"Your Philadelphia's showing, Sam." He grinned. "Take my word for it, branding is a good deal more unpleasant for the branders than the brandees."

She decided to ignore his comments and changed the subject abruptly. "Bree told me your ranch borders Dan's. This place must be huge for it to have taken us three hours to get here."

Jake's deep, rich laughter filled the room, and she

decided unwillingly that she liked the sound very much. "It's a pretty big spread, Sam, but if you take the straight road north for the Lazy L, you can be here in twenty minutes on horseback. I took you on a big circle today," he explained. "Just a small taste of our part of the Laramie Basin."

They lingered over coffee, relaxed in each other's company.

"We'd better get started back," Jake said after a while. He rose and extended his hand. Her own slipped without hesitation into it as he pulled her to her feet. When she looked up at him, her smile was warm and spontaneous.

"Annie was right, that's a pretty thing." He lifted his hand and traced his fingers over the curve of her mouth. She started. "Now don't go skittish on me, Sam, I'm not going to use spurs and a whip."

His mouth lowered, gentle and persuasive. One hand held hers while the other circled the back of her neck to soothe with coaxing fingers. She had only to sway forward to feel his body against hers, had only to lift her hand to bring his mouth firmer and warmer on hers. Before the choice could be made, he drew her away and the decision was taken out of her hands.

"Sam." He shook his head as if exasperated and lightly amused. "You're enough to try a man's patience."

With this, he pulled her through to the kitchen.

"Well, so you're off again." Annie wiped one hand on her apron and wagged the other at Jake. "And don't be keeping her out in that cold too long."

"No, ma'am," Jake returned with suspicious respect.

"Thank you, Annie," Samantha broke in. "Lunch was wonderful."

"Well, now, that's fine, then." She gave Samantha a friendly pat on the cheek. "You just come back real soon, and you say hi to Sabrina for me, and that young rascal Dan, too. As soon as she's fit again, I'll be coming by to see her. Oh, Jake, I clean forgot." Annie turned to him and sighed at her absentmindedness. "Lesley Marshall called earlier, something about dinner tonight. I told her you'd give her a call, then it went straight out of my mind."

"No problem," Jake said easily. "I'll get back to her later. Ready, Sam?"

"Yes, I'm ready." She kept her smile in place, though a large black cloud seemed to have suddenly smothered the sunshine.

Lesley Marshall, she mused, automatically going

through the motions of securing her hat and coat. That was the woman Bree had predicted would marry Jake when he decided to settle down. Why should it matter to me? She straightened her spine and accompanied Jake to the waiting horses. I have absolutely no interest in Jake Tanner's affairs.

He's probably had dozens of girlfriends. Well, it's no concern of mine. Vaulting into the saddle, she followed as he set off down the hard-packed road.

They spoke little on the return journey. Samantha pretended an engrossment with the scenery that she was far from feeling. Unhappily, she realized Wyoming's magic was not quite enough to lift her flagging spirits. Snow-capped peaks glistened just as brightly in the late afternoon sun, and the land still spread and beckoned, but as she surveyed them now she felt strangely depressed.

It had been an unusual day, she concluded. Jake had annoyed her, charmed her, angered her and delighted her, all in a handful of hours. His kiss had aroused excitement and a deeper feeling she could not explain.

The knowledge that he was dining with another woman that evening depressed her beyond belief. She stole a sidelong look at his lean, tanned features.

He was undeniably attractive, she admitted, pulling

her eyes away from him before he could sense her study. There was a powerful aura of virility about him, which alternately intrigued her and made her wary. Perhaps it would be wise to avoid his company. He confused her, and Samantha liked to know precisely where she stood with a man. She wanted to call the shots, and she realized that this man would never allow anyone to call the shots but himself.

She would keep her distance from now on. Let him spread his charm over this Lesley Marshall, or any of the other women who were undoubtedly thirsting for his attention. Samantha Evans could get along very easily without him. As the Lazy L grew closer, she resolved to be polite and casually friendly to her escort. After all, she reflected, there was no reason to be rude. He was perfectly free to dine with whomever he chose; his life was most assuredly his own. Besides, she added to herself, if she had anything to say about it, they would be seeing very little of each other in the future.

When they reached the ranch, she dismounted, handing Spook's reins to a waiting cowboy. "I had a wonderful time, Jake." Samantha's smile was faultless in its social politeness as he walked her toward the ranch house, leading his stallion behind him. "I appreciate your time and hospitality."

Jake's mouth lifted at one corner. "It was my pleasure, ma'am."

If there was a mockery in his tone, Samantha chose to ignore it. Reaching the back door, she turned to smile at him again as he stood, tall and lean, beside the gleaming chestnut.

"Would you like some coffee before you go?" she invited, determined to be polite.

"No, thanks, Sam." He continued to watch her, his eyes shaded by the brim of his hat. "I'd best be getting along."

"Well." She breathed a small sigh of relief when her hand touched the doorknob and safety was in easy reach. "Thanks again."

"Sure." He nodded briefly and turned to his horse, paused and turned back to look at her with a penetrating intensity that turned her legs to water. When he spoke, it was soft and final. "I mean to have you, you know."

Several moments of silence passed before she could summon up an answer.

"D-Do you?" Her voice was a shaky whisper, unlike the coolly flippant tone she would have wished for.

"Yes, ma'am." He vaulted onto the chestnut's back and pushed the Stetson back on his head so that she had a disturbingly clear view of his eyes. "I do," he confirmed, turning his mount and galloping away.

Chapter 5

Often over the next few days, Samantha told herself that her reaction to Jake's kiss had been merely a passing physical attraction. She was a normal woman, wasn't she? So why feel guilty about it?

Jake Tanner *was* a very attractive man. *Too attractive,* she added to herself. And he knew too much about charming women. The fact that Jake was abrasive, smug and irritating had nothing to do with the way she had acted. It had just been a passing fancy. *And would certainly not occur again.*

* * *

Finally Sabrina was allowed up from the confinement of her bed. Samantha decided it was safe to leave her sister for a few hours. With a light heart, she saddled Spook and set off from the ranch at a brisk canter. For a while she enjoyed the feeling of Spook's hooves pounding the hard road. The sky hung low above her, and heavy, leaden gray clouds draped the distant mountains in mysterious gloom. There was a stillness, a waiting in the air, unnoticed by Samantha in her eagerness to escape the close confines of the house.

She rode swiftly past the bored, white-faced cattle and the stretches of barbed wire, eager to explore new territory, tasting the joy of motion and freedom. The mountains, grim sentinels above her, stood stone-gray under the unbroken sky. Remembering Dan's instructions, Samantha took care to mark her route, choosing a clump of rocks, a cottonwood tree with a broken limb, and a gnarled stump as landmarks for her return trip.

She led her mount to a crest of a hill, watching as a jackrabbit, startled by her intrusion, darted across the road and out of sight.

Nearly an hour passed before the first flakes began to drift lazily from sky to earth. She stopped and watched their progress in fascination. The snow fell slowly. Lifting her face, she let it caress her cheeks and closed lids. The air was moist, coming to life around her, and she stirred herself out of her dream.

"Well, Spook, this is my first Wyoming snow. I'd like to stay here all day and watch it fall, but duty calls. We'd better head back." Patting the horse's neck, she turned back toward the ranch.

They rode slowly. Samantha was enchanted with the fairyland that was forming around her. Cottonwoods and aspens were draped in white, their branches a stark contrast to the brilliant etchings of snow. The ground was cloaked quickly. Though the beauty was breathtaking, Samantha began to feel uncomfortably alone.

She took Spook into a canter. The sound of his hooves was soft and muffled. The quiet surrounding her was unearthly, almost as though the world had ceased to breathe. She shivered, suddenly cold in the warm confines of her jacket. To her annoyance, she saw that in her preoccupation with the landscape she had taken a wrong turn, and she began to backtrack, berating herself for carelessness.

The snow increased, plunging down from a sky she could no longer see. She cursed herself for having come so far, fighting down a sudden surge of panic. "Don't be silly, Sam," she spoke aloud, wanting the reassurance of her own voice. "A little snow won't hurt you."

The cold became more intense, piercing the layers of her skin. Samantha tried to concentrate on steaming coffee and a blazing fire as she looked around for a familiar landmark. Nothing was the same as it had been. She clamped her lips tight to still the chattering of her teeth, telling herself that it was impossible that she could be lost. But it was a lie. The trees and hills around her were strangers blanketed in white.

The snow fell thickly, a blinding white wall blocking her vision. A wind had sprung up, breaking the silence with its moans and tossing snow, hard and bitter, into her face. She was forced to slow the gelding to a walk, afraid of tangling with the sharp teeth of barbed wire she was unable to see. Her teeth savaged her lips in an effort to control a growing terror.

It's so cold, she thought as she began to shiver convulsively, so unbelievably cold.

The snow had soaked through the wool of her slacks and slipped mercilessly down the neck of her coat. She hunched her shoulders against the driving wind. Snow was everywhere, blocking her in and seeping into her clothing.

She let the reins hang limp, praying that the horse's instinct would guide him back to the warm shelter of his stables. They trudged on, the vortex of white that had begun so innocently now whirling around her. Time and direction had lost all meaning, and though she tried calling out, her voice was soundless against the fierce breath of the wind.

Now she felt the cold. Her body was numbed into submission. Her mind was following suit. The swirling snow was hypnotic, and a growing lethargy was creeping over her. In a small part of her mind, she knew her survival depended on remaining alert.

Horse and rider plodded on. There was no time, no world beyond the unbroken curtain of white. Samantha felt her eyelids growing heavy, but she willed them open with all her strength. The snow piled onto her back, weighing her down until she slumped onto the gelding's mane and clung to him. Staring down at the gelding's front hoof, she began to count each drudging step that Spook took as he continued his slow progress through the blinding storm.

Samantha's concentration on the horse's halting steps began to fade.

If I close my eyes, she thought dimly, I won't see all that white and I can sleep. Oh, how I want to sleep....

The snow was talking, she mused deliriously. Well, why not? It's alive. Why should it sound like Jake? Helplessly, she began to giggle. Well, why shouldn't it? *They both play to win.*

"Samantha!" The snow was shouting at her. "Open your eyes. Stop that insane laughing and open your eyes!"

Wearily, she forced herself to obey the command. Dimly she saw the blur of Jake's features through the flurries of snow. "You would be the last thing I see before I die." With a moan, she closed her eyes again and sought the silence.

"Tell Dan we've found her," Jake shouted against the howl of the wind. "I'm taking her back to the Double T."

The darkness was comforting. Samantha gave herself over to it, feeling herself falling slowly into a hole with no bottom. She burrowed deeper into it. Her consciousness swam to the surface.

Bemused, she looked around a dimly lit room. The snow that pooled around her was not snow at all, but a bed with a thick, warm quilt. She allowed her heavy lids to close again.

"Oh, no, you don't." The lids opened fractionally, and Samantha saw Jake standing in the open doorway.

"Hello."

His mouth thinned as he advanced to the bed to tower over her. It seeped through the misty reaches of her brain that he was angry. She stared at him with lazy fascination.

"What in heaven's name were you doing out in such a storm? I've seen some dumb stunts, but taking a joyride in the middle of a blizzard tops them all."

She wanted to ask him to stop shouting at her, but lacked the energy. "Where am I?" was all she could find to say.

Sitting on the edge of the bed, he drew her head from the pillow, then held a cup to her lips. "Here, drink this first, then we'll talk."

The brandy was warm and strong, and she sputtered and gasped as he poured it down her throat. Its power spread through her, pushing back the mists of unconsciousness.

"Now, to answer your question, you're at the Double T." Jake set the empty cup aside, and laid her head back on the mound of pillows.

"Oh."

"Is that all you can say?" He was shouting again. He

Song of the West

took her shoulders as if to shake her. "Just 'Oh'? What in heaven's name were you doing out there?"

"It seems so long ago." She frowned in concentration, closing her eyes with the effort. "It wasn't snowing when I left," she said in weak defense.

"Wasn't snowing?" Jake repeated, incredulous. "Samantha, didn't you see the sky? Where are your brains?"

"There's no excuse for insults," she retorted with a small flash of spirit.

"No excuse for insults? Are you stark raving mad? Do you realize what nearly happened to you?" His hands retreated to his pockets, as though he could barely prevent them from throttling her. "Out here in the middle of a blizzard, half-frozen and helplessly lost! It was a miracle we found you. A little longer, and you'd be lying somewhere buried in it, and no one would have found what was left until spring. Dan was half out of his mind when he got through to me and told me you'd gone out in this."

"Bree?"

"Knew nothing." He whirled to face her again. "She was taking a nap. It never occurred to her that you had gone out with a storm brewing." He laughed harshly.

The memory of the snow and the terror washed over her, and she began to shake. "I'm sorry," she managed through the tears that threatened to flow. With a brief oath, Jake ran a hand through his hair. He closed the distance between them and gathered her in his arms. "Samantha," he murmured against her hair. "What hell you put us all through."

"I'm sorry," she repeated, and she began to sob in earnest. "I was so scared, so cold."

He rocked and murmured words she could not understand, his lips brushing through her hair and over her damp cheeks until they met hers. The kiss mingled with the salt of her tears. "I've gotten your shirt all wet," she murmured after a while.

He let out a deep breath. She saw his smile begin to spread before he rested his brow against hers. "That is without doubt the worst calamity of the day."

"It's dark," she said with sudden realization. "How long…?"

"Too long. What you need now is rest."

"Spook?" she began as he lay her down on the pillows.

"Is sleeping off his adventure in the stables. He looks a lot better than you, I might add."

"I want to thank you for everything." Samantha reached for his hand. In that instant, she discovered there was nothing covering her save sheets and blankets. "M-My clothes," she stammered, drawing the quilt higher in a purely feminine gesture that caused Jake's mouth to twitch.

"Soaked through, Sam." Rising, he stood, rocking gently on his heels. "It was necessary to get you warm and dry."

"Did Annie?" she managed a smile at the thought of the matronly presence of Jake's housekeeper. "I seem to have put everyone to a lot of trouble. Will you thank her for me?"

"Well, Sam, I'd like to oblige you, but Annie left yesterday for Colorado to spend a week with her nephew." Jake's grin broadened.

"Then who—?" The question caught in her throat, and her eyes became round and impossibly dark. "Oh, no," she whispered, closing her eyes in humiliation.

"No need to be embarrassed, Sam, you have a beautiful body."

"Oh, no." With a moan, she squeezed her eyes tighter.

"Now, don't you fret." His tone took on the light insolence of the cowboy she'd met a month before in the cold March sunset. "When I took off your clothes and rubbed you down, it was strictly medical. I'd do as much for any stray." He patted her hand, and her eyes opened warily at his touch.

"Yes, of course." Moistening her lips, she attempted to see the practical side. "I, well…thank you."

"'S all right, don't give it a thought." He moved toward the door, then paused and turned back. "Now, the next time I get your clothes off, my purposes'll be completely different."

He strolled casually from the room, leaving a speechless Samantha.

Chapter 6

Samantha looked around her. She remembered with a shock that she was in Jake's house—and, worse yet, *naked* in bed. She was debating the wisdom of wrapping the quilt around her and searching for more appropriate attire when footsteps sounded down the hall outside her room. She pulled the covers to her chin as Jake strode through the open door.

"So, you're awake. How do you feel?"

"Fine." Her respiratory system behaved erratically as he continued toward her and dropped onto the bed. "I'm just fine," she repeated, then added unnecessarily, "It's still snowing."

"So it is," he agreed without taking his eyes from her face. "Slowing down, though."

"Is it?" She forced herself to look out the window.

"The worst'll be over by midday." He reached up and pried one of her hands loose from the death grip on the blanket. "Calm down, Sam, I'm not going to ravish you, I'm going to check your pulse."

"I'm fine," she repeated again.

"Far from fine, Samantha," he corrected. His fingers brushed against her cheek, as if to test its substance. "The first thing is to get some food into you." Rising, he held out a large flannel robe that he had dropped at the foot of the bed. "You'd probably feel better if you had something on." His smile was gently mocking. "Can you manage to get into this by yourself?"

"Of course." Plucking it from him, she kept a cautious grip on the blankets. "I'm not an invalid."

"You best think like one. Put that on, then get back in bed. I'll bring you some breakfast."

"I don't…"

"Don't argue." The two words were swift and final. He was gone before she could say another word.

He had shut the door, however, and grateful for the concession, Samantha tossed back the covers and slipped her arm into the robe. When she stood, the room swayed and spun around her. She sank back onto the bed and slipped her other arm into its sleeve, pulling the robe around her before attempting to stand again. Her limbs felt heavy and weak, and she noted with puzzlement that her ankle was throbbing lightly. Gripping one poster of the bed until the room steadied, she rolled up the sleeves of the robe several times until her hands became visible, then moved to the bathroom to study herself in the mirror.

The sight of her own face caught at her breath. Her skin seemed nearly transparent, her eyes darker and larger in contrast. The breath of color that resulted when she pinched her cheeks faded instantly. She ran a hand through her hair falling on the shoulders of the dark green robe.

It must be his, she realized, looking down at the sleeves, which swallowed her arms, and the hem, which fell nearly to her ankles. A strange sensation flowed over her as she felt the material on her skin. Turning away from the mirror, she studied the bed.

"I'm not getting in there again," she muttered, and with a small gesture of defiance belted the robe more securely. "I can eat at the table like a normal person."

After a moment, her progress down the hall seemed

more of a crawl than a walk. Her legs were heavy with a weakness which infuriated her. The stillness of the house vibrated around her, playing havoc with her nerves, and the need to hear the natural, everyday movements of another human being became increasingly important. She cursed the waves of giddiness that swam around in her head, forcing her to stop time after time to rest her hand against the wall.

"This is ridiculous."

"You're right."

The harsh agreement came from behind as Jake's hands gripped her shoulders.

"What are you doing out of bed?"

"I'm all right." She swayed against his chest. He gripped her waist to support her, and she rested her hands on his arms.

"I'm just a bit wobbly, and I'm having some trouble with my ankle."

He let his gaze travel down to rest on her bare feet. "Probably turned it when you fell off the horse."

"I fell off Spook?" Her expression was incredulous.

"You were unconscious at the time. Now, get back in bed and stay there." Effortlessly, he swept her into his arms, and she laid her head against his shoulder.

"Jake, don't make me go back to bed. It's so quiet in there, and I don't feel like being alone now."

He bent and brushed lips that parted in confusion. "If you think you can sit in a chair without sliding on your face, you can come in the kitchen."

She nodded, sighed and closed her eyes. "I hate being so much trouble."

She felt him shift her in his arms before he began the journey down the hall. "I knew you were trouble the minute I set eyes on you."

"Don't tease, Jake, I'm trying to thank you."

"What for?"

She lifted a hand to his cheek, turning his face so that he would look at her. "For my life."

"Then take better care of it in the future," he suggested.

"Jake, please, I'm serious. I owe you…"

"Nothing, you owe me nothing." His voice had hardened with annoyance. "I don't want your gratitude." They had reached the kitchen, and he placed her in a chair at the table. "Which ankle did you hurt?" He crouched down by her feet.

"The left one. Jake, I— Ouch!"

"Sorry." He grinned up at her, then rested his hand with friendly ease on her knee. "It's not swollen."

"It still hurts," she said stubbornly.

"Keep off it, then," he advised with simple logic, and turned away to finish breakfast.

"You've got some bedside manners, Dr. Tanner," she observed sharply.

"Yes, ma'am, so I've been told." When he turned to face her, his smile was bland. "Tell me, Sam, does Sabrina have a mole on her left hip, too?"

Color flooded her face. "You...you..." she faltered, and clutched the robe tight at her throat.

"Around here, we call that locking the barn door after the cow's got loose. Have some coffee," he invited with sudden graciousness, pouring a cup and setting it on the table. "Start on this bacon," he ordered, sliding a plate in front of her. "That color didn't last long, you're pale as a ghost again. When did you eat last?"

"I...at breakfast yesterday, I guess."

"Toast and coffee, I imagine," he said disgustedly. "It's a wonder you can manage to sit up at all. Eat." He plucked a piece of bacon from the plate and held it out to her. "I'll have some eggs ready in a minute."

Obediently, she accepted the bacon and took a bite. "Are you going to have something?"

"In a minute," he answered absently, involved with breaking and beating eggs in a bowl.

With the first bite of bacon, Samantha realized she was ravenous. Through her preoccupation with food, she watched Jake cook with a deftness that amused and surprised her.

In a moment, he sat across from her, his plate piled high. She wondered how he could eat with such abandon and remain hard and lean.

She watched him under the cover of her lashes, and the thought came unbidden into her mind that never before had she shared the breakfast table with a man. The intimacy of their situation washed over her; the scent of bacon and coffee drifting through the air, the house quiet and empty around them, the soft flannel of his robe against her skin, the faint masculine scent of him clinging to it. It was as if they were lovers, she thought suddenly, as if they had shared the night, and now they were sharing the morning. Her face grew warm.

"I don't know what thought put roses back in those cheeks, Sam, but keep it up."

Her eyes lifted to his, and she had the uncomfortable feeling that he knew very well what road her thoughts had taken. She dropped her eyes to her plate. "I should call Bree and let her know I'm all right."

"Phones are out," he said simply, and her eyes flew back to his.

"The phones are out?" she repeated.

No telephone, her mind said again. Without a telephone, they might as well be on an island a thousand miles from anyone. Their isolation was complete, and the snow was still falling as though it would never stop.

"With a storm like this, it's not surprising to lose the phones. Power's out, too. We're on generator. Don't worry about Sabrina, she knows you're with me." His words did nothing to erase her tension.

"When…when do you think I'll be able to get back?"

"Couple of days," he returned with an easy shrug, and sipped his coffee. "The roads'll have to be cleared after the storm lets up, and you're not in any shape to travel through a mess like that yet. In a day or two, you'll be more up to it."

"A couple of days?"

He leaned back comfortably in his chair, his voice smooth as a quiet river. "Of course, by then you'll be hopelessly compromised, not a scrap of your sterling reputation left. Alone with me for two or three days, without Annie to add a thread of decency to the situation." His eyes traveled down her slim figure. "Wearing my bathrobe, too." He shook his head. "Not too many years back, I'd have had to marry you."

"Thank goodness for progress," she retorted smartly.

"Oh, I don't know, Sam." His sigh was convincing. "I'm an old-fashioned sort of man."

"It's only a matter of circumstance that we're alone here in the first place." With great dignity, she folded her arms. "And I've hardly been compromised, as you so quaintly put it."

"No?" He watched her through lazily narrowed eyes. "So far, I've undressed you, tucked you in and fixed your breakfast. Who knows what that might lead to?"

His smile might have been lazy, but it was full of meaning. Suddenly Samantha found it difficult to swallow.

"Relax, Sam." His laugh was full of arrogant enjoyment. "I told you I mean to have you, but it's not in my plans to take on a pale child who barely has the strength to stand." He paused, lit one of his long, thin cigars and blew smoke at the ceiling. "When I make love to you, I want you to have your wits about you. I don't want you passing out in my arms."

The man's arrogance was amazing! "You conceited mule," she began. "How dare you sit there and tell me you're going to make love to me? You seem to think you're irresistible! Well, you have another thing coming—"

"I'm going to remind you of that one day, Sam," Jake

said mildly as he crushed out his cigar. "Now, I think you better lie down again. You're not quite up to sparring with me yet."

"I do not have to lie down. And I certainly don't need you carting me around. I can manage." She stood up, then was forced to grasp the table as the room revolved around her.

"You don't look ready to turn cartwheels, teacher," Jake observed as he took her arm.

"I'm all right." Her hand, which she had lifted to push him away, lay weakly on his chest for support. He tilted her chin, and he was no longer smiling. "Samantha, sometimes you have to be strong enough to let someone else take care of things. You're going to have to hand over the reins to me for a couple of days. If you fight it, you're only going to make it harder on yourself."

With a sigh, she allowed her head to fall against his chest, not protesting as his arms encircled her. "Do I have to like it?"

"Not necessarily." He gave a short laugh and lifted her easily and carried her back to bed.

Her small spurt of energy deserted her. With an odd feeling of contentment, she settled down under the covers. She was asleep even before his lips had lightly touched her forehead in a farewell kiss...

"I was beginning to think you'd sleep through the night."

She turned her head quickly. Jake was sitting across the room, the smoke of his cigar spiraling upward, the flickering lights from the fire shooting specks of gold into his eyes. Samantha brushed the tousled hair from her face and struggled into a sitting position.

"It's dark," she said. "What time is it?"

He glanced at the gold watch on his wrist and took a slow drag from his cigar. "It's a bit past six."

"Six? I've slept for hours. I feel as if I've slept for weeks."

"You needed it." Tossing the stub of his cigar into the mouth of the fire, Jake rose and moved toward her. His concerned eyes roamed over her sleep-flushed cheeks and heavy eyes. Gradually, his expression lightened, the angles of his face moving into a satisfied smile. "Your color's coming back." He took her wrist, and her eyes dropped from his to study the dancing flames of the fire. "Pulse's a bit jumpy." The smile reflected in his voice. "Strong though. Hungry?"

"I shouldn't be." She forced her eyes to meet his.

"I've done nothing but lie around all day, but I'm starved."

He smiled again, lifting her without comment. She felt small and vulnerable in his arms, a sensation that was both pleasant and disturbing. She found it difficult to resist the impulse to rest her head against the strong curve of his shoulder. Instead, she concentrated on the sharp, clean lines of his profile.

"I'm sure I can walk. I really feel fine."

"I doubt it." She could feel his warm breath on her face. "Besides, you seem to fit in my arms pretty well."

Finding no quick comeback to this comment, she took the journey to the kitchen in silence.

Leaning back in her chair, replete and content, Samantha sipped the cool white wine in her glass and gave Jake a nod of approval.

"You're going to make some woman a terrific husband. You're an outstanding cook."

"I think so." He nodded smugly. "My wife wouldn't have to be a gourmet cook," he added with casual consideration. "I'd demand other qualities."

"Adoration," Samantha suggested. "Obedience, unswerving loyalty, solicitude."

"That's all right for a start."

"Poor woman."

"Of course, I don't want her to be a doormat. Let's say I like a woman who knows how to think, one who doesn't pretend to be anything but who she is. Of course," he added, finishing off his wine, "I'm also partial to good looks."

"Well, so far it doesn't sound as though you're asking for much," Samantha giggled. "Just perfection."

"The woman I have in mind can handle it." He smiled broadly as he rose to pour coffee. Samantha stared at his back, feeling as though her heart had been dropped into a deep hole. *Lesley Marshall.* Her mind flashed the name like a neon sign in bright red letters.

Jake squelched her offer to do the dishes and swooped her from her chair and deposited her on the living room sofa.

"I feel useless," she muttered, helplessly cocooned by blankets and pillows. "I'm not made for lying around. I'm never sick." She gave Jake a sulky glare as if the entire matter was his fault. "I don't know how Bree coped with this sort of thing for a month."

"Could be you got her share of strength, and she got your share of patience," he considered, then shrugged.

"Of course, I could be wrong." She heard his chuckle and the quiet click of his lighter as he lit a cigar.

Well, Samantha, she chided herself, you've really done it this time. Not only are you isolated with a man who constantly confuses you, but you can't even stand on your own feet. They say people learn about each other quickly when they live together, but I think it's going to take much more than one day to learn what this man is all about. *Living together,* she repeated, finding herself more amused than embarrassed. If Momma could see me now, we'd need a gallon of smelling salts.

Chapter 7

Dawn was breaking. Pink and gold streaks split the hazy blue of the sky, and light tumbled through to rest on Samantha's closed lids.

Morning? Sitting up with a start, she shook her head vigorously to dispel the last remnants of sleep. Pulling on the borrowed robe, she set her feet on the floor, took three deep breaths and stood. When both the room and her head remained stable, she let out a long sigh of relief. Her legs were weak, but they no longer felt as if they would melt from under her, and the stiffness in her ankle had disappeared.

Mobility, she thought with arrogant glee. I've never

truly appreciated it until now. Coffee. One thought followed swiftly on the trail of the other, and she deserted the room with the intention of making fantasy fact. A door opened as she passed it, and with a cry of surprise, she fell against the opposite wall.

Jake stood in the doorway, rubbing a towel briskly through his damp hair, a terry-cloth robe tied loosely around his waist. "Morning, ma'am."

"You startled me." She swallowed, over-powered by the lean, bronzed maleness that the terry cloth did little to hide. He took a step toward her, and her breath caught instinctively. "I—I'm much better." She began to babble, unconsciously cowering against the smooth paneling. "I can actually walk a straight line."

Her voice died to a whisper as he stood directly in front of her. Her eyes were on a line with the tanned column of throat revealed by the open neck of the robe. His hand lifted her chin, and she trembled.

"Relax, Sam." His laughter sounded deep in his throat. "I just want to look you over. You must have the constitution of an elephant," he concluded with unflattering candor. "You look as though you've been on vacation instead of battling blizzards. One day's rest after nearly freezing to death. Most women would have been stretched out for a week."

"I'm not most women." She pushed his hand away from her face. "I'm not fragile and delicate, and I'm not going back to bed. I'm going to fix breakfast." She nudged him out of her path and started down the hall.

"Coffee's already on," he called after her.

Samantha had breakfast under way by the time Jake joined her. Clad in the less disturbing attire of corded jeans and flannel shirt, he watched her prepare the meal as he silently sipped at the coffee at the kitchen table.

"I'm getting used to having a pretty face across from me at breakfast," he commented when she sat down to join him.

"I'm sure I'm not the first," she commented with studied indifference. Nor, she added to herself, will I be the last.

"Nope," he agreed easily, "but there's something to be said for big blue eyes first thing in the morning."

"Blue eyes are common enough," she muttered, and lowered them to the contents of her plate. "Besides, this is hardly a long-term arrangement." He did not speak for a moment, and her fork moved restlessly among her eggs.

"We should have the road clear enough sometime tomorrow."

"Tomorrow?" she repeated. A hollow feeling spread through her stomach.

"There's a lot of snow out there, some of the drifts are small mountains. It's going to take a little time to move it."

"I see."

"Do you think you could manage on your own for a while today?"

"What? Oh, sure, I'll be fine."

"There's a lot I should see to. My foreman was in charge yesterday, but the men need all the help they can get." He was frowning. "Cattle need hay brought out to them. They haven't the sense to dig through to the grass. They'll just stand there and starve to death."

"I suppose the storm did a lot of damage."

"It's only minor from the reports I've gotten. We were hit worse a couple years ago."

"Reports?"

"One of my men came by yesterday afternoon to fill me in." Pouring more coffee in his cup, he reached for the cream. "You were asleep."

"Oh." Strange, she thought, there had been a ripple in their isolation and she had been totally unaware of it.

Lifting his cup, he studied her over the rim. "I don't like leaving you alone, especially with the phones out."

Her shoulders moved. "Don't worry about me, I'll be fine." Glancing up, she met his speculative gaze.

"I don't know how long I'll be gone."

"Jake, stop fussing. I feel fine."

He tilted his head to the side, his eyes still narrowed. "Stand up. I want to see how you feel for myself."

Before she realized his intent, his arms were around her, and his mouth was on hers. Her legs buckled.

His mouth was light, teasing, his teeth nibbling at the fullness of her bottom lip until she moaned from the exquisite agony. She gripped his shoulders as a dim light of control seeped into the darkness. Pulling away she shook her head in refusal.

"Now, Sam…" His voice was soft and persuasive, but the hands that descended to her hips were firm. "You wouldn't send a man out in the cold without something warm to remember, would you?"

Insistently, he brought her closer, molding her hips, exploring the soft roundness until she was pressed against him with exciting intimacy. His mouth closed over her protest, his tongue moving with slow devastation to tease hers until she felt the room spinning as wildly as it had the day before. Slowly, his hands ascended, his thumbs circling the side of her breasts while his mouth and tongue destroyed all resistance. She was straining against him, moving against him, reason forgotten. Her body heated urgently at his touch.

Her sigh was a moan as his mouth descended to her throat. His lips tasted, lingered, traveled to new territories, the tip of his tongue moist and warm against her skin, erotic and devastating against her ear, until her mouth was desperate for its return to hers.

Her mouth was to go unsatisfied. He pulled her away with the same arrogance as he had pulled her to him. Dazed and limp, she could do no more than stare up at him as her body throbbed with a myriad of newly discovered desires.

"You're learning fast, Sam. That was enough to keep any man moving through a six-foot snowdrift."

Furious, and humiliated by her own response, she drew back her hand.

"Now, Sam." He caught her wrist easily, holding it aloft, ignoring her efforts to escape. "You're not strong enough yet for wrestling. Give yourself a couple more days." Turning her hand over, his lips brushed her palm, causing her struggles to cease abruptly. "I'm going to bring in Wolfgang to keep an eye on you. Take it easy today, and try to remember, you're not as tough as you'd like to think."

Ruffling her hair as though she were a child, he disappeared into the adjoining mudroom.

* * *

Later Samantha indulged in a hot, steaming shower, attempting to forget, as she soaped her skin, the feel of Jake's hands running over her. In the bedroom, she noticed her clothes piled neatly on the spoon-back chair. She slipped them on and wandered through the house in aimless exploration, the Saint Bernard lumbering at her heels.

The house abounded in small, delightful treasures, an oak rolltop desk, a wall box with Friesian carving, a Windsor cradle. With a small sigh, she wondered if the latter had rocked the baby Jake. Opening yet another door, she found Jake's library.

It smelled of leather and age, and her fingers ran over volume after volume. She pulled out a small volume of love poetry and opened the cover. Light, feminine handwriting adorned the top corner, and her mouth turned down at the inscription.

Darling Jake... To remind you.

Love, Lesley

Shutting the book with a snap, Samantha held it for one heat-blinded movement over the wastebasket, then, grinding her teeth, stuck it firmly back in place.

"It makes no difference to me," she informed Wolfgang.

"She can give him a hundred books of poetry, she can give him a thousand books of poetry. It's her privilege."

She nudged the big dog with her toe. "Come on, Wolfgang, let's get moving."

She returned to the living room and built up the fire, which had burned down to a hissing pile of embers. She curled up beside it.

One hour slipped into two, two slipped into three. Surely, Jake should be home by now, she told the silent clock as the hands crept past six. It was getting dark. Rising, Samantha stared out into the diminishing light.

What if something had happened to Jake? Her throat went dry, fear creeping along her skin. Nothing could happen to him, she told herself, running her hands over her arms to combat the sudden chill. He's strong and self-reliant.

But why am I so worried about him?

"Because," she said aloud, slowly, *"I love him. I've lost my mind and fallen in love with him."* Her hands lifted to cover her eyes as the weight of the knowledge crushed down on her. "Oh, how could I be so stupid? Of all the men in the world, I had to fall in love with this one."

A man, she remembered, *who had chosen Lesley*

Marshall to be his wife. Is that why I've felt pulled in two? Is that why I responded to him when I've never responded to anyone else? Looking out into the darkness, she shuddered. I might as well admit that I don't care about anything except his getting home....

When finally the sound of the outside door slamming reached her ears, she ran into the mudroom and threw herself at an astonished, snow-covered Jake.

"Sam, what's going on?" He tried to pull her away from his cold, wet jacket.

"I was afraid something had happened to you." Her voice was muffled against his chest, her cheek oblivious to the frigid dampness.

"Nothing's happened, except I'm half-frozen and soaked to the skin." Firmly now, he took her shoulders, disentangling himself from her arms. "You're getting covered with snow." His grip was gentle. She stared up at him with huge, swimming eyes. "I'm sorry I was gone so long, but things were piled up, and it's slow working in a mess like this."

Embarrassed by her outburst, she backed away. "You must be exhausted. I'm sorry, it was stupid to go on like that. It must come from being alone in the house all day." As she babbled, she was backing purposefully toward the door. "You probably want a shower and something hot to drink. I—I've got dinner on."

"Something smells good," he commented. His eyes roamed over her flushed face, and a smile spread over his features.

"S-Spaghetti," she stammered and despised herself. "I'll go finish it up."

Retreating into the kitchen, Samantha kept her back toward him when he emerged and announced casually that he would have a hot shower before dinner. She mumbled a vague reply, pretending a complete involvement with her dinner preparation. Listening to his receding footsteps, she let out a long, pent-up breath.

"Oh, idiot that I am," she sighed, and pushed her hair from her face in an angry gesture. The type of behavior she had displayed in the mudroom would only lead to trouble. She took a solemn oath to keep her emotions on a tight leash as long as Jake Tanner was around.

Tomorrow, she remembered, with a mixture of relief and disappointment, she would be back with her sister, and avoiding Jake would be a great deal easier. She had only to get through one more evening without making a fool of herself, and then she would sort out her thinking.

She was setting the table when Jake returned.

"If that tastes as good as it smells, I'll die a happy man." He lifted the lid on the pot and gave a sigh of approval. Grinning, he disappeared for a moment, then returned with a bottle of wine just as she was placing the pot on the table.

"A nice burgundy," he said, opening the bottle and setting out two glasses.

"Samantha, this is fantastic." He broke off eating long enough to give her a smile. "Where'd you learn to cook like this?"

"More of my mother's famous lessons."

"What else can you do?"

"Well, let's see. I do a rather superb swan dive, a very graceful arabesque, I can walk on my hands as easily as some walk on their feet, whip up an incredible quiche, and waltz without counting the time."

"I am suitably impressed. How did a woman of your talents spend the day?"

She sighed and grimaced and began to toy with her spaghetti. "Sleeping, mostly."

"Hmm." His cough did not quite cover his laugh.

After dinner, Samantha insisted on seeing to the washing up herself. She wanted to avoid the intimacy of working side by side with him in the confines of the kitchen.

When the last signs of the man had vanished, she walked down the hall to the living room. Jake was adding another log to the low, shifting blaze. As she entered, he turned to smile at her. "Want some brandy?"

"No, no, thank you." She took a deep breath and willed her legs to carry her to the sofa.

"Not in training, are you?" He moved from the hearth to join her on the sofa.

Smiling, she shook her head. "The fire's wonderful." Grasping the first topic that came to mind, she riveted her eyes on the flames. "I always wanted one in my apartment. We had one at home, and Bree and I used to pop corn over it. We'd always burn it, and…"

The rest of her rush of words was lost as Jake placed his finger under her chin and turned her face to his. His face moved closer, and when she jerked back in defense, his brow lifted in amusement. He bent toward her again, and again she started.

"I'm only going to kiss you, Samantha." His grip tightened on her chin. Sliding from her chin, his hand framed her face as his lips moved over hers, soft as a whisper. In spite of herself, she relaxed against him. Her lips parted, inviting him to explore, begging him to take.

"Samantha." Her name was a sigh.

"Kiss me again," she whispered slowly as she lifted her mouth to his.

With a low groan, he brought his lips down on hers. She clung to him, her body throbbing with heat, her heart desperate against his, while a part of her looked on, aghast, as she answered his kiss.

Her mouth clung, avid and sweet, to his. Dormant passion exploded into life until there remained only man and woman and the need, older than time, to love and be loved, to possess and be possessed.

He opened her shirt and claimed her breast. The first desperation mellowed into slow exploration as his fingers trailed lightly, drugging her with a new, delirious languor. His mouth moved to sample the taste of her neck, his face buried in the spreading lushness of her hair. She pressed against the rippling muscles of his back as his mouth and tongue and hands raged fire over her.

She felt rather than heard him say her name against her mouth, sensed rather than felt the tension enter his body before her lips were set free. Dimly, she heard the strident insistence of bells ringing as she groped to bring heaven back within reach.

"Hell of a time for them to fix the phones." She

opened her eyes, dark as sapphires, and stared without comprehension. "There's nothing I'd like more than to ignore it, Samantha, but it might be important." Her lids fluttered in confusion. She could feel the warm raggedness of his breath against her cheek. "The phones have been out for two days, and there's a lot of damage out there."

His body left hers and took the warmth with it. She struggled to sit up, pulling her shirt closed. The hands that worked at the buttons were unsteady and, rising on weak legs, she sought the warmth of the fire. Pushing at tumbled hair, she wrapped her arms around her body and closed her eyes.

What had she done, losing herself that way? Tossing away pride like damaged goods! What if the phone hadn't rung? Her arms closed tighter. Does love always hurt? Does it always make a fool of you?

"Samantha." She whirled at the sound of her name, her arms still tight in protection. "It's Sabrina." Dropping her eyes from his, she moved into the hall.

Samantha picked up the phone and swallowed. "Hi, Bree." Her voice sounded strangely high-pitched to her ears, and her fingers gripped hard on the receiver.

"Sam, how are you?"

Taking a deep breath, she answered. "Fine. How *you* are is more important."

"Stronger every minute. I'm so glad you had the sense to head for the Double T when the snow started. The thought of you getting caught in that blizzard makes my blood turn cold."

"That's me, a steady head in a crisis." Samantha nearly choked on a gurgle of hysterical laughter.

"Are you sure you're all right? You sound strange. You aren't coming down with a cold, are you?"

"It's probably the connection."

"I thought they'd never get the phones fixed! I guess I just couldn't really relax until I'd talked to you and made sure you were safe! Of course, I know Jake would take care of you, but it's not the same as hearing your voice. I won't keep you, Sam, we'll see you tomorrow. By the way, I think Shylock misses you."

"Probably indigestion. Tell him I'll see him tomorrow." After replacing the receiver, she stared at it for a full minute.

"Samantha." She whirled again at Jake's voice, finding him watching her from the living room archway.

"I…ah…Bree seems fine." She avoided his eyes and toyed with the ink pot by the phone. She took a step backward as Jake advanced. "She said she thought Shylock misses me. That's quite an accomplishment, he's so self-sufficient and aloof."

"Samantha. Come, sit down." He held out his hand for hers. She knew if he touched her, she would be lost.

"No, no, I think I'll go to bed, I'm still not quite myself." Her color had ebbed again, leaving pale cheeks and darkened eyes.

"Still running, Sam?" The anger in his tone was well controlled.

"No, no, I…"

"All right, then, for the moment we seem to be at a stalemate." He captured her chin before she could avoid the gesture. "But we haven't finished by a long shot. Do you understand?"

She nodded, then broke away to flee to the sanctuary of her room.

Chapter 8

As each day passed, Sabrina became more cheerful. Her features took on a roundness that gave her a contented appearance. And as Samantha watched her, she wondered if Sabrina possessed more strength than she had ever given her credit for. It was a sobering experience to see her usually dreamy sister grabbing life with determination and purpose while she herself couldn't seem to stop day-dreaming. Jake Tanner, she had to admit, was disturbing her days and sneaking into her dreams.

Stuffing her hands in her pockets, she scowled and continued her morning trudge to the mailbox. He meant to have her, did he? Well, Samantha Evans had no intention of being had by anyone, especially some annoying cowboy with too much charm for his own good…and fascinating green eyes, and that beautiful mouth….

Now the days began to lengthen. The sun grew in strength. Spring began to drift over the basin greening the grass and teasing the crocuses to push their heads from the earth.

Scurrying down the hall as the doorbell interrupted her latest project—painting the nursery—Samantha wiped a few streaks of canary yellow on her jeans and opened the door.

The woman in the doorway smiled, her almond-shaped dark eyes making a thorough survey. "Hello, you must be Samantha. I'm Lesley Marshall."

The introduction was unnecessary, for with an instinct she had been unaware of possessing, Samantha had recognized the woman instantly. "Please, come in. It's still rather cold, isn't it?" She smiled, refusing to acknowledge the effort it cost her, and shut the nippy May air outside.

"I'm so glad to meet you at last." The dark eyes

swept down, then up Samantha briefly. "I've heard so much about you." There was light amusement in her voice.

"Oh, really? I'm afraid I can't say the same." Her smile was faintly apologetic. "But, of course, I've been rather busy."

"I would have been by sooner, but I wanted to wait until Sabrina was more up to company."

"Bree's feeling much better these days. I'm sure she'll be glad to see you. Let me take your coat." Samantha hung the soft fur in the hall closet. Turning back to her visitor, she needed all her willpower to keep the social smile in place. The oatmeal slacks accentuated Lesley's sleekness; the trim cerise blouse set off her delicately feathered ebony hair and the perfect ivory of her skin. Desperately, Samantha wished a miracle would transform her navy sweatshirt with its Wilson High School banner and her paint-streaked jeans into something smart and sophisticated. As usual, her hair was escaping from its pins. She resisted the urge to bring her hand up to it and jam them in tightly.

"Bree's in the living room," she announced, knowing the pale gray eyes had studied her and found her wanting. "I was just about to make some tea."

Sabrina appeared at that moment, and Samantha gladly relinquished the role of hostess and escaped to the kitchen.

"So, she's beautiful," she grumbled to an unconcerned Shylock as she set the kettle on to boil. "So, she's smooth and sophisticated and makes me feel like a pile of dirty laundry." Turning, she lowered her face to his and scowled. "Who cares?" Shylock scowled back and went to sleep. Her thoughts wandered on. "I don't imagine he's ever laughed at her and patted her head as though she were a slow-witted child," she muttered as she gathered up the tea tray.

"Sabrina, you look wonderful," Lesley commented sometime later, sipping from a dainty china cup. "I'm sure having your sister with you must be very good for you. I don't have to tell you how concerned everyone has been."

"No, and I appreciate it. Sam's made everything so easy. I didn't have anything to do but sit and heal." She shot her sister an affectionate glance. "I don't know what we would have done without her these past two months."

Lesley followed her gaze. "Jake was telling me that you're a gym teacher, Samantha," she purred, managing to make this sound faintly disgusting.

"Physical education instructor," Samantha corrected, slipping into a vague southern drawl.

"And you were in the Olympics, as well. I'm sure it must have been fascinating. You don't look the sturdy, athletic type." The shrug of her shoulders was elegant, as was the small gesture of her hand. "I suppose one can never tell." Samantha gritted her teeth against a biting retort and was vastly relieved when, glancing at a slender gold watch, Lesley suddenly rose from her chair. "I must run now, Sabrina, I have a dinner engagement." Turning to Samantha, she offered a small smile. "So happy to have met you. I'm sure we'll be seeing each other again soon."

She left amidst a swirl of fur and the drifting scent of roses. Samantha sat back in the cushioned chair, relaxing for the first time in more than an hour.

"Well, what did you think of Lesley?" Sabrina questioned, shifting into a more comfortable position on the sofa.

"Very sophisticated."

"Come on, Sam." Sabrina grinned, her hands folding across the mound of her belly. "This is Bree."

"I don't know why I should have to comment, since you seem to be reading me so well. But—" her mouth curved into a rueful smile "—I suppose she's a bit smooth for my taste, and I didn't much care for the way she looked down that aristocratic nose at me."

"Actually, you really don't appear very sturdy." The observation was made with wide-eyed innocence. Samantha grimaced, pulling pins from her hair with a sharp tug until a cascade of golden brown tumbled in confusion about her shoulders.

"She'd have gotten her own back on that one if you hadn't sent me that 'Don't make a scene' look."

"Oh, well, Lesley can be nice enough when it suits her. Her father spoils her dreadfully. Her mother died when she was barely into her teens, and he transferred all his attention to Lesley. An overabundance of clothes, the best horses, and, as she grew older, cars and European tours and so on. Whatever Lesley wants, Lesley gets."

"Poor thing." The sarcasm caused her to feel spiteful and unjust. She sighed. "I suppose too much is as bad as too little. It was nice of her to come and see how you were getting along."

Sabrina's laughter floated through the room. "Sam, darling, I've never known you to be so slow." At her sister's puzzled expression, she continued. "Lesley didn't come to see me, she came to get a look at you."

"At me?" Finely etched brows disappeared under a fringe of bangs. "What for? I wouldn't think a lowly gym teacher from Philadelphia would interest Lesley Marshall."

"Any teacher who caught Jake Tanner's attention the way you have would interest Lesley. He wouldn't have gone out of his way to show just anyone around the ranch, you know."

A light color rose in Samantha's cheeks. "I think Miss Marshall's mind was put to rest after she got a good look." Her hand moved expressively down her sweatshirt and jeans. "She'd hardly see any danger here."

"Don't underestimate yourself, Sam."

"No false modesty." Samantha's sigh came from nowhere. "If a man's attracted to silk and champagne, cotton and beer are no competition. I'm cotton and beer, Bree," she murmured. Her voice trailed away with her thoughts. "I couldn't be anything else if I wanted to."

The following day, Samantha's continuing battle with her paints and brushes was interrupted by a more welcome visitor. Annie Holloway arrived at the ranch's kitchen door with a beaming smile and a chocolate cake.

"Hi." Samantha opened the door wide in welcome. "It's nice to see you again, and bearing gifts, too."

"Never like to come empty-handed," Annie announced, handing the thickly frosted cake to Samantha. "Dan always had a partiality for chocolate cake."

"Me, too." She eyed the cake hungrily. "He's not here right now, and I was just going to make some coffee. Do you suppose we could start without him?"

"Good idea." Setting herself comfortably in a chair, Annie waved a wide-palmed hand. "I reckon it wouldn't hurt for us to have a slice or two."

"Bree's taking a nap," Samantha explained as she put down the mugs of steaming coffee. "The doctor says she still has to lie down every day, but she's beginning to grumble about it a bit. Very quietly, of course."

"You're keeping an eye on her." Annie nodded and added two generous spoons of sugar to her coffee. "Dan says she's up to company now."

"Oh, yes, people have been dropping by now and again. Ah…" Samantha added cream to her own cup. "Lesley Marshall was by yesterday."

"I wondered how long it would be before Lesley hauled herself over to get a look at you."

"You sound like Bree." Sipping her coffee, Samantha shook her head. "I don't know why Lesley Marshall would want to meet me."

"Easy. Lesley's a mite stingy with her possessions, and she'd like to group Jake among them. She hasn't figured out yet that Jake is his own man, and all her daddy's money can't buy him for her. When my Jake picks his woman, he'll decide the time and place. He's always been an independent rascal. He was barely twenty when he lost his folks, you know." Samantha lifted her eyes to the warm brown ones. "It wasn't an easy time for him, they'd been close. They were a pair, Jake's folks, always squabbling and loving. You're a bit like her when she was a young thing." Annie smiled, her head tilting with it as Samantha remained silent. "Nobody's going to ride roughshod over you, at least not for long. I saw that straight off. She was stubborn as a mule with two heads, and there's times, though it's been better than ten years, I still miss her."

"It must have been hard on Jake, losing his parents and having all the responsibility of the ranch when he was still so young," Samantha murmured.

"Seemed to change from boy to man overnight, just out of college and still green. 'Course," she continued, "he'd been in the saddle since childhood and what he hadn't learned about ranching from his father and that fancy college, he learned from doing. He picked up the reins of that ranch with both hands. There's not a man who works for him wouldn't wrestle a long-horned bull if he asked them to. He can fool you with that easygoing way of his, but nobody gets the better of Jake Tanner. He runs the ranch like his life, and Lesley's going to find him a hard steer to rope and brand."

"Maybe it's more the other way around," Samantha suggested. Annie's response was prevented by the appearance at the kitchen door of the man in question.

He entered with the easy familiarity of an old friend.

"Howdy, ma'am." He broke the silence with a cocky smile, removed his battered Stetson and glanced at her attire. "Been painting?"

"Obvious, isn't it?" Samantha said sharply.

"Nice colors." He helped himself to a cup of coffee. "Are you going to part with another piece of that cake?"

"Jake Tanner!" Annie exclaimed in disgust. "You should be ashamed, gobbling Dan's cake when you've got a perfectly good one of your own at home."

"Somebody else's always tastes better, Annie." He slipped off his jacket, tossing it over a hook, and grinned boyishly. "He won't miss it, anyway. I brought you and the cake over, didn't I? You're not going to begrudge me one little piece?"

"Don't waste those eyes on me, you young devil." Annie attempted to sniff and look indignant. "I'm not one of your fillies."

Jake's appearance had successfully shattered Samantha's peace of mind. After a reasonable period of politeness, she excused herself to Annie and Jake and went back to her job in the nursery.

Samantha's artistic talent was decidedly impressionistic. The floor, protected by plastic, was splotched and splattered, but the walls were coming to life with a joy of brilliant colors. Of the four walls, two were yellow and two were white, and each was trimmed with its opposite's color. On the one wall that was unbroken by door or windows, she had begun the construction of a wide, arching rainbow, carefully merging blues into pinks into greens.

Time passed, and in the quiet concentration of her work she forgot her preoccupation with Jake. Sitting on the ladder's top step, she paused, brushing the back of her hand across her cheek absently as she viewed the results.

"That's a mighty pretty sight."

She jolted, dropping the brush with a clatter, and would have fallen from the ladder had Jake's arms not gripped her waist and prevented the tumble.

"Sure spook easy," Jake commented, removing the dangerously sloshing paint bucket from her hand.

"You shouldn't come up behind a person like that," she complained. "I might have broken my neck." She wiped her hands on the legs of her jeans. "Where's Annie?"

"With your sister. She wanted to show Annie some things she's made for the baby." He set the bucket on the floor and straightened. "I didn't think they needed me."

"No, I'm sure they didn't. I need that paint, though, and the brush you made me drop." She glanced down, but his eyes remained on hers.

"I like the blue, especially that spot on your cheek," Jake said.

She rubbed at the offending area in annoyance. "If you'd just hand those things back to me, I could finish up."

"Green's nice, too," he said conversationally, and ran a finger over a long streak on her thigh. "Wilson High." His eyes lowered to the letters on her shirt. "Is that where you taught back east?"

"Yes." She shifted, uncomfortable that the name was prominent over her breasts. "Are you going to hand me my things?"

"What are your plans for tonight?" he countered easily, ignoring her request. She stared, completely thrown off balance by his unexpected question.

"I, ah, I have a lot of things to do." She searched her mind for something vital in her schedule.

"Things?" he prompted. His smile grew as his finger began to twist through a stray curl that had escaped its confines.

"Yes, things," she retorted, abandoning the attempt to elaborate. "I'm going to be very busy, and I really want to finish this room."

"I suppose I could let you get by with that, even though we both know better. Well." He smiled and shrugged. "Come down and kiss me goodbye, then. I've got to get back to work."

"I will not kiss you goodbye…." she began, the words trailing off as he gripped her waist. Her hands automatically went to his arms, and he plucked her from her perch.

He lowered her slowly, his eyes never leaving hers, and her mouth was roughly claimed before her feet could reach the floor. His hands slipped under her shirt to roam the smooth skin of her back, pressing her closer as her body betrayed her and dissolved against his. Slowly he explored her soft, firm breasts, subtly rounded hips, lean thighs.

Every time, every time, her mind murmured. Every time he kisses me, I go under deeper, and one day I'll never find my way back. His teeth moved to nip at her ear and neck, searching and finding new vulnerabilities before returning to ravage her mouth again. Without will, without choice, she rested in his arms, surrendering to forces she could never defeat.

He drew her away, breaking the intimacy, but his mouth returned to hers to linger briefly before he spoke. "About tonight, Samantha."

"What?" she murmured as his tongue traced the softness of her lips.

"I want to see you tonight."

Jerking herself back into reality, she pressed her hands against his chest, but did not manage to break away. "No, no, I'm busy. I told you."

"So you did," he acknowledged, and his eyes narrowed in speculation.

His words were cut off by the sound of Sabrina's laughter drifting down the hall. Samantha wiggled against Jake's hold. "Let me go, will you?"

"Why?" He was grinning now, enjoying the flood of color in her cheeks.

"Because…"

"Don't ever play poker, Sam." The warning was curt. "You'd lose your shirt."

"I…I…"

"Sabrina's due in September, right?"

The sudden question caused her to blink in confusion. "Well, yes, she…"

"That gives you a little breathing space, Samantha." He leaned down, and his kiss was hard and brief and to the point. "After that, don't expect to get away so lightly."

"I don't know what…"

"You know exactly what I mean," he said interrupting. "I told you I meant to have you, and I always get what I want."

Her eyes flashed. "If you think I'm going to let you make love to me just because you say so, then you…"

The suggestion she would have made died as his mouth took hers again. She went rigid telling herself she would not amuse him with a response this time. As she told herself she would not, her arms circled his neck. Her body became pliant, her lips parted with the hunger she had lived with all through the past month. As he took, she offered more; as he demanded, she gave. Her own mouth was mobile, her own hands seeking, until it seemed the month of fasting had never been.

"I want you, I don't have to tell you that, do I?"

She shook her head, trying to steady her breathing as his eyes alone caused her pulse to triple its rate.

"We'll settle this in September, unless you decide to come to me sooner." She began to shake her head again, but the fingers on the back of her neck halted the movement. "If you don't come to me, I'll wait until after the baby's born and you've got that much off your mind. I'm a patient man, Sam, but…" He stopped talking as Annie and Sabrina stepped into the room.

"Well." Annie shook her head at the two of them. "I can see he's been giving you a hard time." She turned to Sabrina with a half-exasperated shrug. "He's always been fresh as a new-laid egg. This is going to be a beautiful room, Sam." She glanced around at Samantha's handi-work, nodding in approval. "Let go of the little lady now, Jake, and take me back home, I've got dinner to fix."

"Sure. I've already said what I came to say." He released Samantha with a last, penetrating look and strode from the room, calling a goodbye over his shoul-der.

"Fresh as a new-laid egg," Annie reiterated, and echoing his goodbye, followed him.

When the guests had departed, Samantha began to gather up paint buckets and brushes.

"Sam." Walking over, Sabrina placed a hand on her sister's arm. "I had no idea."

"No idea about what?" Bending, she banged the lid securely on rose pink.

"That you were in love with Jake." The truth she had avoided for so long was out in the open now: She had fallen hopelessly, irrevocably in love with Jake Tanner! Standing, Samantha searched in vain for words of denial.

"We know each other too well, Sam," Sabrina said before she could answer. "How bad is it?"

Samantha lifted her hands and let them fall to her sides. "Terminal."

"Well, what are you going to do about it?"

"Do about it?" Samantha repeated. "What can I do about it? After the baby comes, I'll go back east and try to forget about him."

"I've never known you to give up without a fight," Sabrina spoke sharply. At the unexpected tone, Samantha's brows rose.

"I'd fight for something that belonged to me, Bree, but I don't move in on someone else's territory."

"Jake's not engaged to Lesley Marshall. Nothing's official."

"I'm not interested in semantics." Samantha began to fiddle with the paint cans. "Jake wants an affair with me, but he'll marry Lesley Marshall."

"Are you afraid to compete with Lesley?" Bree asked.

Samantha whirled around, eyes flashing. "I'm not afraid of anyone," she stormed. Sabrina's lips curved in a smug smile. "Don't try your psychology on me, Sabrina! Lesley Marshall and I don't belong in the same league, but I'm not afraid of her. I *am* afraid of getting hurt, though." Her voice wavered and Sabrina's arm slipped over her shoulder.

"All right, Sam, we won't talk about it any more right now. Leave those brushes, I'll wash them out. Go take a ride. You know the only way to clear your head is to go off by yourself."

"I'm beginning to think you know me too well." With a wry smile, Samantha wiped her hands on her jeans.

"I know you, all right, Samantha." Sabrina patted her cheek and urged her from the room. "I just haven't always known what to do about you."

Chapter 9

During the months since their first meeting, Samantha had grown to know Jake Tanner, and to realize that when he wanted something, he made certain he got it. And she knew he wanted her.

If, when she rode out on horseback, she kept closer to the ranch than had been her habit, she told herself it was not fear of encountering Jake that prompted the action, but simply her desire to spend more of her free time with Sabrina. Now Sabrina was growing cumbersome in her pregnancy, there was a grain of truth to this, so Samantha found it easy to accept the half-truth.

Every day she fell more under the spell of Wyoming. Bare branches were now fully cloaked in green. The cattle grew sleek and fat. The land was fully awakened and rich.

"I think you may just have twins in there, Bree," Samantha commented as the two sisters took advantage of golden sun and fragrant warmth. Sabrina glanced down to where Samantha sat cross-legged on the wide front porch. "Dr. Gates thinks not." She patted the mound in question. "He says there's only one, and I'm just getting fat. One of us should have twins, though."

"I'm afraid that's going to be up to you, Bree. I think I'll revive the tradition of old-maid school teachers."

Sabrina was sensitive to the wistfulness in the words. "Oh, no, you'll have to get married, Sam. You can't let all those lessons go to waste."

This brought the light laugh it had intended. "I'm perfectly serious. Remember what Madame Dubois always said: 'Von must reach for ze stars.'"

"Oh, yes, Madame Dubois." Samantha smiled at the memory of their former ballet teacher. "You know, of course, that accent was a phony. She came from New Jersey."

"I'm suitably crushed. She did think she had a genuine protégé in you."

"Yes, I was magnificent." Samantha sighed with exaggerated pride.

"Let's see a few of your famous leaps now, Sam."

"Not on your life!"

"Come on, cutoffs are as good as a tutu any day. I'd join you in a pas de deux, but it would actually be a pas de trois."

Samantha rose reluctantly from her seat on the porch. "All right, I don't mind showing off a little."

With quiet dignity, Sabrina began to hum a movement from *Swan Lake,* and Samantha lowered into a purposefully dramatic body sweep before exploding with an energetic series of grand jetés, stage leaps and cabrioles. She concluded the performance with a group of pirouettes, ended by dropping in a dizzy heap on the grass.

"That's what you get," she said, closing her eyes and shaking her head at the giddiness, "when you forget to spot focus."

"Is this show open to the public?"

Samantha glanced sharply toward the sound of the all-too-familiar voice.

"Dan!" Sabrina exclaimed. "I didn't expect you back so early."

"Ran into Lesley and Jake out on the north boundary,"

he explained, striding over and planting a firm kiss. "I thought you and Sam might like some company."

"Hello, Lesley, Jake." Sabrina included them both in her smile. "Have a seat, I'll bring out something cool."

Samantha had been sitting, praying without result for the ground to open up and swallow her. "I'll do it, Bree." She jumped at the opportunity to escape. "Don't get up."

"I'm up," Sabrina pointed out, disappearing inside before Samantha could argue.

"Do you teach ballet, as well, Samantha?" Lesley asked. She surveyed Samantha's outfit of semiragged cutoffs and T-shirt with dark, mocking eyes.

"No, no," Samantha muttered, feeling once more desperately at a disadvantage next to the slim woman in elegantly tailored breeches and silk shirt.

"I thought it was real nice," Dan commented, innocently turning the knife.

"Samantha's just full of surprises," Jake said.

Now that he had spoken again, Samantha was forced to give Jake a portion of her attention. He looked devastatingly male, the denim shirt rolled past his elbows to expose bronzed, corded arms, the low-slung belt in his jeans accentuating his leanness. She concentrated on a spot ap-

proximately six inches to the left of his face, in order to
avoid the smile that had already mastered his face.

"Yeah," she returned. "I'm just a bushel of surprises."

"Anything you can't do, Sam?"

"A few things." She attempted a cool sophistication.

"You're so energetic," Lesley commented, slipping
her hand through Jake's arm. "You must be horribly
strong and full of bulging muscles."

For one heady moment, Samantha considered flight.
She was opening her mouth to make her excuses when
Dan effectively cut off all hope.

"Sit down, Sam, I want to talk over a little idea with
you and Sabrina." Sinking down on the porch steps,
Samantha avoided any glimpse of Jake's face. "Do you
think Sabrina's up to a little party?" Samantha looked
up at Dan's question and attempted to marshal her
thoughts.

"A party?" she repeated, drawing her brows together
in concentration. "I suppose so. Dr. Gates says she's
doing very well, but you could always ask to be sure.
Did you want to go to a party?"

"I was thinking of having one," he corrected with a
grin. "There're these twins I know who have this
birthday in a couple of weeks." Bending over, he tugged

at Samantha's loosened locks. "Seems like a good excuse for having a party."

"Oh, our birthday." Samantha's response was vague. The impending anniversary had slipped her mind.

"Did I hear someone say party?" Sabrina emerged through the screen door with a tray of iced tea.

Samantha sipped the cool, sweet tea her sister handed her and watched Sabrina's face light up with anticipation.

"A birthday party, Sam." She turned to her sister, eyes shining with excitement. "When's the last time we had one?"

"When we were twelve and Billy Darcy got sick all over Mom's new carpet." Leaning back against the porch rail, Samantha unwittingly lifted her face to Jake's.

"Well, then, it's high time for another," Dan said. "What do you say, Sam? I know it means extra work for you."

"Huh." Tearing her eyes from Jake's smile, she endeavored to pick up the threads of the conversation. "What? Oh, no, it's no trouble. It'll be fun." Concentrating on Dan's face, she blocked out the sight of Lesley lounging intimately against Jake. "How many people did you have in mind?"

"Just neighbors and friends." He reached up to rub

his chin. "About thirty or forty, I'd say. What do you think, Lesley?"

The full mouth pouted a moment in thought. "If you want to keep it small, Dan," she agreed after a short deliberation. Samantha's eyes grew wide. These people definitely had a different idea of small than she did.

"Oh, Lesley, come take a look at this punch bowl I've got, see if you think we should use it." Rising, Sabrina took Dan's hand. "Come, get it down for me, Dan." Throwing her sister an innocent smile, Sabrina disappeared inside and left her alone with Jake.

"How's the painting coming?" Jake stretched both arms over the back of the swing.

"Painting? Oh, the nursery. It's finished."

That, she recalled with a frown, was just one of many times he had come upon her in a ridiculous situation. Sleeping on stumps, covered with paint, and now leaping across the lawn like some crazed ballerina. Samantha, she told herself, you have class.

"What do you want for your birthday, Sam?" He prodded her with the toes of his boot and earned a scowl.

Blowing a wisp of hair from her eyes, she moved her shoulders. "Fur, diamonds."

"No, you're not the type for furs." Taking out a cigar,

he lit it and blew a lazy stream of smoke. "You'd be thinking about all the little minks that were scalped to make it. And diamonds wouldn't suit you."

"I suppose I'm more the quartz type." She rose, irritated.

"No, I was thinking more of sapphires." He caught her wrist. "To go with your eyes, or maybe rubies to go with your temper."

"I'll be sure to put both on my list. Now, if you'll excuse me." She glanced at her captured hand, then back at him. "I've got to go feed my cat." She gestured to where Shylock lay on the far side of the porch.

"He doesn't look very hungry."

"He's pretending to be dead," she muttered. "Shylock, let's eat."

Amber eyes opened and blinked. Then, to her pleasure, Shylock rose and padded toward her. However, upon reaching his mistress, he gave her a disinterested stare, leaped into Jake's lap and began to purr with wicked enjoyment.

"No, ma'am." Jake glanced down at the contented cat. "He doesn't look hungry at all."

With a final glare, Samantha turned, stalked to the door and slammed the screen smartly behind her.

* * *

The sun shone warm and friendly on the morning of the twins' birthday. Samantha carried a large parcel into the kitchen. Dumping her burden on the table where her sister was enjoying a cup of tea, she nudged Shylock away with her foot. She had not yet decided to forgive him for his treacherous advances to Jake.

"This just came, it's from the folks."

"Open it, Sam." Sabrina poked an experimental finger at the package. "Dan refuses to give me my present yet, and I've searched everywhere I can think of."

"I bet it's six books on child rearing for you, and six on etiquette for me."

"A present's a present," Sabrina stated, and tore the mailing paper from the box.

"Here's a note." After breaking the seal, Samantha produced a sheet of paper and read aloud.

"To Samantha and Sabrina:

A very happy birthday and our love to you both. Sabrina, I do hope you are taking good care of yourself. As you know, proper diet and rest are essential. I'm sure having Samantha with you during the last weeks of your confinement is a great comfort. Samantha, do look after your sister and see that she takes the necessary precautions. However, I hope you're not overlooking your own social life. As your mother, it is my duty to remind you that you are long past the marriageable age. Your father and I are looking forward to seeing you and our first grandchild in a few weeks. We will be in Wyoming the first part of September, if Dad's schedule holds true.

With love,
Mom and Dad

"There's a postscript for you, Bree.

"Sabrina, doesn't Daniel know any suitable men for your sister?"

With a sigh, Samantha folded the letter and dropped it on the table. "She never changes." Dipping into the box, Samantha plucked out a smaller one with Sabrina's name on it and handed it to her. "Marriageable age," she muttered, and shook her head.

"Did you peek in here before?" Sabrina accused, dumping out volumes on infant and child care.

"No," Samantha denied with a superior smirk. "I just know Mom." Drawing out her own package, she ripped off the concealing paper. "Good grief." She let the box drop to the table and held up a brief black lace negligee.

"I thought I knew Mom." Both sisters burst into laughter. "She must be getting desperate," Samantha concluded, holding the negligee in front of her.

"Now that's a pretty thing," Jake observed as he and Dan entered the kitchen. "But it's even prettier with something in it." Samantha bundled the garment behind her and flushed scarlet.

"Presents from Mom and Dad," Sabrina explained, indicating her stack of books.

"Very suitable." Dan grinned as he glanced through the volumes.

"Doesn't look like Sam feels the same about hers." Jake smiled. Samantha felt her already alarming color deepen. "Let's see it again."

"Don't tease, Jake." Sabrina turned to her husband. "Mom says they'll be here the first part of September."

"I'll put this stuff away." Samantha tossed the gown into the box and began to bury it under books.

"Leave that till later." Dan took her hand and pulled her away. "I need you outside for a minute."

She went willingly. Escape was escape. Imagining it had something to do with Sabrina's gift, she was surprised when Dan slowed his pace and allowed his wife to join them in their walk toward the ranch buildings. He kept her involved in a running conversation about the party until they came to a halt at the paddock fence.

"Happy birthday, Sam." Sabrina kissed her sister's cheek as Samantha's eyes focused on the golden Arabian mare.

"Oh." She could manage no more.

"She's from a good line," Dan informed her, his arm slipping around Sabrina's shoulders. "She's out of the Double T stock, no finer in Wyoming."

"But I…" Words faltered, and she swallowed and tried to begin again.

"What do you give someone who packs their own life away for six months without hesitation, without asking for anything in return?" Dan's free arm slipped around Samantha and pulled her to his side.

"We figured if you insisted on going back east, we'd always have a hold on you. You'd have to come visit us to ride your mare."

"I don't know how to thank you."

"Then don't," Dan ordered. "Go try her out."

"Now?"

"Now's as good a time as any." Not needing a second urging, Samantha was over the fence, stroking the mare and murmuring.

"We may convince her to stay yet," Dan commented, watching as she slipped into the saddle and took the mare around the paddock. "I could have a word with Jake."

Sabrina shook her head. "No, Sam would be furious if we interfered. She'd bolt back to Philadelphia before we could take a breath. For now, we'd better keep out of it." She lowered her voice as a beaming Samantha trotted around to them and slipped off the little mare.

"She's a real beauty," she sighed. "I don't know how I can ever bear to leave her…"

Sabrina's eyes met her husband's in silent satisfaction. *Perhaps it will not be necessary,* their unspoken message said.

"Come, little sister," Dan said. "If you can tear yourself away from your new friend, I sure could use a cup of coffee now."

As the trio trooped back toward the house, Jake swung through the back door. "Delivery just came. It's in the living room."

"Oh," Dan murmured, looking entirely too innocent. "Come on, Sabrina, we'd best see what it is."

"Is it the piano?" Sam asked Jake, and Dan and Sabrina disappeared inside.

"Looked like one to me. I guess that's another present that'll go over big. Walk to the truck with me," Jake commanded, and captured her hand before she could protest.

"Really, Jake, I have a million things to do." She trotted to keep pace with his loose, lanky stride.

"I know, you're indispensable." Stopping by his truck, he reached in the cab and produced a package. "But this seems to be the time for gift giving. I thought I'd let you have your present now."

"You didn't have to get me anything."

"Samantha." His drawl was lazy, but his eyes narrowed in annoyance. "I never do anything unless I want to." Taking her hand from behind her back, he placed the box in it. "Open it."

Lifting the statue from its tissue bedding, she examined it in silent amazement. The alabaster was smooth and cool in her hands, carved into the shape of a horse and rider in full gallop. The artist had captured the fluid grace, the freedom of motion. She ran a hesitant finger over the delicate features.

"It looks like me." She lifted her eyes to Jake's.

"And so it should," he answered easily. "It's supposed to be you."

"But how?" She shook her head, torn between pleasure and confusion.

"A man I know does this kind of thing. I described you to him."

For the second time that day, Samantha found herself at a loss for words.

"Why?" The question was out before she could swallow it.

Slowly, a smile drifted across his face. He pushed back his hat. "Because it suits you better than furs and diamonds."

She braced herself to meet his eyes again. "Thank you."

He nodded, his face solemn. He took the box from her hands and placed it on the hood of the truck. "I think a birthday kiss is traditional."

Swallowing, she took an instinctive step in retreat, but he gripped her arms and held her still. She offered her cheek, and his laughter broke out, full and rich on the summer air. "Sam," he turned her face to his, and his eyes sparkled with humor, "you're incredible."

His lips met hers. His hand moved from her arms to her hips, drawing her firmly against the hard lines of his body. She submitted to the embrace, as long as his arms held her, as long as they were mouth to mouth, as long as the heat from his body infused hers, he owned her, and she could not run.

Finally he drew her away, bringing his hands to her shoulders while hers rested on his chest for support.

"Happy birthday, Sam."

"Thank you," she managed, still breathless from the impact of his embrace.

He lifted the box from the hood of the truck and placed it in her hands before sliding into the cab. "See you tonight." With a salute, he started the engine. The truck moved down the road, leaving her staring after it.

Chapter 10

Party sounds filled the house. Laughter and voices and music mingled and drifted through open windows to float on the night air.

On this evening, the twins were dramatically different in their appearance. Sabrina's pale blue gown floated around her, cunningly disguising her pregnancy. Her hair was a glinting halo around rose-tinted cheeks. Samantha's black-striped satin clung to her body, her halter neckline plunging deep to a wide, gathered waist. Her hair was free and thick around her shoulders.

As she moved and mingled with the crowd, Samantha

searched for a tall, lanky form, noting with increasing despair and a gnawing jealousy that a slim, dark woman had also as yet failed to put in an appearance.

Cornered by an enthusiastic young cowboy, Samantha was feeling her attention begin to wander from a detailed account of horse breeding when her eyes met dark jade across the room.

He was standing with two men she did not recognize, and Lesley Marshall stood beside him. She was elegant in an oyster-white gown. Her fine-boned ivory hand was placed from time to time on Jake's arm, as if, Samantha thought grimly, she were flaunting her possession.

Furious with the sudden feeling of inadequacy, Samantha turned to her companion with a dazzling smile. He stammered over his lecture, his words grinding to a halt. She tucked her arm in his and used her eyes without shame.

"Howdy, Tim." Jake appeared from nowhere and placed a hand on the young man's shoulder. "I'm going to steal this little lady for a moment." He paused and smiled easily into Samantha's mutinous face. "There's a couple of people she hasn't met yet."

Without waiting for an assent, he had her unwilling hand in his, propelling her through the crowd. "Tim won't be the same for weeks," he whispered close to her ear. "A woman could get run out of town for using her eyes that way on susceptible young boys," he warned, pulling her through the sea of people.

"You don't have to drag me."

"I know a stubborn mule when I see one," he countered, without bothering to lower his voice. Her furious retort was swallowed as Jake presented her to the two men who flanked Lesley.

"Sam, I'd like you to meet George Marshall, Lesley's father." Samantha's hand was enveloped in a hearty grip. "And Jim Bailey," he continued, nodding toward the second man.

"Jim only works with cattle on paper. He's a lawyer."

"My, this is a mighty pretty girl!" George Marshall boomed. Giving Jake a sly wink, he patted his daughter's shoulder.

"You always manage to rope in the pick of the herd, don't you, Jake?"

Jake slipped his hands easily into his pockets. "I do my best. But then, roping them's one thing, getting them's another."

"Well, now, little lady," George's genial voice continued, "Les tells me you're a gym teacher."

"That's right, Mr. Marshall."

"Now, you just call me George," he instructed, squeezing her shoulder with a genial affection. "Tell me, why isn't a pretty little thing like you married and settled down instead of running around some gymnasium?"

Jake was grinning with obvious enjoyment. Samantha tossed her hair behind her back, but before she could think of a suitable answer, George's laughter boomed through the room.

"I like this girl," George announced to the group. "Looks like she has spirit. You come over to our ranch any time, little lady, any time at all."

In spite of herself, Samantha found herself liking his expansive hospitality. "If you'll excuse me now, I've got…got to get a tray out of the kitchen." She gave the group an all-encompassing smile and melted into the crowd.

In the kitchen, she pulled a tray from the refrigerator to give her excuse credibility and was glad she had when Jake followed her in a moment later.

"George is a good man. He has the right ideas when it comes to women." Smiling knowingly at her, he leaned against the door watching her every move.

"That's your opinion," she returned tartly, bustling around the kitchen in an attempt to ignore him.

"Sit down a minute, Sam."

She glanced up, immediately wary, then lifted the tray as a defense. "No, I've got to get back."

"Please."

Despite herself, she lowered the tray to the table and herself into a chair.

"I ran into Jack Abbot, the school principal, the other day."

"Oh?"

"He told me the girls' phys ed. instructor isn't coming back next term." Leaning back in his chair, Jake studied her. "He's going to offer you the job."

"Oh," she repeated before she could stop herself.

"He wants you pretty bad. He really needs someone this fall. I told him I'd be seeing you, and that I'd mention it. He's going to call you officially, of course."

How simple, Samantha thought.

How simple it would all be if I didn't love this man. I could stay where I want to stay, work where I want to work. But now, I've got to refuse, I've got to go away.

"I appreciate your telling me, and I appreciate Mr. Abbot wanting me, but…"

"Don't appreciate it, Samantha, think about it."

"You don't know what you're asking me to do."

He rose to pace the room, his hands seeking the depths of his pockets. "I'm just asking you to think about it. You like it here. You've made friends. You like being near your sister. You'd still have the satisfaction of doing what you feel you're suited for. Is it so much to ask that you consider it?"

"Yes, it's quite a lot. Jake, I don't want to argue with you. There are things I have to do, the same way there are things you have to do."

"All right." He nodded, then repeated slowly, as if coming to a decision. "All right, there *are* things I have to do." Moving over, he captured her chin between his thumb and fingers.

His arms slipped around her waist to bring her close, his mouth lowering to brush her cheeks and the corners of her lips. "Come home with me now, Samantha. We can be alone there." His voice had become low and seductive, as his fingers trailed over the bare skin of her back.

"No, please don't." She turned her face away.

"I want to make love to you. I want to feel your skin under my hands, all of you. I want to hear you sigh when I touch you."

"Jake, please." She dropped her head to his chest. "It's unfair, here, like this."

"Then come home with me."

"No, I can't." She shook her head without raising it. "I won't."

"All right, Samantha." He framed her face and brought it up to his. "I said I'd give you until the baby was born. We'll stick to that. We won't argue tonight. Let's call it a truce for your birthday. Agreed?"

He kissed her once, briefly, and turned to lift the tray. "Then we'll both do what we have to do when the time comes."

Leaving her confused, Jake moved through the doorway.

Rejoining the festivities, Samantha moved from group to group, but her thoughts were only about Jake. Why was he so interested in her career choices? Why did he want her to take the job in Wyoming? *Maybe he cared for her.* For a brief moment, she allowed hope to shimmer. Her eyes swept the room to find him. Finally she spotted him. He was dancing with Lesley. The shining cap of her raven hair brushing his cheek, the ivory of her hand entwined with the bronze of his. Samantha winced as he threw back his head and laughed at something Lesley had said for his ears alone.

Care for me? her mind repeated in a scathing whisper. Grow up, Samantha, *caring* and *wanting* don't always mean the same thing. In a few weeks, she comforted herself, she would no longer be subjected to this constant pain. When the ache had eased, she could visit Bree again. Jake would probably be too busy with his wife to spare time for visits to the Lazy L. Samantha felt her heart contract with pain.

She turned away and bumped solidly into Jim Bailey.

"Sorry." He took her shoulders to steady her. "I didn't see you."

"It's all right," she returned, offering a smile. "Besides, I think I ran into you."

"Well, no harm done either way." She watched his eyes slide past her and focus on Jake and Lesley. "They look nice together, don't they?"

Embarrassed that he must have seen her staring at them, Samantha nodded, and looked down at her empty glass. "Come on, we better get you a refill."

A few moments later, they joined the group around the piano as Sabrina played.

"So, you're a lawyer." She smiled at Jim. "I don't think I've ever met a lawyer before."

Jim returned her smile. "And you're a gymnast."

"No, actually, I'm a gym teacher now."

He lifted his glass in a toast and drank. "I remember you. I've always been an avid fan of the Olympics. I thought you were fabulous."

"Well, that's nice to hear after a decade."

He tapped his glass to hers. "Well, Olympic star, would you like to dance?"

"I'd love to."

Samantha enjoyed Jim Bailey's easy conversation. She learned during their two dances that he was interested in getting into politics. His dark good looks and ready wit would certainly be assets, she decided.

"Sam." Sabrina motioned to her as they moved back toward the piano. "It's your turn. Union rules."

"Okay," Samantha agreed, sliding onto the bench.

She played with practiced ease, moving from one song to the next. Time slipped through her fingers. As in a dream, she was aware of the voices behind her, the faint, drifting breeze of Wyoming through the opened windows.

Someone sat beside her. Recognizing the lean fingers that lifted to turn the page of her sheet music, she faltered and missed a note.

"You and Jim seem to have hit it off." Samantha heard the click of his lighter over the sounds of the party.

"He's a very nice man. Have you known him long?"

"Oh, only since we were about eight and I gave him a black eye and he loosened a few of my teeth."

"Sounds like a loving friendship."

Jake again turned the page before she could do so herself. "Well, after that we sort of stuck together." He pushed the curtain of hair behind her shoulder, and Samantha struggled not to break the thread of the melody. "The two of you seemed to have a lot to talk about."

"He's very charming, and we have a few mutual interests."

"Hmm." Jake shifted slightly in his seat. His thigh brushed hers, and her fingers responded by hitting three wrong notes.

"You play very well."

Was he being ironic? She turned to look at him, but found no mockery in his jade eyes.

"Pleasantly," she corrected. "I get the general melody, but the details are a bit fuzzy."

"I've noticed that you have a tendency to shrug off your own capabilities. Are you aware of that?"

"That's not true. I just know what I do well and what I don't."

"You're a very tough critic, and you're inclined to underestimate."

"Honesty," she countered, finishing the song with a flourish. "I am a totally honest person."

"Are you, Samantha?" he said softly. "That's what I plan to find out."

Chapter 11

The days grew hot and sultry. The skies were improbably blue, rarely softened by clouds.

Long hours in the sun had deepened the honey of Samantha's skin, teasing out the gold in her hair. As long as she was occupied, she had no time for soul searching. She could enjoy the long summer days without thinking of the fall. As Sabrina wilted like a thirsty rose in the searing heat, Samantha confined her own activities to the early-morning hours. In the long, hot haze of the afternoon, Sabrina moved slowly through the house, her body clumsy. Samantha did not dare leave her. The baby was due in two weeks, and Samantha wanted to remain within calling distance of her sister as much as possible.

One particularly humid afternoon, the two women were sitting idly in the living room. Sabrina got up heavily from her chair to look out the window. "Sam," she said, "before Dan left for town, he said a storm was brewing. From the looks of the sky, I'd say he was right."

Before Samantha could answer, there was a sudden flash of lightning. A blast of thunder rolled in on the wind, and the rain began to fall in sheets.

"It's coming down fast," Samantha agreed. "It should cool us off a bit." She looked sympathetically at her sister's bulky form.

The storm built in power. Jagged flashes of lightning illuminated the room and an angry wind hurled the rain against the windows. The two women watched in fascination as the storm exhausted itself. Soon rain dripped tentatively from the eaves and the thunder was a mere grumble in the distance.

The sun struggled to reappear, breaking through the gloom with a hazy promise of light.

"That," Sabrina commented with an enormous sigh, "was a mean one."

Samantha turned from her place by the window and again slumped into a chair. "Remember when you used to hide in the closet whenever we had a thunderstorm?"

"All too well." She gave her sister a pained smile. "And you used to stand on the porch, loving every minute of it, until Mom dragged you in, soaking wet. On that note from the past," Sabrina announced, and struggled to her feet, "I'm going to take a nap, Sam." She turned at the doorway and studied the woman slouched in the chair, bare legs and feet stretched out in unconscious grace. "I love you."

With a rather puzzled smile, Samantha watched her walk away.

Wandering out to the porch, Samantha drank in the rain-fresh air. Everything sparkled. Raindrops clung like jewels to blossoms and leaves. Though the flowers had drooped with the weight of the storm, their colors had been washed into brilliant life. A bird, flying by on a shaft of light, trilled above her. She could hear the steady dripping of the rain off the eaves above the whisper of the dying wind. Satisfied, she curled up on a porch rocker and instantly fell asleep.

She had no idea how long she had drifted in the soft twilight world when, with reluctance, she woke at the touch of a hand on her shoulder. She looked up drowsily and yawned. "Oh, Bree, I must have fallen asleep. It's so wonderfully cool out here."

"Sam, I think the baby's decided to put in an unscheduled appearance."

"Huh? Oh!" Springing to her feet, she was instantly awake. "Right now? Dan's not here, and it's not time yet. Sit down, sit," she ordered, running agitated fingers through her hair.

"I think the first thing to do is to calm down," Sabrina suggested.

"You're right. I'm not going to fall apart, it was just a shock. I wasn't expecting this for another week or two."

"Neither was I." Sabrina's smile was half amused, half apologetic.

"All right, how long have you been having contractions, and how far apart are they?"

"Only for an hour or so."

"That should give us plenty of time." Samantha patted Sabrina's hand.

"But they've been getting awfully strong, and…" Breaking off, she closed her eyes and began to breathe in a deep, methodical rhythm. "And," she continued, after a final long breath, "awfully close together."

"How close?" Samantha asked, feeling new tension at the base of her neck.

"Ten minutes."

"Ten minutes," Samantha repeated. "I'd better get you to the hospital. I'll bring the car around. Stay put," she told her sister, and raced to the garage.

Upon reaching Sabrina's compact and sliding behind the wheel, Samantha was horrified to find the engine unresponsive to the turn of the key. The little car sputtered, emitted an apologetic groan and died.

"You can't," she insisted, and smacked the steering wheel. "We just had you fixed."

There was no use wasting more time trying to figure out what was wrong with the car. It was clearly not going to start, and Samantha hadn't the first idea of where to look for the problem.

Rushing back to the house, she picked up the phone in the kitchen. At least she could call Dr. Gates. A groan of despair was wrenched from her when she heard the dead silence on the line. Oh, no, the storm must have knocked out the phones!

Forcing herself to appear calm, she returned to the living room where Sabrina was waiting for her.

Reaching her sister again, Samantha knelt down so

their eyes were level. "Bree, the car won't start. All the trucks and jeeps are out with the men, and the storm must have knocked down the phone lines."

"Looks like we've got a few problems." Sabrina took a deep breath.

"It's going to be all right." Samantha took her hand in reassurance. "I'll help you get into bed, and then I'll take a horse and ride toward the Double T. If I don't see any of the men on the way, I'll get a truck there and bring it back. Most of them have radios, and I can call ahead to the doctor."

"Sam, it's going to take time for you to get there, and to get back. I don't think I'll make it in time to get to the hospital after that. You'll have to have the doctor come here."

"Here?" Samantha repeated. Her throat closed on the word. Sabrina nodded. "All right. Don't worry, I won't be long. I'll be back as soon as I can." Samantha raced off to the stables, and without wasting the time for a saddle, she leaped on her mare's back.

The familiar landscape was a blur, as she urged more speed out of the powerful horse. The sound of her own breath was masked by the sound of thudding hooves. Every minute she took was a minute longer that Sabrina was alone. She crouched lower on the horse and dug in bare heels.

When Samantha spotted the men on horseback, she spurred the Arabian over the fence in a fluid leap. As her hooves touched earth, she met the horse's sides again. They streaked across the field, scattering annoyed cattle.

When she reached the group, she reined in sharply. The mare reared, nearly unseating her. Her breath came in gasps as she struggled to keep her seat.

"What are you trying to do, break your neck?" Furiously Jake snatched the reins from her hands. "If you're stupid enough not to care about yourself, think of your horse. What do you mean riding like a fool and jumping fences? Where's your saddle? Have you lost your mind?"

"Bree," she managed at last between giant gulps of air. "The baby's coming, and the phone's out. The car wouldn't start, and there's nobody around. Dan's in town. Bree says there's no time to get her into the hospital now, and I have to call the doctor." She felt tears of fear burning at her eyes and bit her lip.

"All right, take it easy." Twisting in the saddle, Jake called out to one of his men. "Get back to the ranch and get hold of Dr. Gates on the CB radio. Tell him

Sabrina Lomax is in labor and to get to the Lazy L in a hurry." Turning back, he handed the reins to Samantha. "Let's go."

"Are you coming back with me?" Flooded with relief, she gripped tight on the leather.

"What do you think?"

Together, they sprang forward in a gallop.

Speed and thundering hooves were all Samantha ever remembered of the ride back. There was no time for conversation, no time for thought. She was sliding to the ground before she came to a full stop and Jake once more secured her reins.

"Keep your head, Samantha," he ordered, watching her bound up the steps and through the front door.

The house was silent. Her stomach tightened as she rushed to the master bedroom. Sabrina sat up in bed, propped by a mound of pillows and greeted her with a cheerful smile.

"That was quick, did you fly?"

"Just about," Samantha returned, faint with relief.

"We've sent for the doctor. Everything's under control." She sat down on the bed, taking her sister's hand. "How are you doing?"

"Not too bad." Her hand closed over Samantha's, as

much to reassure as seeking reassurance. "I'm glad you're back. Here comes another one."

Samantha looked on with unfamiliar helplessness. Her fingers grew tighter over her twin's, as if to steal some of her pain.

"We can thank Mom for that book on natural childbirth." Sabrina gave a long, shaky sigh and relaxed against the pillows.

"Don't look so worried, I'm doing fine. Oh, hello, Jake." Glancing at the doorway, Sabrina greeted him with friendly cheerfulness. "I didn't know you were here. Come in. It's not contagious."

He advanced into the room, looking tall, male and out of place. His hands retreated to his pockets. "How're you doing?"

"Oh, well, you've seen a cow in labor before, I don't imagine there's much difference." The small hand tightened on Samantha's. "Here we go again."

Samantha lifted the hand to her cheek. *Where was the doctor?* Sabrina should be in the hospital, surrounded by experts.

"This baby's in a big hurry," Sabrina announced with a small moan. "I'm sorry, Sam, it's not going to wait much longer."

I don't know anything about childbirth, Samantha thought in a moment of terror. *What am I going to do? What do I do first?*

Standing, she turned to Jake. "Go sterilize some towels, lots of them, and some string and scissors."

"All right." His hand rested on her shoulder a moment. "If you need me, give a call."

Nodding, she moved into the adjoining bath and scrubbed her hands and arms until they hurt.

"You're going to be fine," she stated as she reentered the bedroom.

"Yes, I am." Sabrina lay back on the pillows and closed her eyes. "I'm going to have this baby, Sam, and I'm going to do a good job of it. You can't do this for me, I have to be strong."

"You are strong." Brushing away the hair from Sabrina's cheeks, she realized with a sudden jolt that it was true. "You're stronger than I ever knew."

Her calm had returned, and she took over the duties of midwifery with an instinct as old as time. She wiped moisture from her sister's face, working with her, breathing with her, uttering soothing encouragements. Sabrina had not gone through all she had to lose now, and Samantha would not allow anything to go wrong.

"All right." Wiping beads of sweat from her own brow, Samantha straightened. "I think she's going to come this time, it's almost over. You have to help."

Sabrina nodded, her face pale and composed. Her hair had darkened with dampness. She shuddered and moaned with the final pang of childbirth. A thin, shrill cry pierced the stillness of the room. Samantha held new life in her hands.

"Oh, Bree." She stared down at the tiny, wriggling form.

Dan burst into the room two steps ahead of the the doctor.

Suddenly, it was all so simple, Dan standing by Sabrina's side, his large hand clutching hers, the small, fresh form swaddled in the curve of her mother's arms.

"Only one." Sabrina sighed, her eyes luminous. "You'll have to handle the twins, Sam. One at a time is enough for me."

Sometime later, Samantha shut the door behind her and walked toward the kitchen. Jake looked up at her approach.

"A girl." She lowered herself into a chair. "The doctor says she's perfect, almost seven pounds. Bree's fine." She pushed at her tumbled hair and ran a hand across her brow. "I want to thank you."

"I didn't do anything."

"You were here." She lifted her eyes, and they were young and vulnerable. "I needed to know you were here."

"Samantha." He smiled and shook his head. "You sure find a man's weak points. I'll get you a drink."

He was back in a moment with a decanter of brandy and two snifters. Sitting across from her, he filled both generously. "It's not champagne, but it'll do." Lifting his glass, he touched it solemnly to hers. "To mother and child, and to Samantha Evans." He paused, his smile fading into seriousness. "She's one hell of a woman."

Samantha folded her arms on the table, laid her head on them and burst into tears.

"I was so scared." She found her voice muffled against his shoulder as he brought her against him. "I've never been so scared. I thought I would lose them both."

He tilted her chin as one hand rubbed the small of her back. "You're a survivor, Sam, and too stubborn to let anything happen to Sabrina or the baby."

Her forehead dropped to his chest as she struggled to stem the flow of tears.

"I always seem to fall apart in front of you."

"Don't much care for that, do you?" She felt his lips descend to her hair and allowed herself the joy of being cradled in his arms. "Most people don't look for perfection, Sam, they find it boring. You," he said, framing her face with his hands, "are never boring."

She sniffed and smiled. "I guess that was a compliment." Giving in to impulse, she leaned over and rested her cheek against his. "I don't think you're boring, either."

"Well." He stroked her hair a moment, and his voice was curiously soft. "That's about the nicest thing you've ever said to me.

"Now drink some of that." He pushed her gently away and handed her the brandy.

Obeying, she allowed the warm strength to seep into her veins and relaxed with a sigh. "Bree certainly came through this better than I did." She drank again. Jake straddled a chair, leaning his arms on the back. "When I left her, she was lying there with the baby, looking like she'd just finished having a picnic. Dan looked like he was about to keel over, I was ready for someone to cart me away. Yet Bree lies there, glowing like a rose."

"Your sister's quite a woman."

"I know." Her eyes dropped to the surface of the table. "She said she has someone to depend on her now. I guess the time's come to stop playing big sister. She doesn't need that anymore."

"So, what will you do now?" His voice was casual.

"I'll stay around a couple of weeks, then I'll go on." She struggled, seeing only a void.

"To what?"

Her fingers tightened on her glass. "To my work, to my life." She drank, and the brandy was bitter.

"Still set on leaving?" He lifted his own glass, swirling the liquid. Amber danced under the kitchen light. "You haven't seen Wyoming in the autumn."

"No, I haven't," she answered, evading his prior question. "Maybe I'll come back next year." She stared down at her hands, knowing she never would.

"She's hungry!" Dan charged into the kitchen, his grin threatening to split his face. "Just had a baby, and she says she's hungry. Sam, I love you." Plucking her from her chair, Dan tossed her into the air. Her laughter ended on a shriek as she clutched at him on her journey down. The shriek was strangled as she was smothered by a bear hug. "I swear, if bigamy wasn't against the law, I'd marry you."

"If I was still all in one piece," she managed, turning her face and gulping for air.

"I ask you, Jake." He consulted the other man as his arms threatened to destroy the alignment of Samantha's rib cage. "Have you ever known another like this one?"

"Can't say that I have." She heard the smile in his voice, though it was impossible in her position to see his face. "I'd say Samantha is unique. One of a kind."

Rising, he lifted his brandy and toasted them both.

Chapter 12

"Sam, you're going to spoil her."

"Impossible." Sitting in the front porch rocker with the week-old Jennifer, Samantha smiled at her sister. "She's much too intelligent to be spoiled. Anyway, it's an aunt's privilege."

As she continued to rock, her lips strayed to Jennifer's soft tuft of dark hair. I won't be able to do this much longer. She looked to the massive peaks gleaming silver-blue in the afternoon sun. A light breeze stirred the air, bringing the sweet scent of freshly mowed grass. She breathed it in, and the soft scent of Jennifer's talc mingled with it. A sigh escaped.

She had not realized such a small creature could wrap her way around the heart so completely. Another love to leave behind. *In just a week, I'll have to say goodbye to all the things that matter: Bree, Dan, Wyoming, and now Jennifer.*

Dents and bruises, she thought again, but not the open wound that comes from leaving the man. Arrogant and gentle, demanding and kind, hot-tempered and easy; the parts that made up Jake Tanner were complicated and many, but to Samantha, it was a simple equation of love.

Blast you, Jake Tanner, if it weren't for you, I could stay. I belong here. I felt it from the first time I saw the mountains. There's nothing for me in Philadelphia. You've left me without anything to go back to.

"Looks like Lesley's coming to pay a visit," Sabrina observed. Samantha jerked back to the present with a snap.

She watched the late-model compact winding down the drive. Ignoring the flare of impossible jealousy, she set her features in casual lines.

"Sabrina, how well you look." Lesley's greeting was obviously tinged by surprise. "It's only been a week, and you look positively…" She hesitated, searching for a word.

"Radiant?" Sabrina suggested, and laughed. "I just had a baby, Lesley, not open-heart surgery."

"But to go through all that here, and without a doctor." She turned to Samantha. "I heard from Jake that you were marvelous and handled everything."

Samantha shrugged, uncomfortable at hearing Jake's praise from Lesley's lips. "It was nice of him to say so, but Sabrina did all the work."

"Well, having a baby is not a prospect I look forward to." Lesley shivered delicately. "I certainly intend to put it off as long as possible." Gliding over, she bent her head over the sleeping infant. "She is quite lovely, Sabrina. Very sweet."

"Would you like to hold her?" Samantha offered.

"Oh, no." Lesley stepped back. "I'm afraid I'm not very good with babies."

As she moved, Samantha caught the glint of the large square-cut diamond on her left hand. Lesley followed her gaze, and held out her hand. "You didn't know I was engaged, did you, Sabrina?"

"No." Sabrina cast a quick glance at her sister. "We hadn't heard."

"Well, you have been rather busy." She moved her fingers, enjoying the changing lights. "And we haven't made any formal announcement yet. We're planning a bit of a party for next week. As a matter of fact, I'm just on my way into town to begin shopping for my trousseau. Of course, I'll have to make a trip into New York for some proper clothes, but I'll just have to make do locally for the time being. We've set the wedding for the end of September." She smoothed her perfectly groomed hair with a well-manicured hand. "I could have done with a bit more time, but men have no idea how difficult things are to arrange properly." She smiled again. "Well, I must fly. I have so much to do. I do hope you'll be able to make it to the wedding, Samantha."

Sabrina glanced again at her sister. "Sam won't be here in September, Lesley."

"Oh, too bad." The regret in Lesley's voice was mild. Her mind had already run ahead to her wardrobe. She opened the door of the compact and slid behind the wheel. Lifting a slim arm in farewell, she drove away.

Rising, Sabrina took the sleeping Jennifer from her sister's arms and went into the house. When she returned, she sat on the arm of the rocker and laid her hand on Samantha's shoulder.

"I knew it was going to happen," Samantha murmured. "I just didn't want to be here when it did. I didn't think it would hurt this much. Oh, Bree." She looked up at her twin with helpless, swimming eyes. "What am I going to do?"

For the first time in their relationship, their situations were reversed, and Samantha was vulnerable, seeking comfort and advice.

"Sam, you can't go on like this. Why don't you talk to him?" Sabrina stroked the thick fall of her sister's hair. "Something is wrong here, and the two of you have to talk things out."

"No. I won't give him the opportunity to feel sorry for me."

"Pride can be a very cold companion," Sabrina murmured.

Samantha stood up. "I'm going back early, Bree. I can have everything arranged by the day after tomorrow, maybe even by tomorrow night."

"Sam, you can't run away from this."

"Just watch me."

"Mom and Dad won't be here for a few more days. They'll be disappointed."

"I'm sorry, I hate to miss them, but I can't handle

this." Pausing, she repeated, the admission surprising her, "I *really* can't handle this."

"But, Sam…" Sabrina joined her at the porch rail. "You should at least talk to Jake. Don't you want to know how he feels? You can't just go flying off without speaking to him, without saying goodbye. Something's not right about all this. I've thought about the two of you. I've seen the way he looks at you."

Shaking her head, Samantha moved toward the door. "No, he hasn't shown his face since the baby was born, and Lesley Marshall has his ring on her finger. A diamond. He has what he wants."

Samantha spent the evening packing, while Shylock watched her in silent accusation from his habitual place in the center of her bed.

Once in bed, she spent most of the night staring at a moon-washed ceiling. When the first pale light of dawn crept into the room, she rose. The mauve shadows under her eyes were a sad tribute to the restless hours.

The house slept on, and she deserted it, making her way to the stables. She saddled her mount with quick, deft movements, then galloped over the faint mist of morning.

As the sky lightened, the air came to life with the sweet song of birds. Sadly, she listened to the song of the west, for she knew that the melody would linger forever in her heart. She watched the mountains transformed by the dawn. Ribbons of rose and gold melted into blue until the peaks were no longer silhouettes, but stood proud in the full glory of the sun. She stayed for a last look at the white-faced Herefords grazing on the short, coarse grass. She knew now that her love for this wild, free country was forever bound up with her love for Jake. In saying goodbye to one, she was saying goodbye to the other. Straightening her shoulders, she turned the little mare back to the Lazy L.

When she returned to the house, she greeted her sister with bright chatter, the meaningless words no disguise for sleep-starved eyes. Sabrina made no comment, and shortly disappeared into the bedroom to tend to the baby.

Alone, Samantha wandered aimlessly from window to window. Tonight, she thought, slipping her hands into the pockets of her jeans, I'll be on a plane. And tomorrow morning, all this will just be a dream.

"Morning, ma'am."

She whirled, nearly upsetting a vase of roses with

the movement. Jake leaned against the door frame, legs crossed at the ankles, as if he had been watching for some time.

"What are you doing here?"

He took a few strides into the room. "Well, now, I came to fetch you." This information was imparted in an irritatingly slow drawl.

"Fetch me? What are you talking about? I'm not a dog or a maverick calf to be fetched."

"Maverick calf sounds pretty close. You're always running off in the wrong direction." Reaching out, he took her arm. "Come on, we're going for a ride." His voice was pleasant, but the steel was there. She jerked away, angry with his arrogance, wary of his tone.

"I have no intention of going anywhere with you. Why don't you just go away and leave me alone?"

"Now, I can't do that, Sam," he returned in a reasonable tone. "We have some unfinished business to attend to. Your time's up."

The fire in her eyes flickered and died. "You can't be serious."

"I'm dead serious."

"What…what about Lesley?"

"She's not invited," he returned simply.

"I'm not going with you," she said, somewhere between terror and fury. "You can't make me."

Stopping, he looked down at her from his overpowering height. "Sure I can," he corrected with easy confidence. With a swift movement, he swung her over his shoulder. "See?" He walked effortlessly down the hall. "Nothing to it."

"Let me down!" Furious fists beat against his back. "This is crazy, it's illegal. I'll have you thrown in jail!"

"No kidding? Sam, you're scaring me to death."

He continued easily down the hall, as if he carried an empty sack, rather than an irate woman who was thumping against his back. Pausing, he touched the brim of his hat as Sabrina appeared in the bedroom doorway, the baby in her arms.

"Morning, Sabrina." His greeting was genial, and he cocked his head to get a better view of Jennifer. "She's a real beauty."

"Thank you, Jake. We certainly think so." She shifted the baby and smiled. "Are you two going out?"

"Thought we'd go for a little ride," Jake informed her. "We may be gone some time."

"It's a fine day for it, hardly a cloud in the sky."

"Bree." Samantha's voice was desperate. "Don't just

stand there, *do* something." She pushed at the hair which hung over her face. "Don't you see what he's doing? He's kidnapping me. Call the police, call Dan." She continued to plead as Jake touched the brim of his hat once more and moved down the hall. "Bree, say something."

"Have a good time" was her sister's surprising response.

Samantha's mouth fell open in dumb astonishment. A stream of imaginative curses was hurled on Jake's unperturbed head as he took the reins of his mount from a grinning cowboy.

"Looks like you got yourself a real handful there, Jake."

"No more than I can handle," he countered, swinging into the saddle with Samantha still held over his shoulder. With a speed that defied his easygoing manner, he had her in front of him in the saddle, spurring the horse into a gallop, before she could think of escape.

"You're going to pay for this," Samantha promised, clutching the saddle horn to keep her balance. "You can't just run off with me this way!"

"I didn't see anybody try to stop me," Jake pointed out.

He followed the road for some time without decreasing his pace, then cut across an open field. At a small grove of trees, he reined in, gripping Samantha around the waist when she attempted to wiggle down.

"Now, don't do that, Sam," he warned in a friendly voice. "I'd just have to catch you, and I throw a mean lasso."

He slid from the chestnut, and before her feet could touch the ground, she was back over his shoulder. Without ceremony, she was dumped under the fragile, bending leaves of a willow while he towered over her, grinning with obvious enjoyment.

"You're going to be sorry," she predicted, smoldering with fury. "I'm going to…" The rest of her words slipped back down her throat as he dropped down next to her. "You—you can't do this, Jake. You're not the kind of man who forces himself on a woman."

"Who says?" Pushing her back on the soft grass, he covered her body with his.

Her body betrayed her with instant response. Her skin tingled as his mouth brushed over it. "You're not really going to do this."

"I told you once—" his mouth moved to her ear, and his words were warm and soft against it "—not to forget your own words. There are some things you just have to do."

His kiss was long and lingering.

When her mouth was free, she drew in a deep breath and spit out with all her strength, "What kind of man are you, to make love to one woman and plan to marry another?"

His eyes lazily narrowed. He propped himself on one elbow, his other arm pinning her down. Lifting his head from his elbow, he undid the top button of her blouse. "Suppose," he continued, moving down to the next button, "you tell me whom I'm supposed to marry."

His fingers trailed a slow line from her throat, down the smooth skin her open blouse revealed, and rested on the next button. The blood began to pound in her ears. His eyes alone held her still as he spread her blouse apart. Slowly, his fingers roamed up the warmth of her skin, moving with casual possession over her. Her eyes clouded with growing need as he explored.

"Tell me who I'm going to marry, Samantha." His body shifted again, molding to hers. His shirt was warm against her naked flesh.

"L-Lesley," she stammered.

"No." His mouth lowered to the curve of her throat, his tongue teasing the vulnerable skin.

She felt the waist of her jeans loosen under his hand. His

finger pushed away the material and moved along her hip. With her last claim to lucidity, she pushed against his chest.

"Please stop."

"Now I just can't do that, Sam." His hands teased the curve of her hip, trailing back up to the side of her breast. "I've waited a good long time to get you where I want you."

"I'm not staying… Did you say you weren't marrying Lesley?"

He frowned down in consideration, winding her hair around his finger. "Seems to me I did mention that. I don't know why you're always piling your hair on top of your head when it looks so good spread all over."

"But she was wearing your ring."

"Not mine," Jake corrected, still concentrating on the hair around his fingers. "Your hair's gotten lighter these past few weeks, you haven't been wearing a hat. Les has a diamond, doesn't she? I told you once diamonds don't suit you. They're cold, and they don't have much imagination. But that's Les." He shrugged and began to move his mouth over her face again. "It doesn't seem to matter to Jim."

Valiantly, Samantha attempted to follow his words. Her head shook with the effort.

"Les is engaged to Jim Bailey. I'm sure you remember

Jim Bailey, you spent enough time with him at the party."

"Yes, but…"

"No buts," he interrupted. "Les likes to have a couple of fish on the line, and when she got it through her head I wasn't in season, she netted Jim without a struggle."

"But I thought…"

"I know what you thought." He cut her off again and smiled. "Running away a few days early, weren't you?"

"I wasn't running. How did you know I was leaving?"

"Sabrina told me."

"Bree?" Samantha whispered. Bree did that?

"Yeah, yesterday. She came to see me while you were packing. I like this spot right here," he stated, planting his lips against the hollow of her throat. "I've had a devil of a time putting things in order since then, so I could take time for a honeymoon. Busy time of year for a cattle-man."

"Honeymoon?" Her skin was trembling where his lips continued to taste.

"I've got a good foreman," he continued, as if thinking aloud. "I reckon he can manage things for a while. I could use another day or two. I had a nice long honey-moon in mind, someplace quiet." He brought his attention back to her stunned face. "You've never been to Bora Bora, have you?"

"Are you talking about getting your ranch in order so you can take time off to marry me?" She attempted to speak slowly and clearly while her emotions whirled like a summer tornado.

"Just being practical," he explained with a bland smile.

"Why you conceited, overbearing… Just what makes you think I'll marry you? You sit back and make all these plans and expect me to run off to Bora Bora with you like a passive little puppy. Of all the chauvinist—"

"How about Antarctica?" he suggested, willing to be reasonable. "Not too many people there, either."

"You're crazy. I never said I'd marry you. What makes you think…" Her tirade was cut off effectively as his mouth coaxed her silence. When he let her breathe, her voice had lost its strength. "That's not going to help you. I'm not in love with you."

"Seems to me I recall someone telling me she was a totally honest person." His gaze was disconcertingly direct. He held her chin, preventing her face from turning away. "You want to look at me and tell me that again? You've been fighting me all along, and I think

I've just about used up my patience." His lips were teasing hers again, and his hands moved over her with more urgency. "Mmm, but you have a nice body. I can't take much more of this waiting around. Six months is a long time, Sam. I've wanted you from the minute you stood there ordering Dan to have his man tend to the horses."

"Yes, you let me know very early what you wanted." She no longer struggled, but lay passive in his arms.

"Gave you something to think about. Of course, you didn't know I wanted you to be my wife, too. It was easy to tell you I wanted you, but a bit difficult to tell you I loved you. Sam, look at me." She shook her head, but the fingers on her chin tightened in authority. "Look at me." She obeyed, her lids opening to reveal eyes veiled with tears. "You stubborn little idiot. Listen carefully, I've never said this to another woman, and I've had to wait too long to say it to you. If you don't marry me soon, I'm going to lose my mind." His mouth took hers, spinning the world into nothing. Her arms flew around him as pain evaporated into unspeakable joy. "Samantha." He buried his face in the lushness of her hair. "It's been quite a race."

"I don't understand." She brought his face back to

hers, needing to see the truth in his eyes. "Why didn't you tell me before?"

"I didn't think you'd believe that a man had nearly been knocked off his feet by a picture of a girl less than half his age, then had completely lost his balance when he saw the woman she'd become. If you hadn't been so wrapped up in Sabrina those first few minutes, you'd have seen how a man looks when he gets hit by lightning."

"Just like that?" Stunned, she traced the angles of his face to assure herself she was not dreaming.

"Just like that," he agreed, bringing her palm to his lips. "Then, after I'd recovered a bit, I knew I had to work around your dedication to Sabrina until you'd figured out there was room in your life for someone else. Then you stood there telling me you were going back home as soon as the baby was born. I nearly strangled you." His fingers tightened on her hand as he brought his eyes back to hers. "How was I supposed to tell you that I loved you, that I wanted to marry you, wanted you to stay in Wyoming? The night of the party, in the kitchen, I made up my mind I wasn't letting you go, no matter what I had to do to keep you."

"But I never wanted to leave." She shook her head

in brisk denial, as if he should have realized it all along. "It was just that I couldn't bear to see you married to Lesley."

"You know, things might have gotten even more complicated if Sabrina hadn't come by and laid things out for me. She's got a bit more of you in her than I had thought." Laughing, he lifted his face from hers. "She told me to sit down and listen. She'd never seen two people run around in circles so long and get nowhere."

"It's not like Bree to interfere."

"She interfered beautifully. First thing she did was ask me what business I had getting engaged to Lesley. I must have stared at her like she'd lost her mind. After I managed to tell her I was definitely not engaged to Lesley, she let me have it with both barrels. Mixed with the buckshot was the information that you were miserable about going home, and that I was a fool for not seeing it myself. Then she folded her arms, stuck out her chin exactly like someone else has a habit of doing and asked me what the devil I intended to do about it."

Samantha stared up at him and shook her head in astonishment. "I wish I could have seen that."

He smiled and lowered his mouth. "Just look in the

mirror sometime." Flesh met flesh with no barriers, and with a small sound of desperation he savaged her mouth. The hard lines of his chest pressed into her breasts. "Let me hear you say it, Samantha," he murmured, unable to resist the curve of her neck. "I need to hear you say it."

"I love you." Her mouth searched for his, her arms urging him closer. "I love you. I love you." Her lips found their objective, and her silence told him again.

"I need you, Samantha." His mouth and hands continued to seek, growing wilder, possessive, demanding. "I never knew I could need anyone the way I need you. I want you for myself for a while, no distractions, no complications, just you. We've got six months of loving to make up for. I'm going to keep you fully occupied for a very long time." Lifting his face, he smiled down at her, running his hand through the hair spread over the grass. "A very long time."

She smiled back, running her hands up his chest to circle his neck. "I intend to keep you occupied, as well. Your cows are going to get very lonely." Removing his hat, she tossed it carelessly aside, then turned back to him with raised brows. "Okay, cowboy." Her arms lifted to lock around his neck, fingers tangling possessively in his hair. "Start occupying."

"Yes, ma'am." With a polite nod, he lowered his mouth and followed orders.

* * * * *

Danger walks in the darkness…

*Don't miss the next thrilling story from
bestselling author Nora Roberts*

Nightshade

is available next month!

**"Some of the stuff they want us to do for the cameras gives
me the creeps. I think they killed one of the girls, so I
am getting out before they kill me."**

*So reads the chilling letter which sends Colt Nightshade on a
private quest for justice.*

*A teenage runaway is caught up in a seedy, terrifying
underworld. Coerced into making sadistic films which end in
violence, even death, Liz is in greater danger than she knows.*

*Colt needs help and is forced to turn to the cops. Partnered
with Lieutenant Althea Grayson, they become an impressive
team. But the clock is ticking for Liz and the trail is going cold.
Can Colt and Althea find her before she winds up dead?*

Read on for a preview!

NIGHTSHADE

Murder scenes, whether indoors or out, in an urban, suburban or pastoral setting, had one thing in common: the aura of death. As a cop with nearly ten years' experience, Althea had learned to recognise it, absorb it and file it away, while going about the precise and mechanical business of investigation.

When Althea arrived, a half-block had been secured. The police photographer had finished recording the scene and was already packing up his gear. The body had been identified.

That was why she was here.

Three black-and-whites sat, their lights flashing blue and their radios coughing static. Spectators – for death always drew them – were straining against the yellow police tape, greedy, Althea knew, for a glimpse of death to reaffirm that they were alive and untouched.

Because the night was cool, she grabbed the wrap she'd tossed into the back seat of her car. The emerald-green silk kept the chill off her arms and back. Flashing her badge to the rookie handling crowd control, she slipped under the barricade.

She was grateful when she spotted Sweeney, a hard bitten cop who had twice her years on the job and was in no hurry to give up his uniform.

"Lieutenant." He nodded to her, then took out a handkerchief and made a valiant attempt to clear his stuffy nose.

"What have we got here, Sweeney?"

"Drive-by." He stuffed the handkerchief back into his pocket. "Dead guy was standing in front of the bar, talking."

He gestured to the shattered window of the Tick Tock. "Witnesses say a car came by, moving north, fast. Sprayed the area with bullets and kept going."

She could still smell the blood, though it was no longer fresh. "Any bystanders hit?"

"Nope. Couple of cuts from flying glass, that's all. They hit their mark." He glanced over his shoulder, and down. "He didn't have a chance, Lieutenant. Sorry."

"Yeah, me too." She stared down at the form sprawled on the stained concrete. There'd been nothing much to him to begin with, she thought. Now there was less. He'd been five five, maybe a hundred and ten soaking wet, spindly bones and had had a face even a mother would have been hard-pressed to love.

Wild Bill Billings, part-time pimp, part-time grifter and full-time snitch.

And, damn it, he'd been hers.

"Forensics?"

"Been and gone," Sweeney confirmed. "We're ready to put him on ice."

"Then do it. Got a list of witnesses?"

"Yeah, mostly useless. It was a black car, it was a blue car. One drunk claims it was a chariot driven by flaming demons."

He swore with inventive expertise, knowing Althea well enough not to worry about her taking offence.

"We'll take what we can get." She scanned the crowd – bar types, teenagers looking for action, a scattering of the homeless and – Her antenna vibrated as she locked in on one man. Unlike the others, he wasn't goggle-eyed with either revulsion or excitement.

He stood at his ease, his leather bomber jacket open to the

wind, revealing a chambray shirt, a glint of silver on a chain. His rangy build made her think he'd be fast on his feet.

Snug, worn jeans rode down long legs and ended at scuffed boots. Hair that might have been dark blond or brown ruffled in the breeze and curled well over his collar.

He smoked a thin cigar, his eyes scanning the scene as hers had. The light wasn't good, but she decided he looked tanned, which suited the sharply defined face. The eyes were deep set, and the nose was long, and just shy of being narrow. The mouth was strong, the kind that looked as though it could thin into a sneer easily.

Some instinct had her dubbing him a pro before his eyes shifted and locked on hers with an impact like a bare-fisted punch.

"Who's the cowboy, Sweeney?"

Passion. Power. Suspense.
It's time to fall under the spell of Nora Roberts.